CHARMIAN STEWART gre'
Highlands, and studied English
as well as History and Fine A
Edinburgh. She now lives in No
her children having fled the nest.

Writing has always been her passion. She started scribbling and illustrating stories when she was barely old enough to hold a pen. Since then, she has written many short stories and poems, and is never without a notebook to jot down ideas.

Ships in the Night is her second novel. Set in the fjords and islands around Bergen, it is a modern-day tale of adventure and suspense. Her first novel, *Highland Enchantment*, tells the story of a ghost grieving for a past love affair and was inspired by her love of the Celtic myths.

SHIPS IN THE NIGHT

CHARMIAN STEWART

SilverWood

Published in 2015 by SilverWood Books

SilverWood Books Ltd
14 Small Street, Bristol, BS1 1DE, United Kingdom
www.silverwoodbooks.co.uk

ISBN 978-1-78132-471-4 (paperback)
ISBN 978-1-78132-472-1 (ebook)

British Library Cataloguing in Publication Data
A CIP catalogue record for this book is available from
the British Library

Set in Sabon by SilverWood Books
Printed on responsibly sourced paper

Prologue

Bergen, Norway

He was alone at the cottage. Nothing unusual in that. His wife and sons knew better than to disturb him when he took his boat and sailed out to the island. Now he sat at his desk in the living room with a log fire sparking and crackling in the grate, his head bowed over the company accounts.

He raised his head and stared out of the half-open window. The black wings of darkness blurred the stark outlines of the trees that surrounded the cottage. The only sound was the restless rippling of the fiord on the pebbly beach below.

Strange, he could have sworn that there were fireflies like pinpricks of light passing the window where he'd left the curtains undrawn. Fireflies…He remembered them from his years when his ships had called at ports in the tropics. But you'd never see fireflies in the chill of a Norwegian night. It must have been a reflection from a passing ship or even an aeroplane. He was getting fanciful as he approached his seventieth year. Elise would have laughed at him.

His laptop on the desk winked irritatingly at him, the figures on the spreadsheet jumping and dazzling his tired old eyes. He rubbed his neck. There was almost two million dollars unaccounted for. Had one of his sons withdrawn such a large sum without consulting him? Or Elise? No, of course not. But no one else had access to the company bank accounts. Had someone hacked into the company computers and discovered the deal he was planning?

The shadows in the room danced insanely in the flickering firelight as a log shifted in the grate. A sudden squall of wind blew in, rattling the windowpanes and carrying with it a fresh salty tang from the fiord. Rising stiffly from his desk, he walked over to the window and peered outside. A single beam of light flashed out and was swiftly stifled.

He peered into the darkness again, telling himself not to get jittery. He'd always been able to hold his own and he'd faced some rough customers on his voyages round the world. There was that deck hand who'd nearly hacked off his hand with a broken bottle. That was a close call. He'd been more careful after that. But still…where was the walking stick he sometimes used when he went walking in the mountains? Last week, he'd read in the local newspaper that marauding bands of foreign immigrants were breaking into isolated small cottages in search of liquor and computers, or anything of value.

The thought propelled him out to the cloakroom where ancient raincoats and sou'westers drooped like tired shadows. He rummaged around and found a ski pole with a point sharp enough to put out a man's eye. Then in the small kitchen, he yanked out a drawer, throwing out old spoons and forks until he found a heavy torch shoved to the back. Armed with his two makeshift weapons, he opened the cottage door.

But there shouldn't be anyone on the island. If it were his sons, they'd knock on the door and call his name, but they seldom bothered to come here. They knew he liked his privacy. Elise never came here, complaining that the island was too desolate and she didn't like the aura.

Uneasily, he stood in the doorway. Down on the shore,

the rhythmic lapping of the waves and a sharp ozone scent wafting towards him helped to slow his heartbeat. He clutched the torch in his right hand and the ski pole in his left. All was quiet save for the flapping wings and mournful cries of a lone bird.

Strange, the shadows seemed to creep closer and the clump of pine trees rustled behind the cottage. Now two figures detached themselves from the trees and walked slowly towards him. They were too small to be his sons. The two figures drew closer and a stink of unwashed flesh floated towards him. His heart thumped faster until he feared he'd have to turn back into the cottage to get his medicine. But he drew himself up to his considerable height, ready to confront the faceless shadows.

'Who's there?' he shouted, pointing into the dark with his thin ski pole.

A swathe of silence hung in the air. 'Who's there?' he shouted again.

Swiftly and silently, three dark-haired men surrounded him. Two from the front and yet another who'd crept up behind him. He stared them down. 'What are you doing here?' he asked calmly. 'This is private property. You've no right to be here.'

The men came together like a living wall and pushed him back towards the cottage. The biggest man moved heavily, his breath coming in panting gasps. The men's faces were pale and gaunt – except for the well-fed, fat one – and their clothes dusty and torn. Roughly, they pushed him over the threshold and backwards into the cottage, resisting his attempts to shut the door on them.

'Get out!' he shouted desperately. 'This is private property.' He slipped and almost fell as the men talked excitedly among themselves.

They moved in closer, trapping him. The sour smell of

sweat coming from their bodies made him gag. Their faces were wolf-like, hungry, feral. Suddenly, a smaller figure, his face obscured by a grey hood, slipped out from behind the others and pointed the muzzle of a pistol at him.

'Get back!' he cried, stabbing violently with the torch. 'Who are you? What do you want?'

A blinding explosion knocked him backwards and a burning pain radiated through his chest. The sound of high-pitched laughter washed over him as he slumped slowly down on his side.

Chapter 1

The large hotel window rattled as if an insistent hand rapped against it. Dropping her mobile on the bed, Silver Fairfax ran across to look out. Rugged mountains ringed the Norwegian city of Bergen. Like black bears, crouched ready to spring, they loomed over the city. Silver studied them for a moment, then pushed the fantasy aside. Here she was in the land of the midnight sun and the long light of the evening beckoned her outside. Not bothering to unpack, she seized her small rucksack, slung it over her shoulder and ran downstairs.

She pushed through the swinging glass doors of the Hotel Norge and stepped out into the street ready to explore. People strolled along the pedestrian street, enjoying the balmy weather. The outdoor tables of the cafés were filled with groups of chattering young men and women. Silver strained her ears trying to pick out a familiar word from the cheerful sound of the raised Norwegian voices. She turned away and hesitated, wondering which direction to choose. Ahead of her, the compelling glimmer of a lake in the distance pulled her towards it.

For the first time in weeks after her break-up with Mike back home, the stinging tension in her shoulders eased and, secure in the knowledge that there was no chance of bumping into him on the streets of Bergen, she stepped out eagerly.

Her eye was caught by the statue of a violinist standing on a pile of rocks, his bow stroking his violin in a still and timeless melody. Then she walked onwards through a green park until she reached a smooth, artificial lake, glassy in the sun's rays. A few small rowing boats bobbed around on its surface. Farther away, she caught the jingling music of a circus or perhaps a fairground and, impulsively, she turned in that direction.

Entering through the red wooden gates of the fairground, Silver sauntered along, her camera bumping gently on her side. A fluttering of butterflies seemed to have invaded her stomach, but she forced herself to relax and to avoid thinking of the huge task she had ahead of her tomorrow.

Close up, the amusement stalls were tarnished and tawdry, red paint peeling off their flimsy walls. But the scent of sweet pink candyfloss wafted towards her, making her mouth water. Resisting the temptation to stop and taste some, she pressed on. The brightly painted horses of the carousel nodded as they circled round. Blond-haired children screamed with joy as they clutched the manes of their whirling horses. She raised her camera to catch the scene.

Old hit tunes from the sixties blared out from the carousel, while some of the stall-holders in the surrounding booths had gone hi-tech, wearing headsets with microphones to call out and attract customers. Their voices crackled and jarred in the soft evening air.

The jumbled noise hurt Silver's ears and her mind flashed back to the conversation she'd had with her boss Tom, the editor of *The Ocean Observer* in London, before she got on the flight to Norway.

'You've got to be extra sharp, Silver,' he told her. 'Dig up all the dirt on what's going on in the Rosenholm cruise business. It's a very classy outfit, but the word is that there are some far murkier dealings going on. The father of the present owner died recently under very suspicious circumstances, which they're trying hard to hush up. And they're running a nice little sideline that they don't want anyone to know about, so it's up to you to find out what that is. We'll run it as a front page story if you can sniff out enough facts.'

From the very moment Silver called Mr Rosenholm's secretary to set up the appointment for the interview, she was involved in a subterfuge. She'd claimed to be researching an article on the cruise line, the kind of smooth piece that would celebrate the company's accomplishments and focus on the new routes they were planning, so Mr Rosenholm certainly wouldn't expect an exposé!

He'd expect her to write a puff piece about how well the company was doing, not an article by an undercover reporter.

Well, Mr Rosenholm, you're in for a surprise! The butterflies in Silver's stomach began to flutter again.

Certainly from his picture, which the Rosenholm Company had sent her, the new young owner, Alexander Rosenholm, was a man of startling good looks – not that that would influence her at all.

She counted herself lucky that Tom had given her this special assignment and it was a great chance to boost her career. Not easy though. Tom warned her that this man was known for guarding his privacy zealously and he would hide his secrets well.

Perhaps she should've stayed in her hotel room to prepare some more before she met the man. Well, even if he were a hard nut, full of his own importance, she'd drag a story out of him. That reminded her that she hadn't yet checked out the street where the company's office was located. It must be quite near the lake as far as she could remember from the map, which annoyingly she'd left behind her on her bed.

She stepped quickly back as a ghost train with jiggling skeletons and thick gray cobwebs rattled across in front of her. She raised her camera again and pressed the shutter. As a child, she'd loved riding on such trains with their harmless scariness, her hand tightly clutched in her mother's. How she missed her now that she was gone. Her ever-absent father was no comfort. Always away in Peru, or was it Bolivia? Never there when she needed him. But she was twenty-eight and she'd got to stand on her own feet. She straightened her shoulders, pushing aside her sadness.

'Hello, pretty lady,' called a stallholder.

Silver jumped. Word must have got round that she was English. But how could they know that? She hadn't yet spoken to anyone. It must be her clothes. Hello, hello, hello…their amplified voices reverberated round the fairground, mingling with the thumping music.

Another dark-haired stallholder tried to cajole her into buying coloured balls to throw at a row of battered tins. At least, that's what he seemed to be saying in his halting English.

'Only three balls,' he cried. 'Very cheap.'

'I don't understand,' she said laughing, once more raising her camera to snap his picture as he stood with two other men wearing black baseball caps, one with a strikingly hooked nose. They were chattering in an unintelligible language in the middle of all the colourful prizes on the stall.

'You win teddy bear,' the stallholder called again, eager to get a new customer.

'No, no. I couldn't possibly carry it home on the plane,' Silver said. 'Even if I won!'

The huge yellow bear seemed to gaze at her mournfully with its dark brown eyes, making a twinge of guilt rush through her as if she had abandoned it.

She moved on to watch a young boy at the shooting booth as he aimed his gun at the white card. His rifle gave a small crack as he hit his target.

Silver raised her camera ready to take a new picture. Suddenly, a sharp elbow jammed into her side. One of the men from her picture had cannoned into her so hard that she almost fell. The camera jerked out of her hands and hit the ground with a hard thunk. Sour breath stroked across her cheek as an unseen person bent over her. A second sharp nudge in her back sent her stumbling against the shooting booth, hitting her head.

She caught a glimpse of her hook-nosed assailant as he dodged quickly away and vanished behind one of the fairground wagons.

Ouch. Silver rubbed her head and bent down quickly to rescue her precious camera. Her hand scrabbled across the hard-packed earth of the path, meeting nothing but emptiness. She dropped to her knees, searching frantically as the sun sank to its rest, casting black shadows between the booths. People surged past, almost trampling her, as they made their way towards the popcorn stall. The smell of roasting popcorn drifted towards Silver, sickening her.

Her breath came in short gasps. Why had he jostled her like that? Didn't he like her taking his picture? How could her large camera be gone? She struggled against the endless tide of people, searching desperately under their feet and trying not to get her hands trodden on. Her fingertips were scraped and bleeding, but there was no sign of the camera. Gritting her teeth in frustration, she scrambled to her feet and ignoring her throbbing head, she automatically checked the zip of her small rucksack to make sure that everything was safe inside.

Her heart jolted. Panic flooded her, making it even harder to catch her breath. A small groan escaped her as she saw that the rucksack was open! 'Keep calm, Silver!' she whispered, telling herself that maybe she'd forgotten to fasten it before she left her hotel. With mounting horror, she saw the inside pocket was gaping wide as well. She slipped her hand inside it, feeling for her credit cards, which she usually kept there. Nothing there. Nothing at all. What a stupid, stupid fool she was – the background notes she had made on the plane were gone too. A chill of fear swept over her. She fumbled deeper into her rucksack looking for her mobile. Surely she hadn't lost it as well. Anyway, who could she call? She hadn't thought to bring the number of the hotel with her. She certainly couldn't call her friends in London. What help would they be?

A cold knot formed in her stomach as the realisation hit her. No mobile either! Frantically, she looked around her. Nothing seemed to have changed except that an eerie twilight now illuminated the scene, while the music of the fair blared on. The children with their parents as well as the groups of teenagers carried on enjoying themselves. She seemed to have become invisible. Nobody seemed to have noticed anything amiss. She opened her mouth to speak to the nearest person, but her throat was dry and no words came out.

She was completely alone. Had it really happened? She seemed to be looking at the world through a pane of glass.

Here she was alone in a foreign country, without any money or hope of getting any. How would she explain her plight? Would the Norwegian police speak English? Could she explain to them what had happened? She was a foreigner in Norway. Suddenly, the language problem seemed insurmountable. With cold sweat trickling down her spine, she tried to calm herself and forced her trembling legs to carry her over to a nearby wooden bench. She sank down on its hard surface, drawing deep breaths and trying to decide what to do.

The music of the fair boomed louder and more hectic, underlining her feeling of isolation. Silver searched quickly through her rucksack again in case she had been mistaken. But the facts were clear: her credit cards and mobile were gone. Worse, her passport too was gone. What on earth had possessed her to bring it out with her? And what about her notes for the interview tomorrow?

Get a grip, she told herself and jumped up from the bench. She must move fast. Rush back to her hotel and get help. But first, she'd take a look around and try to catch sight of the man with the odd-shaped nose. He was the number one suspect as the mugger. Her legs were shaky, but she turned back on her tracks and moved quietly along the sideshows behind which the fairground folk had parked their caravans. As she peered through their windows, a man sprang up from inside a lighted wagon and shook his fist at her. She stepped back quickly, afraid he would come out and chase her. Her heart slammed fast against her ribs as she crept past an old blue bus, battered and rusty, parked under a tree. The low hum of voices floated through the open door and she quickened her pace. There must have been several people inside, but she didn't dare look closer. Ahead were more heavy-leafed trees casting long dark shadows. Goodness knows what kind of sinister characters could be lurking among the branches there. She pushed through the leaves and came back onto the path. For a moment, she stood still trying to decide what to do next.

A tall figure loomed up in front of her, barring her way. A voice spoke to her, but she couldn't understand what the large, blond man was saying to her.

'Hey, get out of my way,' she cried out in a dazed panic as she tried to dodge around him, her hands pushing against his solid form.

He held her arm easily in a light grip. 'An English woman in distress!' he replied in formal English. 'Can I help you?'

Silver was just about to kick his shins, when he dropped her arm. She stepped back and gave him a quick glance. He wore ordinary well-pressed jeans and an open-necked, navy-blue sports shirt, and carried a brief case. Probably he was on his way home from work, though it seemed a bit late. A very attractive man, she thought, sizing him up quickly...the sort that inspired confidence, if she had judged him correctly. He seemed friendly enough, but could she trust him? At least he spoke English.

'Just show me the way out of here,' she cried. 'Where's the Hotel Norge? I've got to get back there.' Then, unable to stop herself, she blurted out: 'Oh God, I've just lost my camera and had my credit cards stolen, as well as my passport.' An uneasy thought struck her. Perhaps he too was involved in pick-pocketing unwary tourists.

The man appeared calm and sympathetic. 'Did you see who did it?' he asked. 'Perhaps I can help you look.' He paused: 'And you've got a nasty scratch on your face too!'

Silver's hand flew up to her cheek and she stepped quickly away from him. She didn't want to linger in the half-light any longer. Even though he appeared so nice, he was a complete stranger. 'No, no. I've got to get out of here and back to the hotel.'

'Don't worry. It's not far from here,' he said. 'Lucky I was passing here on the way home from my office.'

He put his hand gently on her back, propelling her forwards and out of the fairground. Silver's legs were shaky after her traumatic experience and, disquietingly, she felt a spreading warmth in the centre of her back where his large and comforting hand was firmly placed.

She straightened up quickly. She mustn't succumb to weakness even though she had panicked for a moment. She wasn't accountable to any man...or woman for that matter.

As the dying sun slipped down behind the hills, they passed the lake, stopped at the busy traffic lights and turned into a street that Silver now recognised. There was the violinist still fiddling away, standing on his pile of stones.

'Have you just arrived in Bergen?' Silver's new companion asked, slowing his long strides to keep pace with her. 'Are you here on holiday?'

'Yes, yes, a short holiday,' Silver said quickly, reluctant to reveal why she really was in Norway. 'It's a lovely city, Bergen, so clean and pleasant.'

How long had she been in Bergen? Did she like Norway? His questions pounded in her ears. Silver answered in monosyllables. She didn't want to open up to this almost too perfect stranger. Like a mirage, he'd soon be gone.

The large illuminated sign of the Hotel Norge loomed up in front of them. His hand gripped her elbow, sending shivers up her spine as they navigated the revolving door to the hotel lobby. Together they walked up to the reception desk and Silver's companion asked to see the manager.

The manager came rushing out of his office. A smile of recognition spread over his face. 'Herr Rosenholm!' he said.

'*Ja, ja!*' The large, blond man was unmoved. 'We need your help,' he said in English to the manager. 'Miss or Mrs...,' he said looking questioningly at Silver, 'has lost her wallet and her credit cards. And your camera too?' he asked leaning towards her, frowning.

At Silver's nod, he turned back to the receptionist,

saying: 'We need you to report the loss to the police. She'll have to telephone to stop the credit cards being used.'

'Of course, Herr Rosenholm,' the manager said.

'My passport's gone as well,' Silver said in a shaky voice that she didn't recognise as her own. She walked unsteadily towards a red leather sofa and sank down on it, catching sight of a large rip across the knee of her jeans.

She caught herself. What was it the manager had said? 'Rosenholm?' A jolt of surprise hit her and she scrutinised the man's face. Of course! Now she recognised him from the picture which the Rosenholm Company had sent her.

She sat forward and cleared her throat: 'I'm meeting you tomorrow.'

The tall man raised his eyebrows. 'And why is that?' he asked. 'Who are you?'

'You are Alexander Rosenholm from the shipping company,' Silver stated. 'I'm the journalist from *The Ocean Observer* in London. My name is Sylvia Fairfax. We have an appointment tomorrow.'

Chapter 2

'Mr Rosenholm left you some Norwegian kroner as he thought you would need some after your cards were stolen,' greeted the receptionist as Silver came downstairs the next morning. How thoughtful of him. Silver felt a prick of conscience. Probably he believed her to be a scatty, unthreatening tourist, not a tiger reporter who intended to uncover his innermost secrets to advance her own career.

Earlier, she'd spent a long time on the phone in her hotel room, arranging to cancel her credit cards and ringing the British consulate about getting a replacement passport, which it seemed would be extraordinarily difficult to do according to the person on the other end of the telephone. It would take her several days to get a new one, the disembodied person told her coldly.

After all her phone calls, time was getting short and Silver, trying to ignore the throbbing in her head from her fall last night, grabbed some paper from the hotel drawer since she'd lost her notebook. She wasn't sure whether her interviewee would accept her small cassette recorder and, besides, she never liked to depend entirely on a taped interview. Sometimes it took too long to play it back and cut out all the unnecessary chit-chat before getting down to the heart of the matter.

Down in the hotel dining room, Silver didn't allow herself to be waylaid by the tempting spread of food offered by the Norwegian cold table. Turning her eyes away from the centrepiece of the large, pink, mouth-watering salmon and the luscious slices of roast beef, she snatched a cup of coffee and a roll, then dashed out to the hotel reception to ask for directions to the shipowner's office.

'It's just past the fish market,' the receptionist told her. 'It'll take you about fifteen minutes to walk.'

'You'd better call me a taxi then,' Silver said, sending a grateful thought to Alexander for providing her with cash.

The taxi swung down the hill with Silver repressing a shudder as they passed the fairground, now deserted in the morning sun. As they passed, she scanned the caravans and the now motionless carousel. The old blue bus was still there, but all was quiet. Only a few of the fairground people were out and about, sweeping up papers and rubbish from the night before. Of her assailant, there was no sign, although she'd craned her neck painfully to look for him. Later on, she would go back and see if someone had found her camera.

The taxi swept alongside the sparkling blue fiord and past a row of tall, narrow wooden houses with sharply pointed roofs, each house painted in a different colour – blue, red and even bright yellow. Sitting in the back seat of the vehicle, Silver tried to gather her thoughts before she met Alexander Rosenholm again. Leaving the houses behind, the taxi turned into a small street and braked suddenly as it pulled up in front of a large white house which stood secluded in its own garden. Silver got out and checked the number 27 on the gate. She sighed with relief as she saw the name 'Frederick Rosenholm & Co, Shipowners' on the brass plaque.

She swiftly crossed the flagstones which led to a solid oak door and pulled at the heavy, dangling rope of a large ship's bell. It set up a melodious clanging throughout the building. With a click and a whirr, the door opened automatically and she entered a spacious hallway. A blonde-haired receptionist who sat behind a large, curved wooden counter that resembled the bridge of a ship took her name and gestured her towards a group of sofas beside a large sailing ship in a glass case.

She sat down to wait for the shipowner to appear and was deep into trying to read the Norwegian newspaper that lay on the table when a group of dark-suited men walked in. She raised her head and studied the group. It wasn't hard to pick out her new acquaintance from the night before as his blond head ranged higher than those of the other men flanking him. He gave her a brief nod as he passed, while the rest of the group, after staring at her with unconcealed interest, moved away down the hall, disappearing from her view.

Silver searched in her bag to reassure herself that she had all her notes with her. But she couldn't find her pens – were they lying back in her hotel room? No pens, no camera! What an inauspicious start. Well, she'd just have to wing it.

After some minutes, the receptionist came towards her. 'Mr Rosenholm will see you now,' she told Silver and led her upstairs. She opened the door of a large, spacious office and gestured to Silver to enter. 'Here is Miss Fairfax to see you,' she said.

Her rescuer from the night before rose from behind his enormous desk and came towards Silver, his right hand outstretched, but his face unsmiling. He seemed much more formidable today than the evening before. He had changed from the friendly, easy-going man of yesterday into this buttoned-up, overly formal person. Silver searched for a reason for the sudden transformation. Maybe it was because he was at work and his responsibilities lay heavily on him.

Maybe she should make a joke to lighten the atmosphere.

'Thank you very much for leaving me some Norwegian money last night. That was very thoughtful of you. Please allow me to pay you back.' She tried a friendly smile to lighten the atmosphere.

'Miss Fairfax,' he said formally in an only slightly accented English. 'I hope you have recovered from your fright of yesterday. I must apologise on behalf of our city that such a thing should happen to you. I can assure you, it is most unusual. Please sit down.'

'Thank you,' said Silver. 'But I'm fine. I'll look around me more carefully next time.'

They sat down and Alexander Rosenholm leant forward. 'I can only give you half an hour for your interview as we are in the middle of some very delicate negotiations all this week,' he told her. 'My secretary will provide you with brochures and information.' Having dropped this small bombshell, he leant back again and steepled his fingers together, watching her.

Silver was taken aback. Of course! He was expecting a smoothly written publicity piece while she had entirely different intentions. A flash of annoyance swept through her. Her interview with him had been set up over a week ago. She'd travelled all the way to Norway for it. Half an hour was much too short a time to do a good in-depth interview, but she kept her mouth shut and said nothing. Better to hold her fire for later.

The pause lengthened between them. He sat in his chair behind his desk, looking through her as if she was a non-person, then he stirred himself. 'Well, Miss Fairfax?' His tone was only slightly less frosty.

She pulled herself together. She would certainly give him a hard time if that's how he wanted it. No friendliness, no quarter given. She drew out the small recorder and plonked it firmly on the large desk, brushing away his murmured offer of coffee. Notebook in hand, she realised she would have to ask to borrow a pen. A flush of embarrassment rose in her cheeks.

'May I...?' Her hand stretched out, and she lifted a pen from the selection on his desk and moved into reporter mode.

'Well, Mr Rosenholm,' she began. 'I believe that you have just become the owner of the shipping line. I am told you lost your father recently under tragic circumstances? What impact has this had upon you?'

He blinked, suddenly nonplussed.

She studied him, wondering what made him tick. What a beautiful mouth he had, well formed, generous but not too large. His hair was the colour of sun-ripened maize, but perhaps it needed cutting.

She jerked back into the task in hand as she became aware of him speaking. 'I'm only going to talk about our business, of course. Anything about the family is a private matter.'

'But the family is the business,' Silver retorted, as she snapped back into professional mode. Her journalist antennae moved into overdrive. Could the real story lie in what might be a family conflict? What was it that smouldered under the superficial appearance of a successful business? Involuntarily, she glanced up at the large portrait hanging on the wall. A strong-looking man with penetrating blue eyes just like Alexander's and the same thick hair stared back at her.

She pointed to the portrait. 'Is that your father?'

He nodded, and turning back from the portrait, she said: 'How long ago was it since your father died?'

'Three months ago.' His voice was curt and dismissive.

'Are you now the sole owner of the shipping company?'

'No, you are wrong,' he said, his eyes hard as flint stone.

'Since my father's death, my stepmother, my stepbrother and I hold equal shares in the business.'

'But you're the managing director, aren't you?' Silver probed further.

'I may be so, but my mother and my brother together control the board of directors, which is what counts. Very often, I have really very little say in the final decisions made for the company.' His lips closed firmly.

Silver took a few moments to ponder his enigmatic answer.

'Your father's death was very sudden. What actually happened?' she asked.

Alexander Rosenholm's mouth twisted. 'My father was killed in a fire out at our cottage.' He seemed to have to force the words out.

'Killed in a fire?' So Tom's suspicions were well founded. Aloud, Silver said: 'What a terrible thing.'

'The matter is under police investigation, so I have no comments to make on the situation at present.' He spoke stiffly, his face tinged with sadness, lines of strain showing round his eyes.

So now she had confirmation that all was not well in the Rosenholm business. Silver's mind raced. Had Alexander's father been murdered? Was it arson? Why should a respectable, wealthy man out on a remote island be murdered? Was it a burglary? Someone must have followed him there. It must have been planned. She'd have to search for other channels to investigate the facts about the shocking tragedy to circumvent Alexander Rosenholm if he was so determined to keep it under wraps. If she could get the story for Tom, what a coup that would be. Maybe she could even become a chief reporter.

She tried again: 'Was it an accident? Or was your father murdered?'

Alexander's face darkened. 'I told you, Ms Fairfax that the matter is still under investigation. Please do not press me for information.'

He rose suddenly from behind the desk and walked over to the huge window. 'Let me show you the beautiful view out over the harbour.' He stretched out his hand and just touched Silver's elbow as she came to stand beside him, and together they watched the white-winged gulls whirling and swooping in front of the window. She sensed he was struggling with strong emotions.

'What did happen to your father?' she persisted, pen and paper in hand.

Alexander's hand dropped back to his side. 'No comment,' he said. 'I will not be pressed further. I have absolutely no answers for you.'

The silence between them stretched into an empty awkwardness until Alexander said with an effort: 'Silver… that's a very unusual name.'

It was obvious she wasn't going to get anything more out of him at the moment, so Silver replied: 'I was christened Sylvia. Silver is my nickname,' she confided.

'I can see why. Your hair is like spun silver in certain lights.' He smiled at her, seeming to relax his guard for a moment.

They stood together admiring the scene below. A wave of his aftershave touched Silver's nostrils, a mixture of tangy lemon and tweed…and the fresh outdoors. The fiord sparkled under the clear blue sky, its arms reaching out to the distant islands. Down in the harbour, boats ranging from a large, white cruise ship, which dominated the scene, to smaller ferries and fishing boats bobbed on the dark blue waters. Oh, if only she had her camera. She turned towards him. 'Are any of your ships here, Mr Rosenholm?' she asked.

'Yes, the large white vessel over there is ours.' His voice rang with pride as he regarded the ship. 'She's on a summer cruise from New York to Bergen.'

Silver felt his blue eyes lingering on her face. 'Shall we get back to work?' she said too abruptly. Normally, she liked to nurse her interviewees along gently, allowing their confidence in her to grow so that she could lead them to confide more to her than they had originally intended. Her companion gestured towards the chair she had just vacated and they sat down again.

Under his steady gaze, she felt a slight flush spread warmly up her neck and cheeks. What was it about this man that put her off her stroke? She could handle Rottweilers with ease and this man was certainly not one of those.

'I know that your company has been very successful with its cruise ships,' she said, striving for neutral territory as she picked up her pen. 'I believe most of your ships sail in the Caribbean? How many do you own?'

'We have six vessels and, by next year, we shall have nine after the new ships have been delivered to us. They are being built in Japan,' Alexander Rosenholm replied.

'Who took the decision on the building of the new ships?' Silver asked.

'My father, of course, and we continue to work towards their purchase. My brother was in Monte Carlo at the time,' Alexander said. 'He doesn't always find it easy to tear himself away to attend board meetings and take part in company decisions. Then he allows me a free hand.' He gave her an ironic smile.

Silver studied Alexander. He certainly had amazing blue eyes, a mix of sky and sea, reminding her of Viking raids and ravaged women. She moved restlessly blotting out the uncomfortable feeling that he could see straight into her mind. She laid down her pen as her hand felt suddenly sticky.

'I believe your family has been in the shipping business for years,' she pressed on.

'We are third generation,' he said, taking the question in his stride. 'My grandfather started the business. My father carried it on and now it belongs to me and my brother, as well as my stepmother, as I told you before.' He paused for a moment. 'My real mother was the daughter of a sea captain, so the sea is strong in my blood.'

Silver made some quick notes. She was beginning to get a clearer picture.

'I think it would be easier for you if I showed you around our vessel,' said Alexander. 'You can write your article about that. As I said before, and apart from what I told you, I am not interested in talking about our family.'

Silver studied him. Now she knew why he was so reluctant to talk about his family, although he had let a few details slip out. There was a lot more to be uncovered here.

She took a deep breath. 'I would like to have taken some photographs of you down at the ship,' she said. 'But with the loss of my camera, I can't.' She sat forward in the chair. 'Does your company have a spare camera I could borrow?' Inner frustration at having to ask for this favour made her move restlessly in her chair. She jumped to her feet, sensing that she could inveigle more out of him when he was out by the ship.

'Of course,' he said. 'We do have a spare camera which we sometimes use when the tourists are here. We'll pick it up when we go downstairs.'

So easy and so helpful, despite her deceitful intentions. Guilt flushed Silver's cheeks and she kept her face carefully turned away.

Outside, the hot sunshine beat down on their heads as they turned towards the harbour. A fresh, salty breeze rose from the seawater, cooling Silver's hot cheeks as they strolled together across the thick wooden planks of the quay.

'Goodness, it's hot,' said Silver.

Alexander nodded. 'Yes, visitors don't expect the summer to be so warm in Norway. They expect us to have snow all year round!' He took off his jacket and slung it over his shoulder, revealing his white shirt. Then he loosened his tie. Suddenly, he looked more like the man of yesterday evening as he let go of his stuffy image.

Silver studied him covertly. He was a very attractive man, broad-shouldered with a restless energy about him.

'What a majestic ship,' she said quickly, admiring the swan-like lines of the vessel as the tall decks loomed up in front of them, huge anchor chains keeping the ship at rest in the harbour.

'Do you like her name?' asked Alexander.

'*The Guiding Spirit*', Silver read out loud from the blue and gold letters painted on the ship's hull.

'We're very proud of our fleet,' said Alexander. 'I'm looking forward to showing you around.' He seemed to have forgotten the half-hour limit he'd set on the interview.

Silver had the sense to keep her mouth firmly shut.

With Alexander leading, they mounted the narrow gangway. There was only one sailor, clad in white shorts, on watch at the entrance to the ship. He saluted and said: 'Welcome aboard, Mr Rosenholm.'

As far as Silver could see, there were no more formalities in easy-going Norway. Once on board the ship, they mounted the wide staircase, Silver in front, Alexander close behind. As she went up, Silver sensed his gaze on her as if he were drinking in every detail of her figure. That was a surprise. He seemed so unfrivolous and perfectly contained in himself. Had she misjudged him? She'd put him down as a hard-working and dedicated man who had little time for women, probably regarding them as unnecessary frills to his existence.

'Most of our passengers have gone on a tour of the city,' Alexander said. 'So it's a good time to show you around. Perhaps you'll decide to take a cruise with us one day. Come this way.' He gestured towards the elevator on the far side of the deck.

'We'll ride up,' he said. 'There are eight decks to climb up before we reach the restaurant. And then we'll go up onto the sun deck. The view from there is really stunning.'

Silver assented, inexplicably short of breath. As the small heels of her sandals tapped across the highly polished wood of the deck, a tall, dark man wearing well-pressed Bermuda shorts and a crisp, white open-necked shirt strode towards them.

'Knut,' Alexander's voice was full of chill. 'What are you doing here?' he spoke in English. 'I thought you were bent over the tables of Monte Carlo.'

'Well, brother dear,' the man said, his dark brown eyes raking both Silver and Alexander as a smile curved his lips. 'I thought you were bent over your desk, taking care of the family fortunes. It's not like you to be out playing, even with such a beautiful companion. That's more my style!' He winked at Silver.

Even though she wasn't standing very close to Alexander, Silver sensed a surge of controlled anger run through him, disturbing his air of aloofness, but his voice was mild. 'Look, I haven't got time to hang around here chatting with you, Knut.'

Ushering Silver ahead of him, he stepped into the elevator, but Knut put out his hand, barring the door from

29

closing. He shouldered his way inside, so that the three of them stood cramped together in the small space.

Silver stood quietly between the two brothers, watching them unobtrusively. Within the confined space of the lift, she sensed the tension rising in the two men, like two stags waiting to lock antlers. She was glad when the doors slid open silently and she was able to slip out of the cage onto what she guessed was the sun deck from the number of sun loungers and deck chairs spread around.

Quickening his steps, Alexander tried to manoeuvre Silver along the deck away from his brother, but Knut hung on. 'Come on, introduce me to your delightful friend, Al,' he persisted.

'My little brother, Knut. That is, my stepbrother, Knut – Ms Sylvia Fairfax.' Alexander's introduction was perfunctory and Silver's hand was suddenly encased in Knut's bronzed one. He bent his head and just brushed his lips against it. Silver smiled at his flowery courtesy, and Knut threw back his head and laughed, holding her eyes with his.

'Where are you going, brother dear?' asked Knut.

Alexander put his arm round Silver's shoulders. She was so surprised that she didn't draw away. He hadn't seemed like a touchy-feely type. 'We're going to have lunch and you're not invited, Knut,' he said.

Silver kept her head down. Alexander wasn't as cool and assured as she'd thought. He was certainly behaving childishly with his brother.

She shrugged her shoulders and detached herself from the two men. The breeze lifted her hair gently as she leaned against the ship's rail and gazed down at the blue fiord, many decks below. Tree-clad islands clustered around in the huge expanse of water, but only one channel of the fiord led out to the open sea beyond.

The ship's deck stretched invitingly in front of her. In the middle, an enormous turquoise-blue swimming pool beckoned to her. Deck chairs and sun loungers were placed all around it. Wishing that she could take a swim herself in its ozone-scented depths, Silver smiled at the passengers reclining in comfort in the sun loungers, lapping up the bright radiance of the sun.

The two brothers caught up with her. It seemed that their dispute was settled for the time being. Alexander led Silver back to the stairs and they walked down a couple of flights.

They crossed the large circular lobby and entered a small restaurant full of tables already set for an elaborate dinner. The head waiter appeared at once, hurrying forward to greet them. Alexander introduced him to Silver, and he fussed around her, finding her the best seat by a large porthole and handing her the menu.

'Do you know all your employees on board?' she asked, impressed by Alexander's easy and friendly manner with his staff.

'Our head waiter has sailed with us for many years, ever since he was a deck boy,' he told her. 'Besides, our ships aren't so big that we lose track of who's sailing on them.'

Silver leant back in her comfortable chair, relaxing in the atmosphere of well-cooked food and chilled white wine. The delicately prepared starter of pink Norwegian shrimps melted on her tongue.

Knut topped up her wine glass too quickly, despite Silver's protests, a glint of humour in his eyes. She left the glass untouched and sipped at her fizzy water, determined to keep a clear head. Up on the panelled wall hung paintings of stormy, seafaring scenes. The restless swell of the sea in these pictures surely reflected the brothers' relationship.

White-jacketed waiters served the little party unobtrusively and with a small sigh of contentment, Silver began to relax and enjoy herself, while the brothers seemed to have laid down their swords. Both of them were doing their best to entertain her with stories of their ships and life in Norway. She leaned back in her chair, feeling replete with the good food and wine.

A loud clanging noise broke out, startling her out of her pleasant, relaxed state. The ship's siren began to emit deafening shrieks. Everyone sat frozen in their seats.

'What's going on?' Silver grasped the wooden arms of her chair and looked around her. A strange hissing noise fizzed above her head. Two seconds later, an icy cold mist enveloped her, drenching her clothes. Her hair streamed and, for a moment, she was blinded by the thick blanket of moisture. Her nostrils were blocked and it was hard to catch her breath against the watery onslaught. She was drowning! She rubbed her hand over her nose and dashed the water from her eyes. She choked and tried to spit out the strange metallic-tasting water in her mouth, which she'd almost swallowed. Alexander shouted something to her, but the words were blotted out. For a moment, she remained sitting paralysed at the table.

He moved quickly over to her and almost dragged her out of her chair, propelling her towards the door of the restaurant. His warm body served as a barrier between her and the heavy mist sluicing down from the ceiling. Knut stumbled after them, cursing loudly. He collided with Silver, almost knocking her over as he grabbed a large tablecloth from a nearby table, upsetting all the glasses and cutlery with a crash. He wrapped the unwieldy white cloth around him and over his head for protection. Silver hid a smile. He looked like an Arab sheik in fancy dress.

Alexander hustled her out onto the main deck, where

everything seemed to be normal and undisturbed, although several of the cruise passengers strolling on deck turned in astonishment to stare at them.

Silver choked and spluttered. She pushed her dripping hair out of her eyes and looked at Alexander and Knut. 'Are you trying to drown me?' she gasped.

'How could you let this happen? Silver are you okay?' Knut turned away from her to hurl wild accusations at Alexander. 'How the hell did these sprinklers get turned on to drench us all?' The two brothers were so involved in their heated discussion that they quite overlooked Silver's distress as she stood shivering beside them.

'Oh, I'm freezing.' Silver glared at the two brothers, unhappily aware of how ridiculous she looked, with her dress clinging embarrassingly close to the contours of her body. Water was pooling at her feet. 'I can't leave the ship looking like this. Can't you do something about it? You can carry on arguing after we're dry.' She glared at them again.

Alexander took command immediately. He sent one of the scared-looking waiters to fetch the Chief Steward, who appeared swiftly. Knut pushed Alexander aside to address the steward. 'You'll have to come up with a really good explanation for this,' he said angrily. 'You've ruined our party. Is that how you treat the owners of this ship?'

Alexander stepped forward and tried to calm the situation with his more measured approach. 'Have you an explanation for what happened?' he asked. 'Was no one monitoring the sprinklers? And what about the security cameras? Did they pick up anything?'

'Oh, sir, I don't know what went wrong. Our sprinklers are inspected regularly. We'll launch an immediate investigation into the problem. The Captain will be down in a minute.' The Chief Steward's face was full of concern.

'Could it be sabotage?' Silver dashed the water out of her eyes and ventured the question.

Alexander looked taken aback and then brushed the suggestion aside quickly. 'Surely not. What would be the point of that?'

But Silver noticed he was frowning. He beckoned to a young stewardess and asked her to take Silver to a nearby cabin.

'Just look at you,' the stewardess said as she helped Silver to mop herself up in the cabin's luxurious surroundings, which were dominated by a huge bed in the middle with a blue woven silk bedcover. 'What a dreadful thing to happen. Your nice dress is all ruined.'

Silver smiled at her ruefully and towelled herself dry as best she could. She rubbed her hair vigorously with a soft blue towel that matched the bedcover and tried to smooth her tangled locks. 'What a sorry sight I look – like something dragged up from the fathoms of the sea,' she said staring at herself in the mirror. Her mascara had streaked and her hair curled wildly round her head after she gave it an extra rubbing with the towel.

She tore open the plastic packaging of a brand new tee-shirt with an artist's impression of the cruise ship on the front of it. The tee-shirt proclaimed '*The Guiding Spirit – Comfort and Class*'. It seemed to her a nice touch of irony as she pulled it over her head.

She emerged from the cabin dressed in the tee-shirt and some baggy cotton trousers, which were the best option the stewardess could find. She kept on her own underwear, which she was sure would soon be dry. Wiping down her damp sandals, she strapped them on again.

Outside in the passage, she found Alexander waiting impatiently for her. The stewardess reappeared behind him with a plastic bag and helped Silver to put her soaked dress into it.

Silver longed to make her escape and get back to her hotel so that she could change into her own clothes. She was desperate to examine her notes from the interview. Would they still be legible? She was even more worried about her – or rather Alexander's – camera.

'We'll dry and launder your clothes and return them to you later,' said Alexander. 'Look, Silver, I'm really sorry about what happened in the restaurant.' His heightened colour belied his calm demeanour.

'How did you escape the downpour?' said Silver, looking at his clothes. His smart business suit seemed to have withstood the water. She didn't think he'd even had to change his jacket. All she could see were a few large drops of water spattered over his clothing and a splash down the front where he had tried to shield her from the downpour. Silver pursed her lips. Suspicion flooded over her as she realised that only she and Knut had been soaked.

Alexander stiffened at her accusation. 'Just lucky, I suppose,' he said dismissively. 'You took the full blast of it and for that I'm truly sorry.'

He took Silver's arm persuasively. 'Look, say you'll come out with me this evening and we'll go to a restaurant up in the mountains where there is only good food and no sprinklers! Perhaps by then I'll have an explanation for you about what happened.' They stared at each other across a sudden ringing silence.

Silver looked into his intense blue eyes, trying to make up her mind. Was he just trying to butter her up so that she wouldn't make trouble? Was he involved in the murky dealings that Tom was so interested in?

'To make up for the awful thing we've done to you,' he pressed her.

His hand on her arm made her heart skip a beat. She sucked in her breath. If she rushed off like a scared rabbit, she'd never get her story and she was convinced that she was just at the start of a vital discovery.

'I refuse to take no for an answer,' he said stonewalling her in his careful formal English.

'This evening, then,' she nodded.

Down on the quay, she was less certain. Had she done the right thing in agreeing to go out with him? But surely it wouldn't do any harm to have dinner with him. He owed her that!

She hoped that Knut wouldn't appear as well. She'd had enough of the two brothers together, egging one another on to more and more outrageous sparring. It was no fun for an outsider, but perhaps she could get Knut on his own later to ask about his father's tragic death.

But what was she thinking about? She never usually accepted invitations from her interviewees. It was much more professional to keep a certain distance between herself and the person she was interviewing.

She turned away from the harbour and broke into a run, her feet pounding the pavement. Hopefully, no one would notice her too large trousers and bedraggled hair. She'd refused both Alexander's and Knut's offers to drive her back to Hotel Norge as she sure needed some breathing space from them both. The town of Bergen was small, like an old lady, in voluminous skirts, friendly and unassuming. She felt herself getting calmer as she jogged past the brightly coloured wooden houses and the small shops dotted along the waterfront.

Silver whisked quickly through the hotel lobby and into the lift. She didn't want any awkward questions from the hotel receptionist. Why was it that since she came to Norway she seemed to attract bad luck to her like a magnet, falling into one scrape after another?

Back in her room she looked once again at her hair in the mirror. Now it hung in miserable rats' tails round her face. She went into the bathroom and turned on the shower. The water splashing down into the bath reminded her sharply of her soaking in the ship's restaurant. She hesitated for a moment before forcing herself to step in under it. The soothing warm water spurted down as she washed her hair thoroughly to get rid of the strange grittiness from the sprinklers. There must have been some chemicals in the water. She found it hard to work up a proper lather of her shampoo as her hair was so sticky. Afterwards, it seemed to take an extra long time to dry her hair and get it to fluff up again.

In her bedroom, she searched through her meagre wardrobe. She'd only brought a few clothes with her, so she didn't have much choice of what to wear and she had already ruined one pair of jeans at the fair. She didn't plan to get too dressed up anyway for her evening out with Alexander. But she spent a long time putting on her make-up and ended up almost wiping it all off again in her efforts to achieve the fresh-faced natural look.

She looked at her watch and saw that two hours had passed since her unexpected drenching. It was nearly six o'clock in the evening, early to be going out on a date. But it wasn't a date, of course. It was just a generous gesture by Alexander to butter her up after the soaking she'd got. The telephone by her bedside rang and she jumped, smudging the mascara she was so carefully drawing over her lashes.

Her mouth set in determined lines. Right, Alexander, you're in for a grilling!

Chapter 3

Silver walked down the stairs to the hotel lobby. Alexander strode towards her looking casual and relaxed. His deep blue eyes sparkled with suppressed excitement. In a fresh pale blue, open-necked shirt and chinos, he was a very different person from his buttoned-up and stiff-suited image of the morning. Silver was glad she hadn't put on a light dress. Her shirt and cotton trousers were just right. He held out his hand and gave hers a firm shake.

'Hello again, Silver,' he said, a slow smile of pleasure lighting up his face. 'Ready for an adventure?'

Yes, oh yes, very ready for an adventure with you! Silver's inner voice caught her by surprise. Mentally, she slapped herself down and aloud, she said: 'I'm ready. Where are we going?'

'Wait and see!' Alexander said.

They left the hotel and walked out onto the street, Silver automatically looking round for a car.

Alexander picked up on this and laughed. 'No car today,' he said. 'We Norwegians like to walk whenever we can.'

Silver looked at him from under her eyelashes. Yes, he was a really good-looking man. 'How are you? I hope you're none the worse for your soaking,' he said.

Silver gave an airy laugh. She hadn't quite got over the experience. 'I hope you're not going to try that trick on me again,' she said.

'I can't apologise enough for what happened. Our ships are carefully serviced and maintained. I'll get to the bottom of this, I assure you.'

Silver looked at him sceptically: 'Heads will roll, you mean?' She couldn't resist needling him a bit.

'Let's forget it for now.' Alexander's tone was slightly irritated as he strode ahead along the pavement. 'Now I want to show you Bergen from the roof of the city. We're going to take the funicular up the mountainside and then we can eat at the restaurant at the top.'

Silver nodded. 'That should be fun. Is it far to walk?'

'Just around here,' said Alexander, turning the corner and leading the way into a small stone building, full of humming and clicking machinery. A strange-looking red cable car sloped sharply upwards and balanced on the rails leading up the mountainside.

Alexander bought two tickets and they boarded the cable car, which had rows of seats rising above one another like huge steps. It filled up quickly and Alexander moved along the seat to make room for the boarding passengers until he was sitting close against Silver. As his warm thigh pressed closely against hers, he looked into her eyes and smiled. So he was not unmoved either. But she inched further away along the seat, resisting the pull of attraction. She had to keep a professional distance, otherwise she'd find it hard to write an unbiased story.

The red tram car chugged and rattled its way up the steep hill. As it travelled higher, Silver looked down on the red and black rooftops of Bergen. Midway up, the tram paused at a station to allow a black car to cross the rails and pass on its way down to the city. At the top, it clanged to a halt and the passengers disgorged, vanishing swiftly in different directions. Outside, Silver inhaled the clear, sharp air as they walked through the rows of tall pine trees whispering in the breeze. Together she and Alexander climbed higher and higher above the city.

'Let's walk to the top of the hill first so that you can look down,' said Alexander. 'There's a stunning view over the fiord.'

The fiord stretched out far below, with ferry boats and other small craft weaving busily in and out of the islands. The large, white cruise ship still rode at anchor in the harbour, towering over the smaller vessels and fishing boats. Silver suppressed a shudder. The thought of ever taking a cruise on board that ship didn't appeal to her at all.

'What happened? Why did all these sprinklers come on?' The need for an explanation from Alexander nagged at her.

He looked uncomfortable. 'I can't apologise enough,' he said. 'We don't know yet why they came on and we're still investigating. Such a thing has never happened before. Either there was a fault in the system or someone must have got into the control room and turned on the fire alarm, which sets off the sprinklers. That's all we know so far.'

'Someone got into the control room? Don't you monitor what's going on throughout the ship?' Silver spoke sharply, because it seemed very strange that the sprinklers could turn themselves on so easily without a hint of smoke or fire. There must have been a serious fault. Or could it have been sabotage? Alexander seemed very close-lipped about that. But the shipping company would lose all its passengers if it didn't protect its equipment better.

'How often do the sprinklers blast off like that?'

'It's never happened ever before. It's a complete mystery. I told you, we're investigating.' Alexander's tone was curt as if trying to cover his embarrassment. He took Silver's arm and hurried her along the path through the trees. She tried to release herself. She didn't like being hustled along like this, just because he didn't want to talk about something that made him feel uncomfortable. She succeeded in pulling away and turned round to face him on the path.

'Was it Knut?' she asked. 'Was it a trick he played? Perhaps on me or perhaps on you? Maybe he intended to spoil my visit and to make me write something detrimental about your shipping line. Could that be the reason?'

Alexander pursed his lips. 'Maybe it was Knut,' he agreed. 'But remember, it's his shipping line too. Besides, he was with us all the time and he got soaked just like you.'

'But you didn't,' said Silver, her suspicions flaring. 'You kept out of it. You only got a few drops in your hair and some splashes on your clothes, which you brushed off easily. Maybe it was you. It's well known you don't like journalists!'

Alexander's face was hot and furious. 'How can you say that,' he forced out between clenched teeth. 'Why would I invite you up here for a pleasant evening out if I didn't mean to try and make it up to you?'

Silver was momentarily silenced by this argument. Now it was her turn to feel embarrassed. She should have weighed her words more carefully.

'I'm sorry,' she said. 'I'm still a bit jittery about the things that keep happening to me since I came to Norway. I'm not used to being robbed and then half drowned!'

'Truce,' Alexander stretched out his hand and Silver took it. He held her eyes with his until she felt her cheeks flushing and a surreptitious warmth creep through her body. She turned sharply and climbed upwards between the feathery fronds of the trees. Alexander followed and began to point out landmarks.

Across the blue expanse of water, a tall dark stave

church stood like a sentinel on one of the islands. It reminded her of one of the masted schooners of old. To her left was the ferry terminal poised on one of the arms of the fiord, where the ships left for England.

Alexander moved in close behind her. 'There's the cairn of stones marking the highest peak in the mountains round here,' he said. His voice in her ear resonated in places she didn't even want to think about.

Her arm brushed against his, sending an electric current rushing through her. 'You make the perfect tourist guide.' She smiled at him, now feeling free and relaxed as together they looked down on the small city below. It was peaceful standing among the graceful pine trees, with only a few other walkers out enjoying the evening air.

At the top of the path, an outdoor restaurant sprawled over the gravel, with tables covered by snowy white cloths. Several people were already enjoying their evening meal as Alexander led the way to one of the tables.

'You must try our Norwegian beer,' he said. 'It's very refreshing.'

He ordered for them, and they sat there in the evening sunshine. Two tall glasses of light-coloured beer stood on the table in front of them, small bubbles rising. Alexander leaned back and smiled at Silver. He handed her the large menu and as their hands touched, Silver's heartbeat surged.

The harsh ringing of Alexander's mobile shattered their harmony. He picked it up and looked at the display. Jumping up from his chair, he moved a short distance away towards a group of pine trees and turned his back on Silver.

She sat at the table, watching him as he raised one of his shoulders as if to shut her out. It was clear it was a very private conversation. Another woman, perhaps? Someone as attractive as Alexander couldn't be without attachments. He was speaking fast in Norwegian, almost barking into the mobile, so perhaps he wasn't talking to a woman. There were long pauses in the conversation as he listened intently. He turned towards Silver and studied her. It was obvious he was talking about her to the other person on the line.

The conversation ended and Alexander returned to the table. Silver saw his face was grey and drawn. He sat down. 'That's our evening blown away,' he said. 'I'm so sorry, Silver. I have to get back immediately. They're sending a car for me. It's on its way up now.'

Silver was stunned. That wasn't what she expected at all. 'What's wrong?' she asked. 'Is someone ill? Or is there actually a fire this time and the sprinklers don't work?'

Alexander seemed to collect his thoughts and come back from a long way off. 'That was Captain Johansen on *The Guiding Spirit*. They've found some stowaways on the ship. I've got to get back and see what has happened. The police have been called and they're busy searching to find out if there are any more people concealed on board.' His voice was automatic, staccato.

He rose from the table, his gaze raking the open space in front of the restaurant to where there was a small car park. Silver could see that he had almost forgotten her. With what seemed like an effort, he said: 'I don't think you'd better come back with me.' You'd only be in the way...the thought hung in the air between them as clearly as if he'd shouted it.

'Please take the funicular back down to town.' He fumbled in his pocket and thrust both tickets at her. Then he dragged out a couple of notes and threw them on the table to pay for the beers.

'Sorry, Silver,' Alexander's face was strained. Turning away from her, he ran swiftly towards a large Cherokee jeep which was pulling into the car park. The driver's door swung open, and a young man jumped out and ran around to the passenger side. Alexander leapt into the driver's seat, and the big vehicle drove off with a strident squeal of tyres and a scattering of small stones. 'I'll be in touch,' Alexander's voice floated back to her.

Silver stood alone. Stowaways on the ship. Now that really was a story! I'll be right behind you, Alexander – just try and stop me.

She turned back to find the other restaurant guests staring at her with great interest. She felt foolish, as if she had been dumped in full view of everyone. Fun for them, she thought as she picked up the tickets Alexander had flung down.

She rode down on the funicular. Busy with her thoughts, she didn't see any of the fir and pine trees slipping past the window, nor how the mountainside fell away steeply as the cable car rattled down the rails back to the city. Who could these mysterious stowaways be and where had they come from, and why? What kind of people would try to sneak on board a luxurious cruise ship? For a joke? Could it be people looking for work? She wondered if they were Norwegian or if they were from other countries. And the sprinklers suddenly blasting forth – was there a connection there? Of course, people were always trying to board ships to cross the English Channel – illegal immigrants trying to get into England in search of a better life. But a cruise ship – was that possible? And taking a leap in the dark, Silver asked herself if they could have any connection with the death of Alexander's father, Frederick Rosenholm, founder of the shipping line?

Now the Rosenholm story had really been ramped up. There was a lot for her to dig up. If Alexander or Knut wouldn't tell her more about the shipping company or give any explanation about what had happened on board the ship today, she would just have to seek out someone who could. So who could she approach?

What about Frederick Rosenholm's widow? Probably she still lived in Bergen.

The funicular bounced to a stop and the doors slid back. The passengers streamed out onto the platform, drawing Silver with them. She left the little station and ran down the steep hill to the road leading back to her hotel. Her mind was made up. She'd start by asking at the hotel about the widow Rosenholm. There were other ways to find out things without getting Alexander involved, and she certainly wouldn't ask his permission to visit his stepmother. He'd be bound to head her off. Feeling pleasantly rebellious, Silver turned into the lobby of the Hotel Norge.

'Damn, damn, damn.' Alexander didn't often swear. Usually, he managed to keep his feelings under control, his demeanour icy calm.

Just as he was beginning to lighten up and to get things into perspective, that call on his mobile reminded him that he couldn't take time out. Perhaps it was all for the best. He hadn't time to get involved with enticing women journalists. Silver was much too attractive and she seemed sincere, but he wasn't going to be taken for a ride again. He hadn't time for women really. His broken engagement to Mariella had made him very wary indeed.

Now in the passenger seat, the young man who'd driven the jeep up the mountain looked at him uneasily as the car bucketed down the steep and curving road. Alexander knew he was driving much too fast, spinning the steering wheel, his foot hard down on the accelerator as if a set of demons were on his back shouting: 'Faster! Faster! Faster!'

Problems were piling up on top of him. First, the strange business with the sprinklers and now these stowaways on the ship. Damned strange. How could these people have got past the seamen on watch? How many of these unwanted passengers had sneaked aboard? He hadn't managed to drag the actual number out of Captain Johansen. He seemed very reluctant to give even a rough assessment. But at least the man had taken quick action in calling Alexander and the police as well. For once, Alexander hoped that Knut had been dragged away from whatever club or pub he was carousing in and brought in to help.

He braked with a grinding screech and flung himself out of the vehicle, locking it with the remote before he started to run across the quay. There were several police cars parked askew along the quay where the ship was berthed, their blue lights still flashing. The loud buzzing of engines drew his attention to some high-speed inflatable boats spinning in towards them across the harbour. With so many police drafted in, they must be taking the incident seriously.

A policeman in a black leather jacket and peaked cap came towards him. He tried to stop Alexander from breaking through into the area cordoned off with red and white plastic streamers. But Alexander shouldered him off and took the gang plank two strides at a time. Captain Johansen appeared breathlessly and explained to the policeman that Alexander was the owner of the ship.

He ran up onto the main deck. How could the stowaways have got on board? There were security cameras throughout the ship and they were monitored from the ship's bridge. Surely they weren't out of action?

'How many people have you found stowed away here, officer?' Alexander snapped at the policeman standing there.

'A stash of five or six, sir,' said the policeman. 'But we've not finished our search.'

Alexander strode over to the other side of the deck where three policemen were holding a group of dark-haired individuals. Their captives weren't putting up any resistance, and were poorly clothed and undernourished. One of them seemed to be suffering from a heavy cold as his nose was running and he made no effort to wipe it.

'What are you doing here on this ship?' Alexander towered above them, and three of the six men shrank back from him while the others stood stoically, their faces blank.

'We've looked for their papers, sir,' said the policeman. 'But they don't have many of these. As far as we can make out, they're Russian. We don't know what they're doing here or where they're trying to get to. We'll have to take them in for questioning with an interpreter. Perhaps you could come down to the station with us while we sort things out.'

Alexander heard an angry shout. Knut came rushing across the deck, brushing aside the policeman, who was trying to stop him.

'What trouble are you in now, brother dear?' he said insolently. 'Do you know who these people are?' His eyes slid sideways as Alexander tried to hold his gaze.

'And what about you, brother dear?' Alexander retorted. 'Perhaps you know something about these people? We've never had stowaways on board before.'

One of the stowaways stretched out his hand beseechingly to Knut, but Knut pushed it away and turned his back on the man. He strode off angrily as the police officers began to round up the small group and march them out to the waiting police cars.

Alexander hadn't failed to notice the interaction between the stowaway and Knut. What was Knut playing at? Just wait till he got hold of him and dragged it out of him. Alexander tried to reject the thought of Knut being involved, but it preyed on his mind.

There wasn't time to grill Knut about that now. There was too much to be sorted out. There was a long chain of events, beginning with his father's death in the fire out at the cottage three months ago. Now there was this new stowaway problem.

And Silver, she was another pain in the butt. Thank God, she wasn't here. That would really have given her something to write about. It was hard to think of her as a hard-nosed journalist, except when she fixed her green eyes on him with that piercing stare.

He paused in a moment's reflection. He must take care not to get involved with someone with an open line to the newspaper headlines. He wasn't going to let thoughts of Silver deter him from his purpose.

He was sorry he hadn't been able to take Silver back to her hotel, but he was the one who had to take charge at the ship. Knut couldn't be relied on, and anyway he was behaving very oddly. Pushing these thoughts from his mind, Alexander jumped into the waiting jeep and drove off to the police station to see if there were any answers to be found there.

Silver struck out in the direction of the harbour to see what was happening there. There was no way Alexander was going to stop her. She couldn't miss the chance of catching a real story and, if she was quick, she might even get it sent off to Tom in London, showing him that she was really on the job. That would serve Alexander right and show him that she wasn't to be trifled with. Why had Alexander rushed off and abandoned her so quickly? Why couldn't he have offered her a ride down to the city with them? Was he trying to hide something?

Because of Alexander's caginess, she was even more eager to talk to some of the other family members. The widow Rosenholm was her next port of call – to put it nautically! But first to the harbour to see what was going on there.

She walked across the quayside, the small camera which she'd borrowed from Alexander gripped firmly in her hand. In front of her *The Guiding Spirit* loomed ten decks high into the clear blue sky. The police had already cordoned off the area alongside the ship with red and white plastic tape to keep back any too interested bystanders.

She raised the camera to take a shot of the scene. Out of nowhere, a large white car came racing towards her with *Politi* emblazoned in blue letters on the side. Stubbornly, Silver held her ground until the car slid to a stop beside her. The leather-jacketed driver, with his peaked cap, rolled down his window and in a sharp voice said something unintelligible to her.

Silver looked at him firmly in the eye. 'Sorry, I don't understand Norwegian.'

In a milder tone, he said: 'Put that camera away. No unauthorised visitors here. If you have no business here, please leave the area.' He made a shooing movement with his hand.

Silver retreated to the side of the quay. Making herself as inconspicuous as possible, she ducked behind some of the many pallets piled high with provisions waiting to be loaded onto the ship. From her hidden vantage point, she peeked out and saw the police car sweep away. Then she crept out again, pulling out her camera. Tall pallets of polythene-wrapped stores blocked her way, making it hard to get the right angles for the shots she wanted of the ship, so she slipped under a railing and climbed up some stone steps to get a better view.

Despite several other police cars parked on the quayside, their blue lights flashing, the crew in their sky blue overalls, clipboards in hand, went about their work of overseeing and tallying the loading of the stores. Silver came down the steps back onto the quayside, just sidestepping one of the forklift trucks whizzing past.

'Hi, will the ship be leaving soon?' she asked one of the blue-clad sailors who was checking one of the giant packages stacked on the quay.

'Yes, ma'am, quite soon, we've already been delayed,' he said.

'Why's that?' asked Silver.

'A fault in the firefighting system – the sprinklers were faulty. Safety's a top priority for us.' He leaned against the plastic-covered package and smiled admiringly at her.

Silver twinkled demurely at him. 'What was wrong with the sprinklers?' she asked.

'Seems like someone lit a cigarette near one of the fire-detection devices.'

'Someone lit a cigarette?' Silver prompted. 'What do you mean? Who would do that?'

'Yeah, yeah, I shouldn't have told you that,' he shuffled his feet uncomfortably.

Silver's mind made a swift connection. 'Didn't you have some stowaways slip on board?' she asked. 'Was it perhaps one of them?'

'I don't know. I can't tell you that – mum's the word,' he said, tapping his nose. 'Sorry ma'am, I can't tell you any more.' His heightened colour revealed his discomfort.

'How many were there?' Silver persisted.

'Nine or ten. I never saw them all.' He began shoving the pallet towards the next fork-lift truck. 'They were poor creatures. We had a whip-round on board and gave them some clothes and cash. There were women and kids with them as well. They'd taken refuge in the utility rooms on the lower decks.'

'Where did they come from?' Silver followed him across the quayside and shot the next question at him.

'Russia or somewhere like that.'

'How did they get onto the ship?'

'Cunning lot,' he said. 'They came in on a small boat and managed to smash one of the portholes on the sea side. Bold as you please, but the poor sods were shivering with cold and drenched through when we found them. Ship's siren went off.' The seaman stopped abruptly and shuffled his feet. He glanced up at the ship, a look of uneasiness crossing his features.

Had he caught sight of the captain or one of the ship's officers? Hmm, she'd probably pushed him too hard with all her questions. He'd expected a light bantering conversation and here she was grilling him for all she was worth. It sometimes happened that way. People were misled by her looks. Her light fair hair and big green eyes looked so innocent and disarming on the surface. Then they'd find out that they'd got a tiger reporter on their tail.

'Look, ma'am, I'm sorry.' The seaman turned away from her. 'I've got a job to do.'

He was definitely running scared. He turned his back on her and began to tally some more pallets. Silver lifted the small camera again to frame a new view of the ship. If she got her scene properly focused and was very quick, she might get a good shot catching some of the seagulls as they swooped in front of the ship. That would give some movement to the scene. But what a story she had to give Tom.

She broke into a run.

Chapter 4

In the morning, Silver was feeling pleased with the story she had written on her laptop. Last night, she'd emailed it over to Tom who as ever was working late at *The Ocean Observer*. As she was brushing her hair, the telephone at her bedside suddenly shrilled.

'There's a gentleman here in the lobby waiting to see you,' the receptionist told her.

Gentleman? Who would that be? Silver fluffed out her hair and slicked on some lipstick. Humming a light tune under her breath, she descended the stairs. Immediately, her eye caught Alexander, dressed in white shirt and sharply tailored grey suit, pacing up and down in long panther-like strides.

'Alexander, what are you doing here?' She called, feeling slightly uneasy.

Tight-lipped, he stopped in front of her barring her way. 'You wrote an article about our company last night.' He thrust a newspaper in front of her nose.

'Yes,' said Silver, standing her ground. 'I don't think you'll find any mistakes.'

She took the paper from him and studied the article under her byline. The picture looked good, it was just a pity that she hadn't managed to get one of the stowaways.

He seized it back from her and stabbed his finger against it. 'Don't you know you could damage our business irrevocably with your loose talk? The story's quoted in some of the other papers too – and it's your fault. Now it's spread worldwide.' He was almost spitting at her.

'Loose talk?' Silver felt her own temperature rising and took a firm grip on it. 'I assure you that every word was weighed and measured, and the facts were checked. Do you deny there were stowaways aboard your ship last night?'

'Well, that's all dealt with now,' said Alexander, tight lipped. 'The authorities have taken care of them.'

'Don't you feel any compassion for these poor people? Can't you imagine what they have gone through? The discomfort, the cold, the fear – and their hopes must have all fallen to ashes when they were dragged away by the police.' Silver was in danger of losing control of her own emotions. Stick to the facts, stick to the facts, my girl. Her breathing quickened and her heart slammed hard against her ribs. 'There were women and even children as well.' She spoke more calmly than she felt.

'Well, they were illegally on board my ship!' Alexander hissed at her. 'Don't you dare write anything more about us – I forbid you!' He shook his finger threateningly at her.

Turning on his heel, he strode out of the lobby, the glass doors leaping wide at his approach.

Silver stood trembling after his onslaught. No one had attacked her like that ever before. He'd bawled her out as if she was a shivering seaman. She straightened her shoulders. 'I will find out more about your business and I will write a big story to hit the headlines,' she muttered to herself. 'Just wait till I find out more, Alexander Rosenholm.'

Trying to block her contretemps with Alexander out of her mind, she entered the hotel dining room. She realised she was starving as she hadn't had any supper yesterday. She'd been so busy writing her story for *The Ocean Observer* that she'd forgotten to eat. Her mouth watered as she saw the Norwegian breakfast, with its huge array of *koldtbord* spread out over an enormous table. Again, the centrepiece was a large pink salmon, head still on and artistically decorated with tomatoes, asparagus and mayonnaise. Also on the table was the famous brown goat's milk cheese, just like a giant toffee, and all kinds of pickled herring, salami and other sliced meats. An assortment of yellow and white cheeses was laid out attractively. She picked up an apple from the great dish of fresh fruit and filled a glass with orange juice. The guests staying at the hotel, who seemed mostly to be tall Norwegians, were piling their plates high and nearly all of them carried a large glass of milk.

Silver walked round the table trying to make up her mind what to put on her plate. Her attention was on the food and she almost collided with a bespectacled man of about fifty with greying hair.

'I'm so sorry, there's so much to choose from that I wasn't looking where I was going,' she said, moving quickly out of his way. But he followed her anyway.

'It's really neat to meet someone who speaks English. I get tired of hearing nothing but foreign voices!'

'You're American,' she said. 'I'm English. I suppose you could say we were two kinds of foreigners.'

'Chuck Shelton,' he introduced himself. 'You here on vacation?'

'Yes, well no...' Silver paused. Then she thought: What have I to hide? 'I'm here to do an interview with some shipowners,' she told him. 'My name's Sylvia Fairfax, also known as Silver.'

'I get it. It's your shiny fair hair. Very nice,' he said. 'Mind if I share your table?'

Silver sized him up quickly. Probably not a threat, but after her experiences at the funfair and on the ship yesterday, she was much more on her guard. With his brindled hair, he looked like a big shaggy dog waiting for a pat. Surely she was safe enough here in a large international hotel? Besides, she was still trying to shake off the effects of the day before as well as her recent run-in with Alexander. She needed some easy, laid-back company as a change from the Rosenholms and their problems.

'Yes, of course you can sit here,' she said. He collected his coffee cup and newspaper from another table and placed himself on a chair opposite her.

'Shipowners, did you say? Which ones? It's such a small community here in Bergen. We know them all.'

Silver shifted uncomfortably. 'It's one of the big ones,' she said in a non-committal way.

Chuck raised his eyebrows. 'Have you read the newspaper today?'

Silver looked at him questioningly. He spread the Norwegian newspaper out in front of her.

Her breath caught in her throat as she looked at the large picture covering three columns of the front page. In the background, she could see the name *The Guiding Spirit* on the bow of the ship. Several police cars were parked haphazardly along the quay. In the foreground, a group of black leather-jacketed policemen were holding on to some rather shabby looking people. She could just make out what she thought might be Alexander's back on the left side of the picture. He seemed to be in earnest conversation with one of the policemen. She struggled to understand the Norwegian headline of the article. *Blind passengerer?* What on earth was that? She turned questioningly to Chuck.

'Oh, it means stowaways,' Chuck told her. 'That shipowner's in real trouble. They've found a whole stash of stowaways on his fancy cruise ship. Nobody knows how they got there.'

Silver's roll slipped out of her fingers and fell, buttered side down on the tablecloth.

'Hey, hey, don't get upset,' said Chuck. 'It's nothing to do with you. Or is it?' His eyes were shrewd as he studied her face.

'You speak Norwegian, don't you?' said Silver. 'Can you tell me what it says?'

'Yeah, I travel here often to sell life-saving equipment to the fishermen,' said Chuck. 'I've learned a bit of the language so they can't pull a fast one on me when they talk among themselves.' He smirked at Silver.

Pulling the newspaper closer to him, he translated: 'Yesterday, nine stowaways were found on board the cruise ship *The Guiding Spirit* owned by Frederick Rosenholm & Co. The ship is currently visiting the City of Bergen before sailing to the Caribbean. The stowaways appear to be illegal immigrants who have come from Russia or the Ukraine, but it is unclear how they managed to board the ship.'

Well, I explained that in my story, Silver thought. And some other facts as well.

'The problem of illegal immigrants from Russia and the Ukraine is an increasing one as the immigrants have been deterred from crossing the common border between Russia and Finland due to much stricter border controls there,' he continued. 'They have therefore found it easier to cross the border between Russia and Norway, where the controls are less strict.'

Chuck raised his head from the newspaper and looked at Silver, his eyes shrewd and penetrating behind his glasses. 'Is this the shipping line you're writing about?'

Silver looked at him warily, weighing her words.

'Come on now, I can see from your face that you know these people,' Chuck pressed her, once again reminding her of a friendly dog bouncing around, eager for her to drop a bone of information his way.

'Yes, I do,' said Silver, exhaling the breath she had been holding tightly. 'I know about these stowaways, and there was some problem with the sprinklers on board the cruise ship. I don't know the exact connection between them.'

Her lips curved into a secret smile when she remembered how Knut had pulled the tablecloth round him looking like a dishevelled Arab sheik when the sprinkler water poured down on him.

New questions confronted her. How much more did Alexander know about these stowaways? And what about Knut? Could he be involved as well?

She turned to Chuck. 'Since you've been around in Bergen for so long, do you know anything about these Rosenholms?' she asked him. 'Have you ever met any of them?'

'No, never,' he said. 'But I do know the father died about three months ago under suspicious circumstances. Not much was written about it in the newspapers, because the family is very powerful and influential and managed to suppress a lot of information. I think they own a lot of the businesses in Bergen as well as the cruise line.'

Silver sat forward on the edge of her chair. She'd forgotten all about her breakfast. Her plate with its array of food lay untouched on the table. 'Go on,' she prompted.

Chuck took a gulp of coffee. 'There's one hell of a mystery in that family. Ask anyone, but these Norwegians hang together and all you get is a cold stare as they close ranks. There are two sons, who inherited the shipping line, which, under the father, was a very successful one. Everyone is wondering if the sons can carry on his work as successfully as he did. I think the mother is involved too.'

'That's three of them. So the sons have just taken over recently?'

'Yeah, the police are still investigating what happened. It seems the old man died in a fire at a remote cottage.'

'Yes, I've heard that,' said Silver carefully. 'Do you know anything more about it?'

'I told you, the Rosenholms are very powerful and keep what happened as much as possible under wraps.'

Silver's fingers were itching. What a huge story if only she could uncover it. Her professional instincts were in full flow.

'Where do the Rosenholms live?' she asked. 'Do you know that?'

'They've got a great big white house on an island in the fiord. You ought to go there if you want to see how they live.'

Silver was spurred into action. 'Do you know the name of the island?'

'Rosenholm, of course,' said Chuck. 'Why don't you go down to the harbour and see if you can find a boat to take you out there?'

After calling in at the bank to pick up some funds electronically transferred by Tom in London, Silver turned towards the harbour. The tall, white cruise ship still rode at anchor, dominating the scene, but all that remained of the previous night's events was the red and white plastic tape set up to keep out strangers. Two seamen now stood watch at the bottom of the entrance gangway holding special scanners in their hands to check the passenger identity cards. Security had certainly been stepped up since her visit of yesterday.

She turned her back on the ship and, warmed by the sun behind her, she walked quickly along the quayside to where the smaller boats were moored. The blue arms of the fiord stretched into infinity and the Bergen archipelago was dotted with islands of all sizes and shapes. Silver paused for a moment, wondering which one was Rosenholm. She wasn't even sure if it was possible to see it from the shore where she stood. A row of fishing boats bobbed at their moorings, so it shouldn't be too hard to find a boatman to ferry her across.

The seagulls whirled and swooped. And in Silver's nostrils, the smell of fish was overpowering. At last, her eye caught a man who sat on the deck of his fishing boat mending some nets. 'Hello,' she called, waving strongly to catch his attention. 'Hello, hello!'

Reluctantly, he heaved himself to his feet and came towards her.

'Could you take me out to an island in the fiord? I'd pay you well,' she shouted cupping her hands in front of her mouth.

'No speak English,' he said, turning his back on her abruptly and returning to his nets.

Silver's arm dropped by her side, but she pushed herself onwards, picking her way over coils of rope and piles of fishing nets. Her foot slipped on the traces of oil left on the quay as the seagulls screamed derisively at her. The breeze blew in freshly off the sea and she pulled her light blue jacket more closely round her.

Four boats along, another fisherman stood on the deck of his small craft, arms akimbo. Crates containing neat lines of silvery fish were stacked up beside him. The boat rocked rhythmically on its moorings as the fisherman fixed Silver with a deliberate stare. His straggly red beard covered his jutting chin and he didn't seem particularly friendly. But Silver was not going to be put off. She'd nothing to lose.

'Could you take me out to one of the islands in the fiord?' she asked, her voice trailing off as she watched him spit into the water. She tried again: 'Could you…?' She held up some crisp Norwegian kroner bills, thanks to Tom's efficient arrangements, and waved them at him. 'I'd pay you well if you'll take me to Rosenholm Island.'

'*Privat, privat,*' he said. 'No people go.' He too turned his back on her.

Silver stepped away from the edge of the quay and looked around her. It was harder than she expected. How ever was she going to get out to the island if no one would hire out his boat? The fishermen seemed hostile, but perhaps it was the language problem. On the other hand, they didn't seem to be interested in earning extra money. She squared her shoulders, determined to keep asking until someone agreed to take her. Nobody was going to stop her getting out to the island.

'Hiya,' said a voice behind her. She spun round. It was Chuck.

Silver's heart lifted. 'You sent me on a wild goose chase,' she said. 'They don't seem at all keen to take me out to the island.'

'I thought you might be having trouble,' he said. 'As I don't have any meetings until after lunch, I came down to see if you'd got a ride.'

'Just in time,' said Silver. 'I can't get them to budge. I've asked several boatmen and offered them money. I said I'd pay them well. But they all refuse.'

Chuck laughed. 'They're proud, these Norwegian fishermen. They won't be bought.'

'I'm only asking for a boat ride,' said Silver. 'Nothing else. You'd think they'd want to earn a little extra.'

'C'mon then,' said Chuck. 'I know an old guy who's taken me on one or two trips. He's too old for the fishing, but he takes people on trips out on the fiord.'

Chuck led Silver back along the length of the quay and

down into a quieter, older part of the harbour, where the water was green and stagnant. Silver wrinkled her nose. The smell of dead fish was even stronger here.

Chuck put his fingers to his mouth and whistled piercingly. An old boatman popped his head round the tarpaulin of his brown boat several moorings away. To Silver, the man with his bushy white beard looked like an ancient Viking. One eye seemed to look at her, while the other slipped away to the side. His boat looked quite ancient too. It was a nearly round wooden tub with a faded blue tarpaulin folded back over the cabin section. It looked solid enough, but it would probably take forever even to get out of the harbour.

'Here's your Charon. He'll ferry you over the Styx!' said Chuck to Silver.

'Don't frighten me with Greek allusions,' said Silver. 'I don't mean to die first!'

Chuck was fumbling in his wallet.

'I'm paying,' said Silver. 'You just need to do the deal for me. Your Norwegian's much better than my limit of three words.'

With a great deal of talk from Chuck, accompanied by much waving of his arms, the two men seemed to reach an agreement. The boatman smiled, showing he had only three stubs of teeth left, and gallantly held out his hand, streaked with black oil, to help Silver aboard. She wasn't sure if he was looking at her or out to sea.

'Is this going to be all right?' she asked Chuck, suddenly reluctant to leave her new acquaintance behind.

'Sure, you'll be fine,' he said. 'I'm still around to tell the tale after my boat trips with him, hairy though they may have been! See you later.' He laughed and loped off quickly up the quay, disappearing from view.

Silver wiped off a black oil mark from the seat with

a tissue and sat down in the large tub. The breeze was getting stronger. Maybe she should have brought some seasickness tablets in case the breeze should turn to gale force. There didn't seem to be much protection from the elements on the old boat. She breathed carefully through her nose. She wasn't very used to boats, but she supposed she'd manage. She'd bite her tongue off rather than be sick in front of old Charon.

After several coughs and wheezes from the engine, the boatman got it started. He cast off the boat's moorings and they began to chug slowly, backing out from the quay. The breeze was fresher here and the smell of oil from the engine diminished so that Silver began to feel a little better. She wondered if he had such a thing as a lifejacket for emergencies. It seemed unlikely, so she'd just have to take her chances.

The boat ploughed steadily through the waves. They weren't moving fast, but now the sun reappeared and the air was fresh and invigorating. Silver leant back on the hard seat and relaxed. The humped shapes of the islands slipped past and old Charon opened the throttle so that they began to move quite fast, churning up a broad wake of frothy white. Silver tried to guess which island was Rosenholm, but they passed several islands, both large and small, now skimming along at a good clip. The shore receded further and further away until even the cruise ship became a small dot. Silver hugged her knees, trying to decide how she would approach Mrs Rosenholm. What sort of person would she be? Probably grey-haired and dressed in a sky blue frock. Prim and proper, and perhaps not so very pleased to see her. Maybe Silver would just have to turn and go back again. But she was determined to give it a good try. Certainly it was harder to get rid of people when you met them face to face, rather than over the phone. At any rate, she'd get to see Alexander's childhood home from the outside.

Silver tried to communicate with the old Viking, but he only answered in abrupt monosyllables, though she thought he probably understood more than he was letting on. She still couldn't decide which eye was looking at her.

'Do you know the Rosenholms?' She spoke more loudly and slowly than usual. He looked at her and blinked.

'*Ja, ja*,' he said, now managing to focus and looking at her as if he thought she was a tiresome tourist, which she supposed she was.

Silver tried again. 'How many people live on the island?'

'Fru Rosenholm and the old woman.'

'What old woman?'

'Old Christiania, the maid.'

'Are there any other people living there?'

'*Nei...*' and the conversation seemed to be over. He didn't understand any more, or he pretended not to. He kept his head turned away from Silver and looked straight ahead across the water, blocking her out.

They sped across an open stretch of water. Silver looked down at her feet as something cold swilled around them in the bottom of the boat. Water. The boat was taking on water! Her heart jumped up into her throat. She looked round at the islands of the fiord – all vanishing fast as they sailed further out to sea. She'd never manage to swim even to the one that was nearest. Even that distance seemed huge.

Her heart beating fast and her feet freezing, Silver looked at the old boatman. 'Should I bail out a bit?' she asked. 'Do you have a bailer?' The water was now covering her ankles. She stood up suddenly.

The old man looked up startled. 'Down, down,' he said

63

in a hoarse voice, flapping a large hand at her. 'Sit in boat.'

Silver sat down again abruptly, clutching the side of the boat. She wished she'd never embarked on this trip. She looked round for something like a lifejacket, or at least a large piece of wood that she could cling on to.

The wind tore at her hair, and the little boat bounced over the white tops of the swelling waves as water splashed over the bows. Sprays of water shot up on either side of the boat. Silver swallowed. She was about to scream, but the old Viking stood unmoved, holding the tiller, his legs planted sturdily apart and his face unwavering against the rush of the wind, a triumphant smile on his lips.

Silver's hair whipped round her face, almost blinding her. She shivered and wished she'd thought of bringing a thicker anorak or even a scarf, for the wind cut through her thin jacket. She edged over to the side of the boat where there was a little more shelter and lifted her feet up onto the seat across from her to avoid the swirling water. She fixed her eye on a loose plank that lay alongside some coils of rope. If the boat capsized, she would grab the plank to help her stay afloat. She inched toward it still clutching onto the side.

With a last burst of speed, they rounded a promontory and entered calmer waters. The tall cliffs of an island rose above them. High up on the top was a sprawling white house, with a red tiled roof and a clump of dark pines behind it. They continued their course round the island until the old Viking bent down and slowed the engine, and with a heave and a slip of the waves, they entered a channel of quiet waters leading to a jetty. The boatman switched off the phut-phut of the engine and manoeuvred the boat alongside the wooden structure.

'Rosenholm,' he said, with a proprietorial sweep of his hand. He held the boat steady for Silver to disembark onto the small jetty, even offering his greased-stained hand to help her over the side. She scrambled up and then stood on the jetty for a moment, trying to get her bearings. Her eye caught a steep path cut out of the cliffside which led up to a white gate at the top.

With a rumbling roar, old Charon let in the throttle of the boat. He cut a deep swathe of white foam through the water and set course out into the open sea again.

'Hi! Stop!' shouted Silver. 'You have to take me back to Bergen again. Anyway, I haven't paid you!'

She stood watching the boat, which picked up an amazing speed for such an old tub. 'Come back!' Her words blew away on the wind as the boat got smaller and smaller. It rounded a tree-clad island and disappeared.

Well, what was she going to do now? Suppose Mrs Rosenholm wasn't at home? She could be stuck on this island for hours…days, perhaps. Silver shivered and peered up at the house, but from that angle, she couldn't make out if anyone was at home. She gritted her teeth and began to climb up the path to the top of the cliff, hoping for a friendly reception or at the very least to find someone who would take her back to the city again.

Perhaps Mrs Rosenholm would be furious at Silver's intrusion. Perhaps she would be hostile and order her away straight off back to the city before she got to talk to her. Perhaps she didn't speak English. All these unpleasant scenarios beat around Silver's ears.

Come on, Silver, don't hang about. You've got a job to do, she told herself. The path was steep and narrow, so she grasped the rickety railing to steady herself. But as it was so shaky, she was afraid it might collapse and bring her rolling down the cliffside. She realised it was better to trust her own legs and not use her arms for extra leverage. She began to get her second wind and the climb was exhilarating. I should get more exercise instead of sitting in front of my computer or hanging out in coffee bars, she noted to herself.

Now she had reached the top of the cliff. The thought she was trying to suppress burst through. What if Mrs Rosenholm refused to see her?

Chapter 5

At the top of the cliff, Silver unlatched the gate and entered a garden where gnarled old apple trees covered with drifting white blossom spread shade over an expanse of rough-cut grass. Between the trees, the sun was blazing down once more. The air was crystal clear with the sharp scent of pine trees and a hint of winter snows. Silver stood still for a moment, drinking in the peaceful scene.

A woman with long brown hair, lightly threaded with strands of white, popped out suddenly from behind a tree, startling her. She wore a leaf green flowing dress of expensive silk, the colour blending in with her surroundings so that she seemed like the spirit of the place. Only a few fine wrinkles graced her face. Standing framed within the branches of one of the apple trees, she carried several bunches of fresh herbs.

Silver stepped forward. 'I'm sorry if I'm trespassing,' she said. 'But I'm looking for Mrs Rosenholm. My name is Silver Fairfax.' She was glad to hear her voice sounded strong and determined.

The woman raised her eyebrows, and Silver was struck by her extraordinary brown almond-shaped eyes, a strange power emanating from them.

'I'm Elise Rosenholm,' she said. 'How can I help you?'

Under the woman's penetrating gaze, Silver felt compelled to stand still for a minute as Mrs Rosenholm raised her hands towards her in a kind of blessing.

Silver relaxed and heaved an inward sigh of relief. Maybe the first hurdle had been passed as she hadn't been sent packing. But would Mrs Rosenholm tell her anything interesting about the family?

'I'm writing an article about Rosenholm Shipping and, if you can spare me the time, perhaps you could tell me a little about your husband. He founded the shipping line, didn't he?' Silver asked. 'I've been talking to your sons downtown in the office.'

'My husband is dead. He died three months ago,' Mrs Rosenholm said. 'I'm a widow.' Her eyes filled with tears.

'I have been told of his death and I'm so sorry,' said Silver gently, feeling a slight guilt wash over her. 'I lost my mother some time ago and the loss is unbearable, I know.'

Mrs Rosenholm touched her arm and a wave of sympathy passed between them.

Now Silver saw she'd been too eager to get her story. With the loss of her own mother, why hadn't she thought about the grief Mrs Rosenholm would be suffering, caused by her husband's death? She would have to progress more slowly. She'd let herself become much too absorbed in her work, making her careless of other people's emotions. Now she understood better why Alexander didn't want to talk about his father. The wound was much too new. But there was a great mystery about Frederick Rosenholm's death and Silver meant to uncover more about it.

'You'd better come in,' said Elise in her fluent English. 'I'd like to talk about my husband. The boys, that is my son and my stepson, tell me to keep my mouth shut. But that's hard for me to do. They tell me I talk too much. Come in, come in and let's have a cup of tea. Do you like herbal tea? I don't get many visitors to the island. The boys don't come out here so often.'

The entrance to the house was dark and gloomy after the strong sunlight outside. Silver almost tripped over a huge white polar bear rug, which lay stretched out over the polished wooden floor, complete with large head and black nose. That was the nearest she'd ever come to a polar bear and she thanked goodness it wasn't alive. Elise led her through a wood-panelled sitting room and out onto a large wooden-floored terrace like a ship's deck, which extended out into the garden. She waved Silver into a comfortable manila sofa with bright green and red flowery cushions, and drew up a glass-topped table. Disappearing back inside the house, she reappeared after some time with a tray, which she set on the table.

'How pretty your china is with these delicate Norwegian wild flowers. They're all different.' Silver admired her cup and saucer.

'Yes, Frederick liked everything in harmony,' Elise said. 'You see all the cups match the paper napkins, just as he would've liked it. But he left me in turbulence and violence!' She stretched out her arms dramatically.

Silver was brought up short. 'What do you mean – turbulence and violence?' she asked.

Elise's voice deepened to a rich contralto and her Russian accent became more pronounced. Sighing heavily, she took out her handkerchief and wiped away a tear. Her slanting eyes reminded Silver of someone she couldn't quite place.

'I have tried to see beyond, to reach my husband in the next life. But something or someone seems to block me. I must know the answer.' Elise's tears were falling fast. 'After his terrible death, is Frederick at peace?'

'What do you mean – terrible death?' Silver asked.

'It was a truly terrible death,' said Elise. 'He was alone at the small cottage we own, which is situated on one of the other islands in the archipelago here. He liked to go there because he said he could think more clearly away from everyone.'

'So he was all alone,' said Silver. 'What happened?'

'There was a terrible fire. He was burnt to death. He was unrecognisable. They had to identify him from his dental records,' Elise sobbed openly. 'Yes, unrecognisable,' she repeated, her eyes staring at a horror that Silver was glad she couldn't see. 'The police are still investigating what happened. They haven't yet told us if it was an accident or whether the fire was started deliberately.' She peeped over her handkerchief at Silver.

'Arson,' said Silver. 'Could it be that? You poor thing, what a dreadful ordeal you've been through.' She patted Elise's hand, wishing she could give her more comfort.

'That's why I have to get in touch with my husband on the other side,' said Elise.

'Are you clairvoyant then?' asked Silver.

'Yes, it's a gift I have from my Russian ancestors,' Elise said. 'But it's so hard to get in touch with my husband. It would make his death so much easier to bear if I could just get a message from him. But it's all so chaotic just now. It's all blocked.' Two more tears ran down her cheeks. She brushed them quickly away and turned to Silver.

'You've been left too,' she said. 'You have a sore heart.' Her eyes shut and she fell into a kind of trance and began to murmur unintelligibly.

Silver was disturbed. She didn't know what to do. Was Elise a little unhinged after her husband's murder? Should she bring her out of her trance, or should she just wait and see that she didn't hurt herself? The crystal at Elise's throat winked blindingly, dazzling Silver's eyes.

'Elise,' she called softly. 'Are you all right?'

Elise leaned over and grasped Silver's fingers. She held

her hand in a light firm clasp. 'Don't be bitter,' she said. 'You're so tense. You must relax and break free of the past. I see a big upheaval in your life. You must get ready to face it.'

Silver felt an incredible warmth from Elise's touch creep up her arm and seep over her back. She lay back against the cushions of the sofa, tension slipping away from her. Certainly Elise had a very strange power.

Elise jerked out of her trance and knocked over her cup. It rolled across the floor spattering tea, but didn't break.

'There's trouble ahead,' she cried. 'Someone doesn't want us to be together! What was it you wanted to talk about?'

'I wanted to talk about the Rosenholm family,' said Silver, trying to keep up with her hostess's lightning changes of mood.

'Of course, of course,' Elise said. 'I'll get the photographs!' She darted away, her elegant sandals tapping over the decking.

Silver looked at her retreating back. This other-worldly woman was not quite what she expected as the wife of a powerful businessman. A stripey cat had slipped into the room and sprang up onto the sofa beside her, rubbing its head against her and purring loudly.

Elise returned, slightly out of breath. In her arms, she had three large black photo albums. 'Here you are,' she said dropping them onto the table. 'All my boys are in here!'

'All your boys?'

'Yes, yes, my husband, my son and stepson.' She opened the first album.

Silver glanced quickly at the pictures so carefully preserved in the album. 'Are these two boys Alexander and Knut?' she asked looking at a blurry photograph of two young boys both glaring into the camera. 'They're so very different!'

She looked at Alexander's tow-coloured hair, a complete contrast to Knut's very dark head. Just like his Russian ancestors, thought Silver, in a flash of insight.

'Yes, very different,' said Elise. 'They've never really become friends. They're always fighting, even today. I didn't know what to do to stop it. I suppose it was because they are only half-brothers and that makes them bitter rivals, even though I always tried to treat them alike. I'm good friends with Alexander, but Knut's my rebel child. I've never been able to do a thing with him.' Her lips curved in a proud smile.

Silver turned the pages. There were pictures of the boys with fishing rods and pictures of them climbing trees. One picture in particular caught Silver's attention. The two boys, now a little older, sat in a small rowing boat, Alexander in the stern and Knut in the middle, his hands holding the oars.

Elise peeked over Silver's shoulder. 'That picture shouldn't have been kept,' she said shaking her head. 'That was taken on the day when Knut hit Alexander on the head with an oar and then pushed him overboard into the fiord. I suppose Knut was about nine at the time. He was always big for his age. And so unruly.'

'How old was Alexander?' Silver was aghast.

'Oh, eleven or twelve. He was such a strong swimmer that he managed to swim ashore. He had a bump on his head where the oar had hit him, and he had a black eye for weeks! He never forgave Knut for what he did.' Elise glanced sideways at Silver as if judging her reaction. 'I shouldn't have told you that,' she said.

'Don't worry,' Silver soothed her. 'That's not something I'd write about.' It seemed important that she gained Elise's trust. Elise had treated her so well. She was so friendly and open. It would be like kicking her cat to betray her confidence.

Elise smiled at Silver and drew out another album. 'I want to show you my husband,' she said, eagerly turning the pages. 'There were two sides to him – the strict side and the one who loved to play. He was a gambler all his life – that's what the shipping business is all about, you know.' Her eyes were shining and she pointed to the photograph of a tall, unsmiling man carrying a briefcase. He had Alexander's blond cap of hair, though perhaps a little more faded. Of course, that figured. Silver nodded her head as she recognised the man in the portrait in Alexander's office. And in the next picture, Silver saw the same man wearing a loud red check shirt, collar open, and carrying a saw.

'That's Frederick,' Elise said. 'He loved making furniture. The last thing he did was to carve chairs for the dining room. They are beautiful, but there are only seven, he never finished the eighth one.' Her mouth drooped.

Silver patted her hand. They sat in silence for a moment, then there was a quick thudding of footsteps running up the path towards them. Both she and Elise turned in surprise. The stripey cat whisked itself from the sofa and dived underneath it. Alexander emerged onto the terrace, his tie askew and slightly out of breath.

'What on earth are you doing here?' he asked Silver, his brows drawn together and his eyes glittering with anger. 'I never thought I would see you again after all the trouble you made!'

'Trouble *I* made?' Silver jumped to her feet. 'If it's about the illegal stowaways on your ship – it's all over the Norwegian newspapers, and abroad as well I suppose. That's something you won't be able to hide. Don't blame me for your problems. I didn't cause them!'

Silver took a step backwards and sat down again. She and Elise huddled together, making a protective front against him. The photo album slipped off Elise's knee and fell to the floor, spilling out loose photographs of large ships and children playing in boats.

'Then why are you here? Are you planning a new story to make more trouble for us?' Alexander frowned suspiciously.

'Why are you here, yourself, Alexander?' Silver spoke in a cool tone. 'I'm paying a very pleasant visit to your stepmother. She invited me to take a cup of tea with her. You haven't bothered to visit her for ages, she says. You've left her alone too long!'

Alexander's face reddened and then he seemed to get hold of himself. 'Perhaps you're right, Silver,' he said in a milder tone. 'I've been so busy working that I've neglected you, Elise. I certainly didn't mean to.' He put his arm round the older woman's shoulders.

A shout came from the garden. 'What the hell's going on here?' said a voice. Five seconds later, Knut strode onto the terrace.

'What a cosy little party!' he said. 'Mother, brother and you too, Silver! Have you come to take a picture of the Rosenholm family united?'

Alexander stepped forward in front of Silver while Knut measured her with a cool appraising look. Like a naughty child, he peeped round Alexander at his mother. 'Mamma!' he said.

Alexander made a noise of irritation in his throat and stepped aside as Elise sprang up and rushed to embrace Knut. 'Where have you been, Knut, my darling boy?' she said. 'You haven't been to see me for such a long time.'

Alexander and Silver exchanged glances. He drew her back into the house, leaving Knut and Elise together on the terrace.

'How did you get here?' Alexander asked her. 'How did you find my stepmother?'

'I got a funny old Viking to bring me in his boat,' she said. 'I've enjoyed meeting your stepmother and I think she was pleased to see me. The photographs of you both as young boys were very revealing. Did Knut really push you overboard from that boat?'

Alexander's face darkened. 'Yes, he did. But don't remind my stepmother of that. It upsets her. I shouldn't have let it happen, because I was older and stronger, but he caught me by surprise. I don't know yet why he did it.'

'Could he have been jealous of you being the elder son?'

'It must be that. We fought a lot when we were children and we still do. Now you see why I'd never travel in the same boat with him.' Alexander's face was grim and it seemed to Silver that he was only half joking.

'Perhaps, but he has his own mother,' said Silver.

'Yes, of course, my mother was dead by then. She was English like you.'

'That's why you speak such good English then,' said Silver. 'But Knut does too.'

'That was another bone of contention between me and Knut,' said Alexander. 'He didn't like being forced to speak English when he was a child. But my father insisted on it.'

Then with a sudden change of tactics, he asked her: 'What did Elise tell you?'

'About what?' asked Silver.

'About our family. I'm surprised she seemed so keen to talk to you. She's usually very nervous of strangers, especially since my father died.'

Knut appeared behind Silver. 'What's this, Al? Don't be giving away family secrets, even to such a beautiful journalist. You never know what she'll do with them.' He smiled, looking intently at Silver from under his dark lashes. Putting his arm round her shoulders, he pressed her close to him. She tried to break free from his hold, but he gripped her even tighter. 'What a fluttering bird she is,' his slanting eyes gazed deep into hers.

'Are you going to come back with me on my new speedboat?' he asked. 'She's a beauty. She handles just like a sexy woman! Not paid for yet, because Al's dragging his heels as usual. Getting money out of the company is like getting blood out of a stone. It's my company too. Ma sits on the board as well. I'll have to get her to talk to Alexander. She won't let her little boy down!' And he winked at Elise.

Silver twisted out of Knut's hold and ducked under his arm. 'Is it safe to sail in your boat?' she asked. 'I've just heard the tale of how you pushed Alexander overboard when you were young boys.'

Knut's laughter was loud and triumphant. 'He's told you then. How I'm the stronger of the two. He was an idiot to let it happen!' He tried to tilt her chin up towards him.

'Oh, leave me alone, Knut!' Silver turned her back on him. To escape his teasing, she walked over to where Alexander was deep in conversation with Elise. 'We'll just have to get someone to come and stay with you, so you're not alone on the island,' Silver overheard him say.

That was strange. Wasn't Elise happy staying alone on the island? And hadn't the rough old ferryman told her about the old maid who kept Elise company? Silver mulled over this, hoping that her unexpected visit hadn't made Elise even more nervous, but Elise had seemed happy to talk to her.

Elise began setting out tall glasses on the table. A large, fat woman wearing a white overall and apron, as well as an old-fashioned maid's cap, was helping or rather hindering Elise. Elise dodged round her with quick bird-like movements.

'This is Christiania,' said Alexander indicating the woman. 'She's been with our family ever since I can remember.'

'Hello, Christiania,' said Silver.

The fat woman bobbed an old-fashioned curtsey.

Sitting at the table between the brothers with Elise opposite, Silver sipped at her light sparkling wine, worrying all the while how she was going to get back to Bergen. She didn't want to go in Knut's super speedboat. It might be the last thing she ever did, though she supposed he had grown up a bit and wouldn't try to push her overboard, for it was far too far away to swim to shore, battling through the strong waves. Probably she was safe enough, as such a wild action would make too much trouble for him and he seemed to like to glide through life as smoothly as possible. But how was she going to return to the mainland? She chewed her lip.

As if reading her thoughts, Alexander turned to Silver and asked: 'How are you going to get back, Silver? Is your hired boatman going to pick you up?' His eyes held a challenge.

Silver quivered. Despite everything, it was just too easy for Alexander to stir her pulses. She looked away from him before answering. 'Actually, he seems to have dumped me. I don't even know if he's coming back.' She stood up and began to pace restlessly.

'Knut...or Alexander will take you back,' said Elise. 'Knut's got a marvellous new boat. It's a bit large for the channel into the jetty, but he's so clever at handling it.' She gazed fondly at him.

'No, I'm taking Silver back,' Alexander's tone was final.

Silver's head snapped round in surprise. So it was true then. Alexander and Knut didn't travel in the same boat. It was really over the top that they each had to sail their own craft when visiting Elise's island at exactly the same time. The channel was very narrow and the jetty was small. As far as Silver could see from her own trip out to the island, there was only room for one – or perhaps one and a half boats at a pinch – to be moored at the same time.

'Come on Silver, I've got a meeting in town,' said Alexander, picking up his jacket from the chair.

Silver released the breath she didn't know she was holding. Problem solved! She wouldn't have to roar through the water, scared to death in Knut's speedboat, as she had pictured herself doing. She went up to Elise and embraced her. 'Thank you so much for being so welcoming to me,' she said.

Elise nodded and smiled. 'Come back and see me soon,' she said, giving Silver a hug.

Alexander and Silver walked down the steep cliff path to the jetty. As they approached the sea, soft rhythmic thumps came from the two boats bumping against each other on their moorings.

'Damn,' said Alexander. 'Knut has boxed me in.'

Silver stood on the jetty while Alexander untied Knut's mooring lines and untwisted the two boats. He dragged his brother's high-prowed craft further along the jetty, leaving an open space for his own boat to get out.

While Alexander struggled to extricate his boat, Silver studied the graceful racing lines of Knut's boat. She jumped back as her eye met the eye of a man sitting inside Knut's boat – no, there were two men, sitting patiently there in the cabin section of the boat. She bent forward to look more closely, almost hitting her head on the glass window. Both of the men turned away quickly. The cabin interior was murky, but she strained her eyes trying to get a better look at the two poorly clad and skinny men. And was there even a third man, hiding further in the shadows? She couldn't be sure.

Alexander's voice broke in on her scrutiny. 'Come on Silver, shake a leg! We're ready to sail!'

Perhaps the passengers in Knut's boat were none of her business, though her curiosity was raised. But she wasn't going to miss her ride with Alexander. She ran across the jetty and Alexander held out a firm hand as she stepped on board. She sat down quickly as opening the throttle with a roar, he set course out into the open sea.

'You seemed to get on well with Elise.' Alexander's strong hands held the steering wheel steady as they swooped towards Bergen harbour, cutting through the waves, the sun glittering on the water and the islands seeming to float weightlessly on the blue surface. 'I hope she wasn't too indiscreet.'

His remark riled Silver. 'I liked your stepmother a lot. I'm not going to betray any confidences – even to you,' she said.

'Sorry, sorry,' said Alexander lifting his hands from the steering wheel of the boat and holding them up disarmingly.

'Oh please, watch the steering!' Silver's knuckles were white as she gripped the side of the boat. 'We journalists know how to distinguish between public and private. Some of us are ethical – sometimes! Besides, I'm not into uncorroborated scandal stories for the tabloids. I just want the facts and it seems you're concealing things from me.' She looked at him sternly.

Alexander shrugged, letting the matter slide. The wind blew through his fair hair, making him look carefree and tousled. The last meeting between them had ended in disaster. Now she had a new chance to talk to him and she wasn't going to miss the opportunity.

'What actually did happen to your father out on the island? Where did it happen – it wasn't on the island back there where Elise lives?'

Alexander's face set in stern lines. 'It's not for the tabloids.'

Silver swallowed the insult. 'Do they know who killed him? Or was it an accident?' she persisted. 'I can find out if I really want to. I expect the local newspapers carried a big story about it.'

'But you can't read Norwegian.'

'It's not hard to find someone to do the translation,' she said. 'But if you tell me, I'll know I'm getting the true version of events.' She put her hand on his arm and gazed at him, trying to convey her sympathy.

Alexander yielded to her. 'Okay, okay, I'll tell you. You know my father was out alone on that island where there's a large stave church. Quite often he went there to think through problems and to work on new strategies for the business. He stayed as always in our little cottage on the island. Someone attacked him. We don't know who. We don't know why. But he was shot in the head twice, perhaps more. They found at least two bullet holes in his skull, but the police haven't yet finished their investigations.'

'What a dreadful story,' said Silver. 'I'm so sorry. What a terrible shock for you all. But I can't believe that you have no thoughts about who might have attacked your father?'

'Shipping is a cut-throat business, rivalries run high. But it gets worse,' said Alexander, clenching his jaw. 'A fire broke out, which burnt the cottage to the ground. We don't know whether it was deliberately started, possibly to cover up the murder. For it was murder, make no mistake about that. In fact, we don't know whether my father was already dead from the gunshot wounds or whether he burnt to death. The police are still investigating. At least, they say they are, but they haven't come up with much new information recently,' Alexander sighed. 'They've been very slow at finding answers.'

'Are there any suspects?' Silver asked.

'Me, Knut – the obvious ones, the ones closest to the victim. We're always the first suspects. That's how it seems to work. They spent ages questioning us, but couldn't make anything out of it. Except Knut's alibi…and mine.'

'Knut's alibi?' Silver pressed him.

'Forget it. Knut had rather a shaky alibi. But that's all straightened out now.'

'And what about your alibi?'

'You ask too many questions. Forget the whole thing,' said Alexander, his face shuttered. He straightened his shoulders and with a swift change of subject, he said: 'Not another word. Let's take a trip round the islands and see the sun set. It's quite spectacular to see it slide and disappear behind the mountains.'

Silver dissolved under his steady gaze. She was burning with sympathy and she respected his wish not to pursue the subject any further – well at least not for the moment. His father…murdered. How devastating. It was a wonder that Alexander was so calm and level-headed in the circumstances, although his temper flared up quickly enough whenever his brother was around.

Her professional cool was blowing away on the wind. He had such a powerful effect on her however hard she tried to resist it. She stood beside him in the stern as he casually slung his arm around her shoulders, causing her heart to skip a beat. He held the boat on a steady course with one hand. Silver was filled with a longing to comfort him, to sail with him and let the boat speed on into eternity.

Mentally, she slapped herself down. She mustn't let her

undeniable attraction to him get the better of her. She had to admit she had never before been so strongly drawn to a man. Not so quickly and intensely as now. Her two-year affair with Mike back in London was just a thing of the past. Five months back. Anyway, it was over. *Finito*, as if he'd never been. But what of Alexander? How strongly did he feel the pull of attraction between them? But if he was anything like his brother, he probably liked to play around.

She pulled away from his arm. He looked down at her, his blue eyes now slumberous and dark. 'Silver, you're driving me off course,' he said huskily. 'I haven't time to get involved with you.'

It was like a splash of cold water in the face. So he was only playing with her. At least he was honest about it before they went any farther.

Silver went over to one of the cushioned side benches and sat down, her senses reeling. She felt as battered and bruised as if the waves had knocked her down. First, she was shocked at what he had told her about his father. And then, she was upset at his apparent need to warn her off. She took a deep breath and tried to relax. They were sailing smoothly into Bergen harbour. Silver dashed the spray from her eyes. She wouldn't admit that it was mingled with a few tears for herself, or for Alexander's tragedy, she wasn't sure. She was determined to conceal how much he had affected her.

God, she was a fool, susceptible and silly, letting herself be drawn to a good-looking man against the romantic backdrop of sea and mountain. The boat bumped gently along the quayside. Silver clambered up onto the seat, not caring if her sneakers were leaving marks on the cushions. She grabbed at a rope hanging down from the quay and pulled herself up, almost falling onto the stone quay in her haste to get away.

'Sorry, I've just remembered I have some work to do. Thanks for the ride,' she got out between clenched teeth and then started running along the quay.

She heard Alexander's deep resonant voice calling her. 'Silver, Silver, what's the matter? Silver, come back!'

Alexander moved across the boat and restowed the anchor. He fixed the moorings more securely and put out the fenders so that the boat wouldn't scrape against the side. Up on the quayside, he looked back at his boat. Just a small cabin cruiser, she was at least ten years old, but he was fond of her. He liked pottering about in her and giving her a new coat of paint each year to freshen her up. She was big enough to spend a night or two in if he wanted to take a trip along the coast.

But what had he said to upset Silver? Just as he thought they could've spent a nice evening together, she was up and away like a winged bird.

She was so unpredictable. One moment she seemed ready to fall into his arms and set his pulse racing. Then she pulled back and gave him the brush-off. He only intended to warn her that he wasn't ready for a serious involvement. Wasn't that fair play? What was she playing at? Norwegian women were at least more straightforward. If they wanted to go to bed with you, they told you so straight out with no beating about the bush. But he didn't want a Norwegian woman, he wanted Silver – Quicksilver, he should call her. He laughed at himself for having such flights of fancy. She had set his life in turmoil and upset his regular professional rhythm, as if he didn't have enough to worry about just now.

What a flash boat Knut had bought himself. Or rather, he supposed Knut had borrowed out of company funds. That speedboat must have cost a packet. It wouldn't have come out of Knut's own pocket. That was for sure. Yet how the hell had Knut managed to lift a large sum of money out of the company without him noticing and despite all the rigorous checks and controls he'd put in place to stop any unauthorised drain of funds from the company. He'd have to look into that and see what kind of creative accounting Knut had managed to get the Accounts Department to come up with.

It was seldom he felt so tired and washed up. If only he had a brother he could trust and depend on, they could get things sorted out more quickly after their father's death. But he had to spend his time playing cat and mouse with Knut, making sure he didn't drain the company of capital and hamstring its future.

He'd have liked to have talked to Silver about it. She was so quick and intelligent. She probably could've come up with some bright suggestions on how to rein in Knut. He would have liked to get to know her better. But he seemed to have upset her for some reason, although he'd probably expressed himself clumsily. They could have built up a good relationship, if he could spare the time. That is, before she'd turned her back on him and rushed away.

He caught himself. Relationship – what did he expect? He'd only met the woman two days ago and every time they met, things turned out pear-shaped. He must just put her out of his mind and get on with his work. He'd always managed on his own. Even when his father was alive, he had borne most of the responsibility for the company in the latter years. And after his father's death, he'd had to step in immediately to look after Elise, even though she was only his stepmother and not his real mother. In many ways, she depended more on him than on Knut, and it had always been that way.

He remembered his last conversation with his stepmother. She'd complained about strange telephone calls she'd been getting out on the island. She didn't seem unduly worried, and he'd allowed her to lull him into a false sense of doing nothing about it. But perhaps he'd taken it too casually. Then there was the strange business of the stowaways on board the ship. That was something which had never happened before and it should have set warning bells ringing in his head. Perhaps he'd been too dismissive about the telephone calls. He'd have to speak to Elise later and ask if she'd been bothered by any more strange people on the phone.

That reminded him. He'd call in at *The Guiding Spirit* on his way home to see what progress they had made there and whether the security systems were operating as they should. By breaking in through the porthole, the stowaways had neatly managed to dodge the security cameras. Could it be an inside job? Illegal immigrants from Russia. That was something new. In recent years, there'd been a stream of refugees slipping across the border into northern Norway, but it was surprising – shocking even – to find them so far south and now on his ship in Bergen. Someone must have planned the operation. But who?

At least he knew why the sprinklers had released the blinding water mist so unexpectedly when Silver was visiting. It wasn't just a technical fault. Several of these miserable stowaways were hiding in the ship's utility rooms in the lower decks. And one or several of them had lit cigarettes. Silver had made a first-class story about that. At first, he'd thought it was a betrayal, but then he saw it was something that couldn't be hushed up. Several other newspapers had followed her lead.

He'd been too confiding with her too. You'd think he'd have learnt his lesson. With a groan, he remembered what he had confided to her about his father's murder, telling her all about the bullet holes and Knut's dodgy alibi – when only the police knew about that. How could he have been so careless, but with her sweet face and large sympathetic eyes to drown in, he'd allowed himself to be lulled into dropping his guard. That too would make a first-class story for her newspaper if she managed to sniff around and uncover more facts. She would worry at it like a dog with a bone, never letting go.

A first-class story! Why hadn't he thought of that before?

She'd really conned him when she seemed so worried about getting back to the mainland. It was just too easy for him to step in to help her and for her to work her charms on him.

Then why had she given him the brush off? Answer: he'd just presented her with the start of another first-class story and she wanted to chase up more about it.

Stupid, gullible fool that he was. He'd have to catch up with her again. He simply couldn't let her walk off like that. She was trouble on legs. He ran his fingers distractedly through his hair. God knows what she was doing now. And there was more to come, he would bet on it. For a moment, he'd forgotten how dangerous Silver was – with an open line to the world's press. How soon would he see the Rosenholm name splashed across the front pages once again? Surely it was only a matter of time before she betrayed him.

He had to get hold of Silver.

Chapter 6

Back in her hotel room, Silver opened the window to get rid of the stuffy smell of past guests. Outside, the sun had vanished and rain was lashing down, making the air cool and heavy. She sat on the green and blue woven bedcover, and with lacklustre eye surveyed her surroundings. How could she have left Alexander like that? Just when he seemed to need her. He would think she was a complete idiot rushing off like that from the boat. Why did she always overreact whenever she was with him?

She couldn't leave things unfinished like this. She'd have to arrange a new meeting with him when she would be more patient and she'd force a story out of him. But if she wrenched a story out of him and got it splashed all over the front page of the newspaper, that would be a dreadful betrayal. Could she deceive him like that?

It was just that Alexander got under her skin and skewed her normally impeccable judgement. There! She had admitted it to herself. He was the most attractive man she'd ever met. But what did he think about her?

So what – she had more important things to think about. All her old uncertainties came flooding back. Was she up to the job? There was no way she could allow herself to fail – it would destroy her career and, besides, she needed the money. With her mother no longer here and her father up the Amazon or wherever it was, she had to stand on her own feet. She thought of Mike, who'd never respected her enough. He had wanted her to cut down the hours she worked and to spend more time with him, like a tethered woman. Ironing his shirts and cooking weren't her favourite pastimes. She wasn't cut out to be a homebody from another century.

Yes, she could come to terms with the break-up of the relationship with Mike. She had a good career, using her brain and her skills. She loved doing interviews with people and she had a nose for a good story. There was a lot more to uncover about the tragic death of Alexander's father. There must be more about it in the newspaper files – if only she spoke Norwegian.

Kicking off her shoes, she went through to the bathroom. In the mirror above the basin, she saw that her face was hot and red from exposure to the sun and wind out on the fiord. Her hair was frizzing wildly round her head. She picked up her after-sun cream and smoothed it over her skin. She felt as if she had been away for days, and what had she accomplished? One small story only. The interview she'd made earlier with Alexander at his office was so full of holes that it would be unusable in the light of what she had discovered today.

The telephone at the side of her bed rang, making her jump. For a nano-second, her heart leapt with hope that it was Alexander wanting to speak to her again.

'Silver,' barked a familiar voice and her heart sank with disappointment. 'What the hell are you doing? I've been trying to call you for several hours and all I get is a weird, male foreign voice and then I'm cut off!'

Silver sagged. She didn't want to admit that she'd even managed to lose her mobile on top of everything else. Tom would only tease her about being scatterbrained again. She was forever losing things – pens, business cards, notebooks

– in her haste to get things done, but despite all that she usually came up with a damned good story. She sighed. The last person she wanted to talk to was Tom in London. 'Hello, Tom,' she said slowly. 'I'm on the case, but it just takes some time to gather it all.'

'I'll bet,' he said, and she pictured him with his feet on his cluttered desk, the ashtray full of cigarette stubs and about five cups of unfinished coffee ready to be knocked over as his hands shuffled among his piles of paper.

'Anyway, great story about the illegal immigrants on the ship. You certainly scooped that one. There are already some copycat pieces in some of the other papers,' said Tom. 'Have you got anything more on the story? It could be really red hot. You've got a good nose. Stir your stumps! I'm holding two pages for you for Thursday.'

And now I'm just floundering, thought Silver. But she didn't say it aloud. 'Yes, yes, Tom. I've got started,' she said briskly. 'I've got some meetings set up.' She crossed her fingers.

'Well, it's your baby. Get that story written and emailed over to me soonest. And some better pics too. Buy yourself a decent camera and you'll get better results. C'mon girl, get to it!' Then he hung up in his abrupt way.

Silver sat staring guiltily at the telephone for a few minutes. She'd have to move faster. She'd only just scraped the tip of the iceberg of the Rosenholms' secrets, and if she could uncover all the facts, what a story it would turn out to be. She jumped to her feet restlessly and began pacing the room, her thoughts tumbling around in her head. Her mind switched back to Rosenholm Island. What were these men doing on Knut's boat? It was very strange – these miserable men were not like the playboy friends she would have expected Knut to hang out with. Maybe it was quite innocent and they were merely workmen. But the image of the two furtive men on the boat played on her mind.

What a predicament. How could she hang the Rosenholm family out to dry for all the world to read about? Alexander and his stepmother, who had been so kind to her. Well, Knut could swing in the wind. It seemed to her that he would always fall on his feet. But one thing was brilliantly clear to her, if she didn't come up with a story, she'd lose her job. She'd have to get out, talk to people and grab hold of some more information.

Alexander was out of the question. She'd certainly made a hash of that. He wouldn't welcome her after she'd made such a fool of herself running off from his boat like that. She'd learnt a lot about the family from Elise, but she didn't think Elise would know much about illegal immigrants. Out on her island, Elise was totally isolated from what was happening in the city.

But what about brother Knut? She shouldn't have given him the brush-off so bluntly. She'd just have to flutter her eyelashes a little and see what he could come up with. Probably if she played his flirtatious games, he'd talk to her. He liked to boast. He would talk. But where would she get hold of him? She supposed that she'd have to ring the Rosenholm Company again and try to arrange to meet him. What would Alexander say about that? Silver rubbed her hot cheeks. She couldn't always be thinking of Alexander. She must cast him out of her mind. But she'd better get a move on if she wanted to keep her job. Knut was the answer.

First thing next morning, Silver picked up the phone and called the Rosenholm Company. Knut hadn't yet arrived. She should have guessed that it was much too early for him. She was left hanging about in frustration in her hotel room until finally he called back and agreed to meet her at the Café Maritime down on the waterfront.

The rain of yesterday was gone and the sun was shining. Its warmth beat down on Silver's head as she passed along the row of brightly coloured tall-gabled houses on her way to meet Knut. She was looking for the sign with the café's name on it when a large, green open-topped Porsche with Knut at the wheel roared up and swept to a halt a few metres away from her outside some squat grey buildings, probably derelict harbour warehouses. He slotted the car neatly into a parking space. Slamming the door, he jumped out and strode towards her, sweeping her along with him, his arm around her shoulders.

They entered the open-air cafe by the marina. People of all ages sat at the tables, which were covered by cheerful blue and white checked cloths. The waiters ran back and forward carrying large trays balanced aloft their up-stretched arms. The ever-present seagulls wheeled over the harbour mewing loudly, and a salty tang rose from the sea. A cheerful chink, chink rose from the metal wires on the masts of the tall yachts as they twanged in the soft breeze.

They sat down at one of the tables and Knut snapped his fingers at a passing waiter. 'Prawn sandwiches for two and two lagers.'

So he wasn't going to offer her a choice. She hated men who took charge as if she had no mind of her own.

'What if I'm allergic to prawns?' she said, just to needle him a little.

'A beautiful girl like you, allergic? No way,' he said.

Silver studied him. He was wearing a light grey suit that shouted money, but which would be more at home in Paris or Rome than in a small Norwegian town. In fact, he looked like a cross between a banker and a top-ranking Mafia type. That slight air of danger could make him very attractive to some women.

His well-tanned hand flicked a non-existent piece of fluff

from his lapel. They sat for a moment holding each other's gaze, not in a romantic way but in a struggle for power.

Silver frowned. He looked to her like the type of man who always had schemes on the go. The type to chase after glittering prizes that were always just out of reach. Silver's instincts worked overtime, but she was the first to avert her eyes.

The waiter set the cutlery before them along with two large napkins. Two open-topped prawn sandwiches were placed on the table. The waiter poured light tawny lager into two tall glasses. Silver leant forward, determined not to waste time. She drew out her notebook and pen.

'What's this?' said Knut, his voice silken. 'I thought you wanted to see me, not talk about dreary business.' He winked at her and moved his long legs closer.

Silver swallowed. She leant forward and touched his hand, disturbing a waft of his expensive perfume. 'Of course I want to see you, but I also want to talk about your fascinating family,' she said. 'Tell me about yourself, Knut. You must live a really exciting life. What an interesting family you have, owning all these ships.'

Knut stretched out and grasped her hand, studying each finger intently. 'You don't take much care of your hands.' He looked at her bitten nails and untended hands.

Silver snatched her hand back. 'Thanks for the compliment, but that wasn't what we came here to discuss.'

He smiled teasingly. 'What do you think of our cruise ships?' he asked. 'Allow me to invite you on one of our cruises in the Caribbean. It's a perfect setting for a beautiful girl like you. You could get your hands manicured as well! You're a girl that likes a little luxury, aren't you?'

He leaned forward and brushed her light hair from her forehead, making her draw back sharply and almost knock over her glass. She didn't like him touching her at every opportunity, particularly when they most definitely weren't on a date. But then she remembered that she must play his game and stroke his feathers the right way.

'I expect you're very important to the company,' she said, tilting her head to one side to look up at him. 'You must have a lot of responsibility.'

'Oh, I'm the driving force. The company would go bust without me. I buy and sell ships, transact shares and make sure everything runs smoothly,' he said. 'There's a lot of money involved. We'll soon own nine ships, you know.'

'Nine ships,' said Silver with unforced admiration.

'Yes, the company's doing so well that we've ordered three new ships. Much larger than the ones we've got at present.'

'Congratulations. You must work very hard.'

'I do indeed, so sometimes I feel entitled to take a little time off.' Knut stroked Silver's cheek. 'I'll invite you to the launch of the first new ship. It's going to be held in sunny Miami. Say you'll come. You'll love it.'

'What will Alexander say about that?' Silver said, testing him.

'You'll be my guest, so Al will just have to lump it.'

'What exactly does Alexander do in the company?'

'Oh, he does what I tell him. Keeps a few accounts and writes a few letters.' Knut chewed his prawns appreciatively. The sun glinted on his gold Rolex as he raised his glass to drink.

'But I thought he was the older of you two. Isn't he in charge?'

'Alexander? No, of course not. He's just an old stick in the mud. If I didn't prod him on, we'd never have any new ships or new ventures. You've got it all wrong, little Silver.'

A flash of irritation ran through Silver. He hadn't told her anything she didn't know already. In fact, he'd turned some of the facts on their head. She was in no doubt that Alexander was the one at the helm of the shipping line after his father's death, and probably even before that.

She'd have to push Knut harder. 'Tell me about your father, Knut. What happened to him?'

She caught the annoyance rippling through him. Suddenly, another person seemed to look at her out of his eyes. A dark, uncontrolled person. Then he blinked and leaned back in his chair, his smooth manner back in place, his voice still silken. 'We don't talk about that with outsiders.' He closed his mouth firmly.

'Was he murdered?'

Knut half rose from the table. 'Look Silver, I came out here with you to have a bit of light fun. And now you turn all heavy on me. It's none of your business anyway.'

'I'm sorry. It's such a dreadful thing.' Silver put her hand on his arm and smiled at him from under her lashes. At her touch, Knut seemed to relax and sat down in his seat again.

Silver felt Tom's invisible presence behind her, urging her on. But she'd have to handle Knut carefully or he'd be up and away. 'What about the stowaways on board the ship?' she pressed, trying another tack. 'Do you know anything more about that? Where did they come from?'

'Oh, that's police business.' Knut looked mutinous. 'It's out of our hands.'

'But what were they doing on your ship?'

'Look, the security cameras were turned off. We don't know yet. Anyway, there were only about nine that slipped aboard. I thought you knew all that – you certainly shouted it loud enough to the world! They shouldn't have been there, but some of them had the idea of getting jobs on the ship. Okay, are you happy now? Curiosity killed the cat, you know.'

He studied her for a long moment, frowning at her. 'Keep your nose out of it, Silver. It's nothing to do with you.'

'What's happened to the stowaways? Are they still at the police station? Are you sure they've found all of them?'

'You're like a little terrier. Once you get hold of something, you won't let go.' Knut's tone was patronising. 'Wuff, wuff!'

Silver was unmoved by his remarks. 'What nationality are they? Is it true they're Russian?'

Knut sighed noisily. An expressionless mask came down over his face. Suddenly, his mobile rang. Silver could have sworn he'd muttered 'Saved by the bell'. He clicked open the phone and spoke into it, turning his back on Silver to exclude her from the conversation.

'Look, I'm busy. Don't bother me now. I'll get back to you later.' He turned away and spoke in a low tone in English into the mobile.

Silver couldn't hear the other person's reply.

'It's ten thousand dollars for one person.' Knut seemed agitated and cast a glance over his shoulder at Silver. 'Take it or leave it. I don't do cheap deals or cut price rates for couples.'

Silver tried to pretend she wasn't interested by cutting her sandwich up into little bits with the knife and fork provided. But her ears were on stalks. She'd bet a month's salary that it was something to do with the illegal stowaways, and there was obviously big money in it.

Knut put his hand over the mobile. 'Be with you in a minute,' he mouthed at her. He got up and walked away as he continued to speak sharply into the phone: 'Just come up with the money or we'll take someone else. You've already caused me a lot of hassle.'

Silver got up from the table, pretending to look more closely at the boats moored in the marina. She kept Knut within earshot and heard most of what he was saying.

The person at the other end continued to speak. Knut's face grew white and strained as he listened. 'Forty people on a bus! Just forget it!' His tone was sharp. He shut off the mobile abruptly and was silent for a few seconds before he suddenly noticed Silver was right behind him. He looked at her with a 'you think you've caught me out' type of smile. But Silver's instinct was that he was annoyed that she had overheard so much. She was sure as sure that it was all to do with the business of the immigrants trying to get into Norway.

'Who was that? More guests wanting to join your cruise ship?' she asked him, widening her eyes innocently.

'Just someone trying to pull a fast one over me,' he said. 'Look, I have to get back and sort out some things. Sorry and all that.' He threw some money down on the table and was turning away when Silver said: 'Maybe I should come back to your office with you. I want to talk to Alexander.' The words were out even before she realised her own intention.

Knut's face was blank, his eyes half closed as he looked at her. It was obvious he wasn't at all pleased to have her tagging along, but he shrugged his shoulders and moved towards the exit.

Leaving the cafe, Silver and Knut walked along the waterfront towards his green Porsche, which was now standing bumper to bumper with an elderly Volvo station wagon outside the squat grey warehouses. A large, heavy man wearing an ill-fitting suit and a broad, yellow tie emerged backwards from the open door of one of the buildings. He carried a large pile of clothing which he dumped in the back of the Volvo. The car radio blared onto the street in a stream of unintelligible Norwegian.

Knut seemed uneasy and tried to hustle Silver past the

old car. 'I've changed my mind, Silver. You'll have to walk up to the company office alone. There's someone I've got to see.' He made a shooing motion with his hands as the burly man advanced towards them, his face split in a wide grin, showing a gold tooth.

'Knut, my friend!' he purred, arms outstretched to envelop the reluctant Knut in a bear hug. 'We have business to transact.'

Silver stood entranced on the sidelines watching the little scene. What a contrast between the two men. The urbane Knut in his well-tailored suit and the hulking man, his balding head ringed by jet black hair.

'Goodbye, Silver,' said Knut, flapping his hands at her again. He seemed to be desperate to get rid of her. But why? What was it about the big man that upset him so much?

Silver was in no hurry to move on. She was determined to find out what was going on between Knut and the man who stood towering over both of them.

She dodged round Knut and picked up a well-tailored navy-blue jacket. 'Hello,' she said to the large man, holding out the garment to him. 'Are you one of Knut's business associates?' She couldn't resist teasing Knut.

The large man looked at her and a lascivious light came into his eyes. '*Da, da*,' he said. 'Knut and me, we do deals.' He reached out his giant paw to shake Silver's hand.

'You come from England?' he asked. 'Very nice country, England.'

Silver tried to place his accent as he didn't seem to be Norwegian. He was too swarthy skinned. Probably another person from Russia or one of the former Soviet countries, just like Elise. Perhaps he was an illegal immigrant himself.

'Goodbye, Silver. You're holding us up.' Knut's tone was exasperated. He'd lit a cigarette and was drawing heavily on it.

'Are you going to buy a new car, Knut?' Silver cast a mischievous glance at the battered old Volvo, noticing Knut's heightened colour as he struggled to keep his temper. 'A station wagon has more room than a Porsche.'

Knut stepped close to her and a sudden chill of fear ran down her spine. Once again, the menacing stranger looked at her from Knut's eyes. Perhaps she had pushed him too far. She moved away quickly.

'It was nice to meet you, Mr…?' she said to the swarthy man.

'I am called Lazlo,' he said. 'We will meet again, Miss…?' He leered ingratiatingly at her and his gold tooth glinted in the sun.

Silver turned on her heel and began walking back. As she passed the old Volvo, she peered inside. A small man with the same swarthy skin as Lazlo's sat down low in the front seat. When he caught her glance, he turned his face sharply away and slid further down in the seat. On the back seat behind him lay heaps of roughly folded clothing. Elegant black dresses with cinched-in waists were jumbled up with perfectly ordinary sweaters and trousers. They all lay strewn across the seats. There were several more piles of quite good clothing lying in the back part of the vehicle, certainly not worn-out old clothes fished out of a dustbin. How strange to see so many garments collected together. And to top it all, there were several pairs of men's brown and black shoes tumbled on top of the clothes.

She heard a step behind her and whirled round. Lazlo had moved stealthily up beside her – so close that she caught the scent of his cheap cologne, which was quite different from Knut's.

There was obviously no point in staying any longer, so with an airy wave of her hand she started along the road leading back to the centre of town. After a time, she turned and looked back over her shoulder. The two cars, the old and the flashy-new, moved along the road in solemn cortege.

Silver planned to call Alexander from the hotel. She clenched her fist in irritation. It was maddening that she'd lost her mobile at the fair. It was so complicated without it. She hadn't had a moment to buy herself a new one. She must get her act together and get it replaced. She began planning what she would say to Alexander when she met him again. She'd apologise for her hastiness in leaving him so abruptly and hopefully that would put things right between them. It'd be great to see him again, but she would be sure to keep her emotions in check. From now on, it would be strictly business.

Chapter 7

Alexander leaned against the door jamb of Knut's office. He surveyed Knut's spacious high-tech office with its clutch of computers blinking idly. The scent of cigars wafted across the room as he regarded Knut and a burly stranger who were occupying the padded leather armchairs in the coffee table section of the office. Each of them was enjoying a fat Havana cigar. Two cut-glass crystal tumblers half full of whisky stood on the table.

Knut looked up, his face full of irritation. 'What are you doing here?'

'I have some things to discuss with you.' Alexander glanced enquiringly at the stranger, but Knut made no move to explain who he was.

Two fat bundles of crisp fifty dollar bills lay on the table. With a quick sleight of hand, Knut bent forward and whisked them into a drawer. He moved so fast that Alexander began to doubt the evidence of his own eyes, but alarm bells rang in his head.

He stepped closer. 'Mind if I join you?' He dropped into the leather couch on the other side of the table before Knut could protest. Maybe he was behaving like an unpaid policeman, but his gut instinct told him he'd better check out Knut's companion.

Knut was silent, his face mutinous.

'I thought you were out of town on business today,'

Alexander pressed on, raising his eyebrows.

'Mind your own business, brother dear,' said Knut. 'Can't I have a meeting, without you barrelling in?'

Alexander's uneasiness increased. 'I don't believe we've met,' he said, turning to the burly man.

The man puffed on his cigar, savouring it as if it was his last before execution. 'Lazlo, at your service,' he said, extending his hand. He bent forward, compressing his heavy belly.

Alexander picked up the foreign inflexion of Lazlo's accent. 'Where are you from?' he asked casually.

'I am from Bergen,' said Lazlo. 'Norwegian citizen.' He smiled ingratiatingly at Alexander and took a further deep puff of his cigar.

A strange new business connection, Alexander thought. Knut's cronies were usually the sharp suits of the Rolex and Cartier brigade. His female friends were a more variegated bunch of lilies and blowsy roses, with a high turnover factor.

'Do you speak Norwegian?' Alexander probed Lazlo. 'What brings you to Bergen?'

'I find work,' said Lazlo.

'And what is that?' Alexander didn't let up on his interrogation.

'Import, export.' Lazlo gave an airy wave and leaned back in his chair, stretching his feet out in front of him in surprisingly well-polished shoes.

Out of the corner of his eye, Alexander caught Knut smirking. 'That must be quite a lucrative business,' he said. 'Which countries do you deal with?'

Knut's face reddened. He jumped to his feet. 'Look, we're just having a quiet discussion, and you come and give us the third degree. Just bugger off!'

Alexander rose. He was increasingly sure that Knut

and Lazlo were involved in some sort of scam, but he'd pushed Knut far enough for the moment. It would be better to get him alone later and force the truth out of him. His gaze landed on Lazlo just as the man took another swig from his whisky glass.

'Where did you say you were from originally?' Alexander pressed him again.

'Ukraina, Russia,' said Lazlo. 'You been there?' His gold tooth glinted as he smiled broadly.

'I think Silver wants to see you.' Knut turned to Alexander with an ironic glint in his eye. 'She knows Lazlo.'

Alexander blinked. 'Silver knows Lazlo…?'

'Yes, yes, very pretty lady,' said Lazlo, smiling at Alexander and waving his whisky glass.

Alexander caught himself. Knut was only trying to needle him. 'Goodbye, Mr…Lazlo,' he said formally.

Back in his office, Alexander sat in the big leather chair, his feet on the desk, unable to concentrate. The computer blinked watchfully at him. Swivelling round, he stared out of the window at *The Guiding Spirit* as she rode at anchor down in the harbour. She'd be leaving tomorrow and now that security had been tightened, he'd make damn sure there were no stowaways aboard when she sailed. But why had they boarded her in the first place? Or were they using her as a temporary staging post to get to the States?

The police had reported back to him this morning that the nine stowaways weren't carrying any papers and they had refused to talk. According to DCI Berg, the officer in charge of the case, they were probably Russian or Ukrainian nationals trying to make their way into Norway and possibly beyond. Ukrainian. Very probably Lazlo had some connection with them – he was Ukrainian – so it didn't need a great leap of imagination to make that connection. Did that mean Knut was involved in the scheme as well? Alexander rubbed his temples, trying to force his brain to think clearly. Uneasiness swept over him. He knew there was a growing problem with illegal immigrants from these countries because the Finns had more or less closed the border between Russia and Finland. With a common border with Russia, Norway, with its more liberal immigration policy and reputedly generous handouts for asylum seekers, was often seen as a softer touch.

Alexander shifted in his chair and picked up his cup of coffee, but it was cold and grainy, so he thrust it from him. He looked at his watch. He'd tried several times throughout the day to call Silver at her hotel. Despite him leaving several messages, she'd never called back. Perhaps he'd catch her at the hotel as he passed it on his way home. God only knew what she was up to. Maybe she'd already sent a new story to her editor. That would be a real worry.

He looked at his watch. Most people would have gone home by now. The long days of the Norwegian summer meant that people usually left work early at three o'clock in the afternoon to catch the sunlight and warm weather to build up their health to face the winter months. He was probably the only one left in the office. He should be on his way home too as he wouldn't achieve anything more today. He heard a door slam at the end of the corridor. That'd be Knut, though he was leaving late today. He normally left the office at three o'clock sharp like a sprung horse in a race. He was good at finding excuses to sidle off early too, despite Alexander's best efforts to keep his brother's reluctant nose to the grindstone.

Alexander needed a break. He shut the door behind him and was halfway down the corridor when he heard the telephone in his office ringing insistently. Squaring his shoulders, he ignored it. If it was Silver, he'd look in at her hotel on his way home. He locked the main door of the building and walked out into the sunshine.

Maybe he'd try to take Silver for another fiord trip in his boat. He'd got to find out if she'd sent off any more stories about the cruise line to London. He was pulled between distrust and his unwilling attraction to her. But first, he'd make an extra check that there was no more trouble aboard *The Guiding Spirit*. The security checks on board had already failed disastrously. Now he'd double-check that all the new procedures which had been put in place were functioning smoothly. He quickened his step.

Chapter 8

Silver walked down to the quayside, with the highly advanced digital camera she'd just bought dangling from her shoulder. Probably Tom would deduct it from her salary as she'd been so careless.

It was quiet in the harbour today, except for a group of guests wearing shorts and sunhats who had disembarked from the cruise ship and were waiting in line to board a large tour bus. A young woman stood ticking off their names on her clipboard and several seamen stood on watch at the end of the gangway as the passengers filed off the ship. Security was much in evidence today.

A hand fell on Silver's shoulder and she jumped, immediately shielding her camera.

'Alexander,' she burst out. 'What are you doing here?'

'Well, it's our ship,' he said mildly, pressing his cheek against hers in an unexpected gesture, so that the slight stubble scraped excitingly against her skin. She stepped back quickly, her pulses spinning.

Alexander's eyes met hers and held them. It was hard to break the current of electricity running between them. Silver was the first to avert her eyes, and she began fiddling with the camera lens to regain her lost composure.

'I've got to talk to a couple of people on board,' said Alexander. 'Would you like me to show you around the vessel – without Knut! I'll personally guarantee that nothing will go wrong this time!'

He seemed in a particularly good mood today, a mischievous sparkle in his eye. His hostility over her article about the stowaways seemed to be a thing of the past.

'Just lead on,' she said, waving him ahead. Passing the security checks, they climbed the gangway up into the ship. The sun glanced off Alexander's blond hair and behind him Silver studied his tall lean body as he moved with long strides upward. A sexy, modern Viking.

Stop there, a nagging voice murmured in Silver's ear. Good journalists don't get involved with their sources.

At the top of the gangway, Alexander stopped suddenly and Silver almost barged into him. 'Would you like to go up onto the tenth deck and look at the ship's bridge?' he asked. 'It's quite an experience with all the modern navigation equipment.'

They strolled across the sun deck, where the red and white sun loungers were now filled with people trying to catch a tan in the warm sunshine. In one of the swimming pools, a boisterous game of water polo was going on. An almighty splash of water jetted up onto the deck almost swamping Silver. She dodged quickly and held up her hand as the red and green ball thudded across the pool. Excited shrieks rang through the area.

'The bridge deck is down here.' Alexander gestured down a broad flight of stairs. 'Have you ever been there before? I'll show you the owner's suite as well.'

The deck below was a haven of peace. They walked along the low corridor towards the bow of the ship. Alexander stopped suddenly outside a large double door. He took out a key card, but the door swung open before he could insert it.

'Strange,' he said. 'Are the cleaners here?' He entered

and looked around swiftly. He beckoned her inside.

'Come on, Silver, there's nobody here. It's more lax security.' His annoyance was clear. But in a lightning change of mood he bowed low with a teasing smile on his face and announced: 'The owner's suite, please come in!' All traces of the uptight and correct businessman were gone. Maybe there was a spark of the buccaneer in him too, like his brother Knut.

What did he want of her?, Silver asked herself, stealing a glance at his face. Her heart beat faster as she felt a strange mixture of recklessness and abandonment in his company.

She slipped past him, feeling he was close, much too close. She could feel the heat of his body and she caught the fresh tang of a citrusy aftershave. What was it about this man that sent her heart into overdrive every time he came within a yard of her.

'A grand piano!' Silver stood transfixed inside the suite. It was spacious and furnished with great luxury in co-ordinated yellows and blues, with the ebony grand piano as the focal point. There were six large curtained portholes so that the lighting came from a crystal chandelier on the ceiling.

'Ostentatious, isn't it,' said Alexander in her ear. 'But we have to show a bit of style for our passengers.'

Alexander's nearness was overwhelming and Silver's throat seemed to have closed up. She sank down on a brocaded sofa, then sprang up again, banging her camera against the elaborate mahogany coffee table. She moved quickly over to a single well-stuffed armchair.

'What do you think, Silver? Is this enough luxury for you?' Alexander's tone was ironic, even deprecating, as he watched her.

'I could get used to it,' she said, leaning in the chair and looking around the room. 'I've never seen such elaborate furnishing. The colours are exquisite.'

'Elise helps with the design on all our ships,' said Alexander. 'These brocades are specially woven to her designs. She's very artistic and she paints as well. Did you notice the paintings in her house?'

He moved over to the drinks cabinet and took out some glasses. 'What would you like to drink?'

'A light white wine, please,' said Silver. 'Life on the ocean waves is no hardship here.' She took the glass from him.

'*Skol*,' he said smiling at her, and she melted in the Nordic blue of his eyes. 'Welcome aboard, Silver. Here's to our better acquaintance.' He leaned forward and clinked glasses with her.

They sipped their wine for a shared moment, but now Alexander seemed restless. He sprang up and prowled around the room. Silver watched him and he threw her a mischievous smile.

'You must see the other rooms of the suite,' he said, striding over and throwing open the door of the adjoining room. Silver preceded him into an enormous bedroom.

'Goodness, it's like an Arabian tent with all the glamorous draperies.' Silver gazed in admiration at the formally luxurious bedroom. A huge yellow bed, with a silken canopy rising above it, dominated the middle of the room. The dressing table had silver-backed brushes, and there was a highly polished mahogany writing desk on which stood an exotic flower arrangement of red and yellow tropical flowers that she couldn't have begun to name. A stateroom for show, with great elegance, comfort and opulence.

Silver's throat tickled and she began to cough. Something was wrong. A heavy stench of cigar smoke hung over

108

the room. It was mixed with a cloying odour which was hard to identify. Some kind of alcohol. Probably a rich cognac.

Such a beautiful room, yet the atmosphere was all wrong. She looked at Alexander who stood as if sculpted from stone. His eyes were fixed on something beyond the bed.

'What the hell's this?' he said. Silver pushed past him to look.

'Who's been in here?' Alexander's voice was raised, though he seemed to be struggling to suppress his anger. 'No one is allowed in here except us, the stewards and cleaning personnel.'

The yellow silk cover on the bed was in disarray. Swiftly, Silver crossed to the other side of the opulent bed and bent down to examine a shabby rucksack, stuffed full of clothes, some of them quite expensive looking. With a jolt, she recognised that the mixture of garments was just like the clothing she'd seen Lazlo loading into his station wagon. Another rucksack stood beside the first one, filled to the brim with loose cigarette packets still in their cellophane wrapping.

Alexander's anger burst forth. '*For fanden*,' he roared. 'Someone has sneaked their way in here. That's why the door was unlocked. But did these bloody intruders get in because of a careless steward or did someone have a special key card? There's no sign that the door was forced.'

The two rucksacks sat there abandoned, yet faintly menacing. Who could possibly have left such things behind? The displaced objects jarred against the silken luxury of the room. Silver was struck by an alarming thought. Could the intruders still be here in the suite? She took a deep breath to steady herself, and her natural instincts came into play. She looked at Alexander and adjusted the lens of her camera. 'Do you want me to take a picture of this?' she asked. 'Good evidence, if someone's broken in and stolen things.' Her hand was shaking slightly, but she forced herself to hold the camera still.

'Yes, go ahead,' said Alexander, stepping back before she clicked the shutter.

He walked round, studying the room. He stared at something on the floor and beckoned to Silver to join him. 'Look at this plate and these crumbs. Here's proof that someone's been here – and not so long ago.'

'Hey and look at these cognac glasses,' said Silver, just avoiding stepping on them. 'And there's a pair of tights. Someone's being living it up.' She tried to take a lighter tone.

'Don't touch anything.' Alexander's large hand held her back. 'I don't want anything moved.'

'Of course not,' said Silver. 'Give me credit for some sense.'

Alexander walked round, sliding open the heavy doors of the built-in closets. They were big enough for a man or even several men to hide in. A shiver ran down Silver's spine. The feeling of malevolence in the room grew stronger and she pushed down her fear that Alexander would flush someone out – perhaps armed with a knife or a pistol. What then? But she forced herself to stand her ground.

He continued shoving back the heavy doors, his face as thunderous as a marauding Viking's. He paused at one of the closets and thrust his head inside its depths. Silver stood stock still, her heart fluttering. He drew out an attaché case and thumped it onto the bed. 'What on earth is this?' he said.

'Oh, do be careful,' said Silver, trying to stop a second shiver. 'Suppose it's a bomb.' With her eye, she measured the distance to the outer door of the stateroom. Her fear escalated, not helped by the furious look on Alexander's face. He looked ready to murder someone. 'Are you sure it isn't someone from your family who's been here?' she offered feebly, more to calm herself than him.

Alexander didn't answer. He was busy trying to snap open the clasps of the attaché case. It wasn't locked and he raised the lid. 'Well, I'll be damned, look at this.' He sat down on the bed beside the case.

Silver peered over his shoulder. The case was full of used dollar bills, with rubber bands round each neat bundle. She lifted her camera swiftly again and took a picture.

Alexander was silent. So silent that Silver gave him a nudge. 'Have you any idea who could have come in here?' she asked. 'Who could have left those bundles of money? Smugglers?' Her voice trailed off.

Alexander's face was pale. He seemed to be searching for words.

'What is it?' asked Silver. 'Why don't you say something?'

With an obvious effort, he regained possession of himself. 'I'll say something and just wait till you hear it! I saw two very similar bundles of fifty dollar bills this morning in my dear brother's office, where I found him with a very slimy individual called Lazlo. I can't believe that I'm seeing a second lot of money like this today. This is serious crime. And I suspect very strongly Knut is involved in it. Damn him. Oh God, what will Elise say? She worships the ground he walks on.'

'Lazlo!' Silver picked up the name. 'I met a Lazlo today – with Knut. Not the sort of man you'd like to meet on a dark night alone, but the type who probably has all sorts of shady schemes going on.' She told him of her meeting with Knut and Lazlo. 'And get this: Lazlo had piles of clothes in his car. Some of them quite good. Just like these clothes in the rucksack.'

Alexander listened intently and frowned. 'It must be a huge operation and it gets worse all the time.'

'It's like those Russian dolls,' said Silver. 'Open one and you find a new problem, and then another, and another.'

Alexander paced across the spacious cabin as if he couldn't bear to be still. Then he wheeled round. 'We've forgotten to look in the bathroom.'

Silver followed close behind him. But the bathroom seemed empty. So was the separate toilet cubicle. She turned towards the glassed-in shower. 'What about here?' She hesitated for a moment, staring intently through the door of frosted glass which separated the shower from the rest of the bathroom. Was there a shadowy figure in the far corner? Alexander pushed swiftly past her and wrenched open the door.

Her heart froze as a shape erupted from the shower room. A thin, dark man rushed forward and headbutted Alexander in the stomach so that he reeled back. With a sideswipe of his arm, the man knocked Silver out of his way and she fell against a bathroom stool, which clattered to the floor.

Alexander was on his feet in a moment and ran to the main door of the suite, which now swung wide open. Silver heard his feet running along the corridor outside. She picked herself up and rushed to the door, but both pursuer and pursued had vanished.

Silver stood uncertainly at the door to the suite, then squaring her shoulders she went back inside. Perhaps there was a second intruder. Her heart in her mouth, she peered under the large beds, then slid open the door of each closet, leaving them gaping. Nothing. She heaved a deep sigh of relief, then bent down to snatch up a dark knife with a wicked-looking blade, which lay under the sofa.

She dropped it immediately. What a fool. Now her

finger prints would be on it. She found a box of tissues in the bathroom and gingerly packed the knife in them. Who was the man who had been hiding here? One of the stowaways? The police must have missed him in their search.

Her thoughts turned to Lazlo. He must be the man behind all this. He must have helped the stowaways to get on board and hidden them in this suite. Knut must be in on it too. Lazlo could never have managed without someone who knew the layout of the ship. She heard feet pounding along the corridor, then Alexander erupted back into the stateroom. He grabbed her by both arms. 'Are you okay?' he asked.

'Don't worry about me. What's happened to that man? Has he got away?'

'I lost the bastard as he slipped down one of the companionways,' he said. 'But the Captain has alerted everyone on board, so there's a big hunt going on for him. We'll catch him sooner or later. We must stop him getting off the ship.' He thrust her back. 'Can you wait here a little longer?'

'Not likely,' said Silver, sidestepping him. 'You're not leaving me alone any longer. The intruder might catch me. Anyway, I checked out everything here and I found this.' She picked up the knife and unpacked the tissues to show him.

He took it from her and shoved it in his pocket. 'Come on then,' he said, pushing through the door and striding along the corridor, Silver behind him. As they walked along, his mobile shrilled. Alexander studied the number on the display before answering. 'Hello, Elise, how are you?' His voice was hurried and reluctant. 'What can I do for you?'

As he spoke, he looked at Silver. She saw his body

stiffen and his eyes darken. 'Yes, Silver's here with me right now,' he said. 'But I'll get out to see you this evening. Don't worry. We'll put it right.'

He ended the short conversation and put his mobile back into his pocket. Silver looked at him questioningly.

'That's Elise,' he said. 'She's frantic because she's had three frightening phone calls. She says she's being threatened. She wants me to go out to see her this evening. Would you like to come with me? She asked me if you'd like to come.' Now his face was tired and drawn. He looked at her, his deep blue eyes almost pleading. There was no sign of the tough Viking now.

Silver put her hand on his arm. 'That's awful! Of course, I'll come with you,' she said. 'I really like Elise.'

Neither Captain Johansen nor the Chief Steward could throw any light on who had sneaked into the owner's suite. They stumbled over themselves to offer apologies that an intruder or intruders had managed to slip into the exclusive suite.

'The police searched the ship thoroughly. I thought we were in the clear.' Captain Johansen's tone was sheepish. 'I shall certainly review our security procedures.'

'You haven't reviewed them thoroughly enough.' Alexander's tone was belligerent.

'But no one has a key card apart from you and Mr Knut,' explained the Captain. 'The Chief Steward delegates the inspection and cleaning of the staterooms every day so that he always knows who has carried out the task.'

Alexander's eyes were cold with disapproval. 'As far as I can see, nothing is missing,' he said. 'Rather the reverse. Things have been brought into the stateroom and left there. I'll give DCI Berg a call and get him up here to see these strange rucksacks for himself, and of course the money. That should particularly interest him.'

'Perhaps the money comes from a robbery.' Silver spoke in a low voice to Alexander as Captain Johansen conferred with the Chief Steward, whose face was flustered red.

'No, it's not in Norwegian kroner,' Alexander answered, his back to the two ship's officers. 'That's what's so strange. So it's obvious some kind of smuggling activity is going on which brings in all these bundles of dollar bills.'

'Yes, and what about the cigarettes,' said Silver. 'Are they smuggled too?'

'A rucksack of cigarettes,' said Alexander. 'How much profit do you think you'd make on that? Not even a small-time smuggler would bother with so little. No, it's not so straightforward. Maybe the police can figure out what's going on. But my first concern is Elise. We have to get out to her.' He turned to the Captain. 'This is your territory, Johansen. You'll have to tighten up your controls. You've been far too slack. Get the police up here. I'll talk to them briefly and then I have to visit my stepmother. You'll have to carry on with the search for that man who's still loose on the ship.'

Alexander pushed Silver in front of him and they left the confines of the owner's suite. The Norwegian police were not as efficient as Silver had believed. But they went about their task examining the staterooms and shooting questions at her and Alexander as well as the ship's officers. Silver could see that Alexander was champing to get away, torn between getting the mystery of the rucksacks and the dollar bills cleared up, and his concern for his stepmother.

The warm wind slicked through Silver's hair as she and Alexander stood on the deck of his speedboat. She thrust her face forward, enjoying the cleansing feel of the breeze as they skimmed over the waves. She shot a look at Alexander, but his profile was stern and distant, as if chiselled from the rocks that surrounded the bay of Bergen. He was no longer the flirtatious companion of the afternoon, but a man with too many cares on his shoulders.

He caught her glance and his face broke into a rueful smile. 'It's not much fun for you, Silver,' he said. 'Every time we try to take time out, something gets in the way.'

He turned the wheel hard and the boat arced in a wide curve to the port side. He cut the engine and they glided into the calmer waters of the channel between the outer rocks of the island. The boat drifted and then bumped gently against the jetty. Alexander leapt onto the wooden platform with a rope in his hand. He drew the boat into its mooring, knotting the rope round a metal stanchion.

His hand was warm as he helped Silver to climb out of the boat. She avoided looking at him. She wasn't going to allow his powerful presence to overwhelm her. She had to get her story, but how far could she remain uninvolved with this family if she was helping Elise?

Chapter 9

Elise came out of the house and met them at the white wicket gate. Her hair was windswept and her eyes were brilliant. Could it be with fear?, Silver wondered.

Elise was wearing another floating dress of leaf green and brown, in harmony with the trees and bushes of the garden. Today she was wearing high-heeled shoes, so that she easily reached up to put her cheek coolly against Alexander's. 'How are you, Elise?' he said looking at her closely. 'What's all this about phone calls?'

Elise shuddered. 'Come into the house and I'll tell you all about it.' Her eyes darted around nervously. She caught sight of Silver and gave her a hug. 'I'm so pleased you came with Alexander, Silver,' she said. 'It gets very lonely out on this island, now that my husband has gone and I'm alone, except for Christiania and the cats.'

Silver looked down and saw two cats weaving themselves around Elise's ankles, tails on high like the masts of a ship. She wanted to be here with Alexander... and Elise, yet she was no further on with her article on the Rosenholms. She was getting too close to them. How ever was she going to backtrack and write an impersonal article? Her stomach clenched as she tried to see a way out of the dilemma.

Alexander led the way into the sitting room where the doors were still open to the terrace outside. It was lighter outside than indoors, and Silver watched how the shadows gathered in the corners of the room. At this time in the evening, the dark-beamed timber in the ceiling had a gloomy effect, vying with the white-painted walls. The three of them sat round the low coffee table and Christiania brought in a large marzipan-covered cake decorated with walnuts. She put down some coffee cups, and Silver noticed her hands were stiff with arthritis as she struggled to set out the china.

'Poor Christiania,' said Elise, as she watched the maid's retreating back. 'She's getting older and shakier all the time. Nor does she hear so well. So I'm in effect on my own.'

'Tell us about the phone calls,' said Alexander, cutting direct to the matter in hand. 'You can speak openly to us. Who was it? Do you know?'

'There have been three, maybe four or five,' said Elise. 'It's always a man's voice and he asks to speak to Mr Rosenholm.'

'To father? Or to me, or Knut?' asked Alexander.

'He won't say. Mr Ros'holm, he says and his voice is foreign. He speaks very bad English.' Elise twisted the hem of her silky dress in her fingers. The cats had slipped under the table and one of them lay curled up against Silver's foot.

'But is that what frightened you?' asked Alexander.

'No, no, of course not. But he says to tell Mr Rosenholm that he'll be along shortly. The job's done and now it's payment time,' he says. 'He has a horrid liquid-sounding laugh, and it rattles in his throat. It makes me so scared. Now I hardly dare pick up the phone. I've told him and told him that there's no Mr Rosenholm here now.'

'Oh Elise, you shouldn't have done that. Told him you're alone, I mean.' Silver sat forward and then bit her lip. She

118

should have kept her mouth shut and not interfered. Now she'd spelt out the danger to Elise and made the situation worse.

'Then the last call was from a man who called himself Frederick.' Tears ran down Elise's face, and she began to sob hard. 'Frederick, my husband!' she repeated. 'My heart almost stopped beating in my chest when I heard it. I called out his name. I thought maybe he was trying to contact me from the other side.' She wiped her eyes and looked defiantly at Alexander. 'I know you don't believe me about that. You never did.'

'Elise, I do believe you.' Alexander took her hand. 'I do believe someone's trying to call you. Not from the 'other side' as you call it, but for some reason.'

'Well, it wasn't Frederick's voice and then that awful liquid chuckle came over the line. Then I knew they were playing with me, trying to frighten me.'

Alexander's brows drew together. 'Did he ring today?'

'That's when I called you,' said Elise. 'I tried to call Knut, but you know him. He's never got time to speak to me.' She dabbed her eyes again and picked up the stripey cat. She stroked her until she settled in her lap.

Alexander moved restlessly. 'I'm sorry, Silver, but I think we'll have to change our plans. I'd better get back to town and check up on the ship before she sails tomorrow. And I want to make sure that the police have taken the money into their safe custody.' He looked at her questioningly. 'Could you possibly stay the night with Elise to keep her company? I know it's a lot to ask, but you see what she's going through.'

'But I've no pyjamas or luggage,' Silver said, a little taken aback. Then she caught herself and put her hand on Elise's. 'Of course I'll stay with you, Elise. Have you a spare bed and nightie?'

Elise jumped up and clapped her hands. 'Oh Silver, thank you. I'd feel much better. I'll go and get the bed in the spare room ready at once.'

'Walk down with me to the boat,' said Alexander to Silver.

They walked out into the garden. 'It's so beautiful here,' Silver said. 'You'd think it would be completely safe and nothing could disturb the tranquillity.' She slipped under the overhanging bough of an apple tree and white blossom drifted over her like snowflakes. She leant up against its trunk and shut her eyes. The evening was warm and she could hear the grasshoppers whirring in monotonous song, just as if they were cicadas far away in the tropics.

Alexander came up close and took her hands, lacing his fingers through hers. 'Thank you, Silver. It's really kind of you to stay with Elise this evening. She's got herself worked up into a bad state.'

'It's not surprising,' said Silver. 'Phone calls like that are terrifying. You don't know what's behind all this. She can't be alone tonight.' She turned her head away from him and kept her words cool and low key so that he wouldn't realise what he was doing to her senses. She was fighting a personal battle of restraint to keep a distance between herself and Alexander.

But Tom in London was waiting. If she didn't write the story, her job would be in jeopardy and in turn her life in London, and her flat.

She gave an awkward laugh and slipped away from Alexander. Opening the white gate, she started down the path in front of him.

The boat loomed up ahead of them. Alexander clasped Silver against him once more. He brushed her lips with his. 'Thanks, Silver,' he whispered. He released her quickly and sprang onto the boat. 'Cast off that rope there,' he shouted and, gunning the engine, he backed out of the narrow space of water into the open fiord.

Silver's heart beat a tattoo of confused feelings. She tried to breathe more evenly as she waved to Alexander. 'When will you be back?' she called, but the breeze snatched her words away, and the boat disappeared into the pearly twilight.

Back in the sitting room, Elise had drawn the heavy curtains. She put two candlesticks on the table and lit the deep red candles. She took out a dark green velvet cloth and a crystal prism, which reflected the candle flame, flashing blue, green and orange. She picked up a pack of large cards. 'Has anyone ever read the tarot cards for you?' she asked Silver.

'No, never,' Silver said. 'But I must warn you, I'm a real sceptic.'

Elise cast her a wary look. The smell of burning incense made the room feel more closed in and intimate as she shuffled and laid the pack of cards down on the table. 'This is for you, Silver. I want to see if your destiny's in Norway.' She pushed the cards towards Silver.

'No, no. Why should you think that?' Silver's head jerked up at Elise's words. 'I've got a home, and family and friends in England. My job's there. I can't just suddenly burn my boats and come over here. Besides, I don't speak the language.'

'You can learn the language,' said Elise, sliding her dark brown eyes sideways to look at Silver. 'And Norway's not so far away from England.'

'But why should I want to leave my own country?' Silver persisted, a wave of uneasiness flooding over her.

'Mix the cards.' Elise's gaze was compelling.

Half reluctantly, yet fascinated, Silver pushed the cards

around on the table. She gathered them up into a pack and handed them to Elise. She watched as Elise laid out the cards in a special pattern.

'Can you really foretell the future?' asked Silver.

'Ssh, just look at the cards.' Elise's eyes were faraway and dreaming as she turned up mystical and colourful figures.

The bright images seemed to speak to Silver with a seductive allure, yet as she watched Elise laying them out, the cards were strangely familiar. Elise gave little cries of satisfaction as she studied the spread of cards. Her soft voice and the ticking of the marble clock on the mantelpiece above the big fireplace were the only sounds in the room.

'The Empress,' said Elise. 'That's a wonderful card to represent you. The life force, creativity and fertility.' She slanted a look at Silver.

Silver regarded the picture of the voluptuous lady, dressed in her flowing robes of red and white. She looked down at her own light beige trousers, covering her slim legs. The queenly figure on the card resembled Elise much more than Silver. And Silver couldn't picture herself wearing a heavy crown either. Elise had a look of majesty which would carry it off.

Silver looked at the spread of cards that Elise had laid out for her. 'What about this card...that doesn't look good for me at all. The Death card – oh, how sinister!' She pointed to the card, which pictured a knight, his face a grinning skull, riding a white horse. Despite her scepticism, a frisson of fear slipped down her spine. But it was all a game, wasn't it?

Elise laughed on a high excited note. 'It's not as bad as you think.' Her long fingers, the nails covered with dark red polish, stroked the card. 'Look at the sun rising between the two pillars. It brings hope. It's the end of the old life and the start of a new one. There are big changes ahead for you, Silver.' She jumped up and began to whirl around, her green dress floating out around her. 'I knew it. I knew you were going to be important to us.' Still whirling around, she began to sing a Russian folk song, stamping her feet and clapping her hands. At least, that is what Silver thought it was, her Russian being non-existent.

'You're going to move to Norway. And let's look at your love life. Who's going to be important to you? Is it Alexander?' She swung away again in her dance, her eyes fixed all the time on Silver. 'Or is it Knut? I know it's someone close to me. I feel the ties that bind you to us.' She clapped her hands again, and her laughter held a trace of hysteria.

The maid, Christiania, appeared from nowhere and spoke soothingly to Elise. Silver couldn't understand what the maid said, but it seemed to have a calming effect on Elise. Christiania led Elise back to her seat, where she subsided, her eyes glittering strangely. Christiania bent down stiffly and picked up the stripey cat, which she deposited in Elise's lap.

Silver moved uneasily. Elise's actions were over the top and she seemed obsessed by the cards. Could she be playing a kind of game with her? 'Elise, maybe you have psychic powers,' she said coolly. 'But they've gone awry here. I have no interest in Knut! No way. He and I don't get on at all.'

'Then what about Alexander?' Elise's hands were busy kneading the cat's fur. She cast a sly look at Silver.

Silver avoided Elise's eyes. 'Elise,' she said. 'I hardly know Alexander and, in two days' time, I'll have gone back to England. He's very charming, of course – at least most of the time.' Silver hoped the dim light concealed the sudden flush to her cheeks. 'But my home is in England.

He's got his life here. Don't match-make. People have careers nowadays. They don't always have time for homes and family.' She spoke sharply to hide her embarrassment.

Again, Elise's laugh had a slightly hysterical note. She seemed nervy and overstimulated. Could she be slightly unhinged? The violent death of her husband could unbalance any woman. Silver watched Elise's hand as it hovered over another card in the spread. 'The Wheel of Fortune,' she said triumphantly. 'Now, Silver, you see...'

The sharp ringing of the telephone in the hall disturbed their contemplation of the cards. Elise clutched Silver's sleeve, her red-painted nails nipping her skin. Her almond eyes were wide and scared. 'Ooh...what shall I do?' she said trembling. 'Maybe it's that awful man again.'

'Don't answer it,' said Silver. 'Just let it ring. If it's him, he'll soon get tired.'

'No, no, I couldn't. Suppose one of the boys has had an accident. I've got to answer it.' Elise was up on her feet, agitatedly twisting her hands.

'I'll answer it for you,' said Silver. 'I won't let him scare me. I'll ask him what he wants.'

She rushed out into the hall, Elise at her heels, and seized the phone. 'Hello, who is this?' Silver spoke hoarsely. She strained her ears, catching a faint far-off melody floating over the phone line. It was somehow familiar and she realised it was the distant strains of the Grieg piano concerto. Someone was playing a CD in the background and the tones were haunting and melancholy. She clutched the phone tightly, feeling her palms sweating. 'Who's this?' said Silver again. 'Speak up.'

Elise hung close to her side, her eyes questioning. After a few moments, Silver put down the receiver. 'It does look like someone's playing a joke on you,' she said. 'And a horrid joke too. You'll have to report this. You have to

124

get a new phone. One that shows who's calling you on the display. Then you'll feel safer.'

The telephone shrilled again under her hand, and they both started in fright. Elise let out a little scream. She pushed Silver aside and grabbed the phone.

'Hello, hello,' she gasped. 'Who is this?' The colour drained away from her face. 'There's no Mr Rosenholm here. Leave me alone, or I'll call the police.' The telephone slipped from her hand and dangled on its cord from the hall table.

Silver picked it up and spoke into the receiver. 'Who's there? Answer me!' But all she heard was a sharp click and the line went dead.

Silver led Elise back into the sitting room. 'Whatever happens, we're not answering the phone again tonight. I'm going to unplug it. I've come here to keep you company. Perhaps we could get something to eat. I'll help you. Perhaps we can make a few of those wonderful open sandwiches.' Anything to distract Elise from the unsettling calls. Silver pushed down her fear. She'd soon be as edgy as one of Elise's stripey cats.

Elise nodded in agreement and they went into the kitchen, which sparkled, all white, with pristine worktops. One solitary teaspoon lay on the worktop.

'Where's Christiania?' Silver asked. 'Does she know about the phone calls?'

'Oh, she goes to bed early. Anyway, she's rather deaf so she never answers the phone.'

'I'll get out the plates and set the table,' said Silver. 'Just point me in the right direction.' She began piling the cups, saucers and plates on a tray, and searching for knives and forks in the drawers.

Elise took down a huge haunch of dark-coloured meat from a muslin bag hanging from a hook in the ceiling

125

in the old-fashioned way. 'It's dried, cured mutton,' she told Silver. 'A real Norwegian delicacy.' She began to slice the dark meat thinly and then put it on a large pewter plate. She took out a crusty loaf, then opening the door of the refrigerator, she brought out butter and the special Norwegian soured cream. She was piling everything on a tray when she stopped, suddenly transfixed. She stared hard out of the window into the fading light. 'There's a man out there,' she faltered. 'A tall man.'

Silver dropped the knife she was holding with a clatter. She came to stand behind Elise. 'You must be mistaken,' she said, striving for calm, as she tried to make out the dark shape of what just might be a person at the corner of the house. Elise stood rigidly, eyes dilated with fright. A corresponding stab of fear swept through Silver, but she tamped it down firmly.

'Look,' said Elise. 'Look, over there.' She leant over the worktop and pointed her finger at something outside. 'I can see his shadow. Now it's my turn to be murdered, just like Frederick.' Her face was as pale as winter snow, her body vibrating with tension.

Silver caught her arm. 'Stop it, Elise. You're terrifying us both. It's nothing but a shadow.' But she wasn't sure if she was right.

'I've got a gun, Silver. Let's get the gun.' Elise dragged Silver after her. 'Upstairs, follow me. Don't leave me alone for a minute.'

Elise's fear was contagious. Silver certainly didn't want to be alone either. They ran upstairs together, Elise clutching Silver's hand firmly. She pulled her into a large bedroom and opened the drawer of the bedside table. A revolver lay there gleaming dully, black and heavy. Elise picked it up and thrust it at Silver. 'Take it, take it,' she cried. 'We've got to protect ourselves. It's Frederick's old navy revolver, but I don't know how to use it. It's loaded, I know. He always kept it loaded.'

'I don't know how to use it either,' said Silver backing away as Elise again tried to thrust the ugly black weapon into her hands. 'Watch out. You'll shoot me, if you're not careful.'

'Take it then,' said Elise. 'You take it.' Her voice was a low scream.

Reluctantly, Silver accepted the gun from Elise's shaking fingers. It felt alien and cold in her hand. She held it behind her back, pointing down to the floor in case she should accidently slip the safety catch and it went off. The isolation of the island closed in on her. There was no way of leaving it except by boat, and she didn't even have a small rowing boat. How could Elise stand being so cut off from other people? Look what had happened to her husband, and now she was a lonely widow. 'Come downstairs now!' said Elise, two high points of colour in her cheeks. Her composure was returning after she'd put the gun into Silver's hand. Silver straightened her shoulders and concentrated on keeping the gun safe.

They went back downstairs again. Elise hovered uncertainly, her eyes on the front door.

'Don't even think of touching the door,' Silver rushed forward and grasped Elise's arm. 'If there's someone out there, you'll just allow him to walk right in.' She was now more frightened of what Elise would do next than of an unseen presence.

'You've got the gun,' said Elise. 'If you see anything move, just shoot!' Her eyes were glittering with excitement, her lips red.

She's totally unbalanced and freaked out, thought Silver. 'What if it's a cat...or a rabbit?' she asked.

'There aren't any rabbits on this island,' said Elise

127

in a cold voice. 'Don't be absurd, Silver. Did you think they crossed over by boat?' Rational Elise was even more frightening.

'A bird then?' Silver's hand holding the gun was slippery with sweat. 'I can't do it,' she faltered. 'I can't shoot...anything.'

'You're supposed to be protecting me,' shrieked Elise. Now she was changing before Silver's eyes, as fear gripped her in its claws.

Outside, a shoe scraped on the stones of the path. 'Shoot!' screamed Elise again. She seized Silver's arm. 'You don't need to shoot at them, just scare them.'

Shaking off Elise, Silver fingered the trigger nervously. The handle of the front door turned. It opened slowly. Silver raised the gun and pointed it. A tall man emerged from the shadows thrown by the house and stood framed in the doorway. 'For God's sake, put down that gun,' said a familiar voice and Knut strode into the light which streamed through the hallway.

Silver erupted into fury. She dropped the revolver like a hot coal and turned on Knut. 'What the hell were you doing skulking about the garden and scaring the living daylights out of your mother and me? Why didn't you come straight in? You could've been shot.' She almost spat out the words in her anger.

Knut's eyes darkened. Beneath his suavity lurked a dangerous wolf. He recovered swiftly from Silver's onslaught.

'Silly little Silver.' He put his arm heavily round her shoulders and led her into the sitting room. Her mouth was so dry she didn't manage to utter a word of protest.

Elise followed, fluttering and murmuring. 'Knut, darling, why didn't you come straight in? You really frightened us.' She dragged at his sleeve.

'Can't a man walk in his own garden, Mother?' he said. 'I was looking at the apple trees. The blossom's so pretty at this time of year.' He threw the cigarette he was smoking into the fireplace.

Why should Knut bother to lie? It was too dark to see the blossom on the boughs, and the apple trees were nowhere near the kitchen window. What had he been doing round the back of the house that he couldn't tell them straight? The shadowy figure had seemed to move around that area, not in the middle of the garden. So what was he trying to hide?

Was he alone or were there several more sinister characters out there?

It was late, but Alexander loved sailing at night, navigating round the buoys and watching the lighthouse beam out its warning of hidden skerries. An inner compulsion had driven him to go down to his boat and set sail for Rosenholm so that he could spend the night there with Silver and his stepmother, even though he was sure that they had probably gone to bed by this late hour. But he needed to check on them just the same. He allowed the boat to nose its way up the channel into the jetty. Straight ahead of him, bobbing gently beneath the jetty, Knut's flashy white cabin cruiser was already filling most of the mooring space.

Damn Knut, what was he doing here? Alexander had expected Silver and Elise to spend a quiet evening, just the two of them together. He'd hoped that Silver had been able to calm Elise's fears. Silver was a resourceful person and unlikely to lose her head. Elise on the other hand was highly volatile since the loss of her husband. That wasn't surprising given the brutal circumstances of his death, but Elise had always been emotionally fragile. Knut had inherited some of his mother's tendencies, and it showed in his roller-coaster style of living and sudden rages.

The police investigation on board *The Guiding Spirit* that afternoon had once more drawn Alexander's thoughts back to the circumstances of his father's death. And he had at last received the coroner's report, which had shaken him to his roots. It confirmed that his father had died from two gunshot wounds fired at close range to his temple. After that, the criminals had deliberately set fire to the little cottage so that they could cover their traces. Even today, Alexander bore the pain of his loss like a stone in his chest. He could never let his thoughts penetrate too deeply into how his father had spent the last hours of his life. That was why he trod on a knife's edge with Silver. That part of his life was closed forever and he wasn't going to let Silver ride roughshod over him just to get her story and send it out worldwide.

It was a burden keeping so much of the truth from Elise in order to spare her. There was no need for her to know all the tragic details. Her husband had been murdered and that was more than enough for her to bear. But it was strange that Knut didn't seem to want to know the details. His policy was simply to shrug it off.

Alexander climbed the steep path up to the house. He knocked swiftly on the front door before entering. A tableau of frozen faces met him as he strode into the sitting room. 'What's the matter?' he asked. 'Have you all seen a ghost?'

Knut was the first to recover. 'No, just a little contretemps with a gun.' His voice was exasperated. 'As I came up the path, your lady friend pulled out a revolver. She could've easily blown my head off.'

'Silver! What's this story? Are you okay?' Alexander strode over to her and grasped her arm. She sagged against him. He noticed her delicate features were strained and her luminous green eyes were huge. 'It was your father's revolver,' she told him. 'Elise gave it to me. But you should rather ask your brother what he was doing crawling around the garden at this hour. He terrified Elise and me. We thought he was a burglar, or worse.'

Knut sneered. 'I was merely in the garden. These silly women panic for nothing.'

Alexander looked out of the window, but the soft bluish light of the night enveloped the garden, and it was hard to make anything out clearly. He sat down beside Silver on the sofa. Too close. With her soft thigh against his, all his senses were set on fire. He found it hard to concentrate on what she was saying, while her nearness set waves of heat coursing through his body. 'Revolver?' he said with an effort, inching away from Silver's distracting warmth. 'For God's sake, Elise, what were you thinking about? How could you put Silver into such jeopardy?'

'It was Silver's fault.' Knut's voice was harsh. 'She was the one who pulled the gun.'

Chapter 10

Silver got up early. Last night, she'd left the Rosenholm family still in heated discussion about what had happened and, in a wave of fatigue, she'd simply gone upstairs to the bedroom Elise had prepared for her earlier. She'd sunk into the black depths of sleep under the goose-down duvet. At least she'd avoided dreaming about strange figures in the garden.

The strong morning sun shone through the white curtains at the window as Silver struggled out of the strange but comfortable bed. She untangled her feet from the flowery nightdress borrowed from Elise and caught sight of herself in the mirror. Now she really did resemble the Empress in the tarot cards that Elise had shown her. The nightdress enveloped her, flowing down to the floor.

She opened the door of the bedroom and peeked out. She'd have to find the bathroom. She really needed a shower to freshen up and clear her head. But which door was the bathroom? As she stood hesitating, the door opposite opened suddenly and Alexander appeared, a cloud of steam rising behind him in the doorway. He was clad only in light blue boxers. He stepped towards her smiling, his hand outstretched.

Silver tingled all over as she surveyed him, fascinated by the golden hairs on his tanned arms. She stretched out her hand to him, but suddenly he withdrew his hand and his expression became shuttered and remote. 'Good morning,

Silver, breakfast will be served in half an hour.' His voice was cool. 'I'll see you downstairs.'

Silver's hand dropped and she was left standing on the landing. Her thoughts were jagged and painful – the dilemma confronting her was still unresolved. Furious at herself for being so easily moved by Alexander's physical presence, she stomped into the bathroom and just avoided slamming the door.

Silver was the last one down. All the others were already gathered round the breakfast table. Alexander, Knut and Elise. Old Christiania carried in fresh coffee and offered Silver the plate of brown caramel-shaped goat's cheese.

Silver stared at it, wondering if she could eat anything at all.

Elise's eyes were tired and she seemed drained, but she brightened when she saw Silver. 'Sit beside me,' she said. 'I hope you slept well.'

Silver slipped into the chair next to Elise, glad she didn't have to sit by Alexander. She felt raw and exposed, but pride kept her calm. She gave him a half nod and lowered her eyes, avoiding his gaze. For once, she was glad of Knut whose social skills seemed to be back in place. His well-defined profile was like that on an ancient Roman coin, and it was clear he believed he was irresistible to females as he leant forward to Silver.

'You look as fresh as the new dawn,' he said, smiling intimately into her eyes as he passed her the basket of freshly baked rolls.

He spread Silver's napkin over her lap, making sure he touched her thighs through the crisply ironed linen. She was left unmoved, except for a jarring feeling of irritation.

'Silver, we have a suggestion to make to you.' Alexander's deep voice stirred her, although he was carefully evading her eyes. An unwelcome flush rose in her cheeks, and Knut seemed to notice her heightened colour. He leaned back in his chair, one eyebrow raised and a mocking smile spread over his face.

'Would you be willing to stay with Elise for this week and the next? Just until we get these nuisance phone calls sorted out.' Alexander's voice was persuasive. 'She really needs company just now. Wouldn't it be a nice holiday for you as well?'

'Holiday? For two weeks? I can't just drop my work?' Her voice came out in a harsh croak. 'It isn't a game, you know.'

'I'm willing to do an interview with you about the Rosenholm Shipping Line,' said Alexander.

So now he was trying to bribe her. But Silver felt sorry for Elise. The island was very remote and the phone calls were frightening. But how could she stay?

'You could call your editor,' said Alexander. 'I'm sure he'd give you time off.' He leaned forward, his eyes pleading her to say 'yes'.

'You're assuming too much,' said Silver sharply, summoning her resistance.

Yet he had blue Nordic eyes to die for. Damn her fluctuating emotions. Yes, she could write a good story, but she'd be sure to resist Alexander's attractions with all her strength.

So Alexander thought he was offering her an inducement or carrot stick to stay. Silver looked scornfully at him, but remained silent. If she stayed for a few days longer to write the story, she would do it on her own terms.

She squared her shoulders and looked at him straight in the eye. 'I'll stay,' she said. 'But for Elise's sake, not yours. I'll have to ask my editor if I can extend my time here. And I'll write my story according to my own judgement! You're not going to fob me off with a smooth public relations exercise.'

Chapter 11

Silver realised she had tied her own hands. Now she was trapped into staying on in Norway for several more days. But there was a story to be uncovered here, and though it was not his intention, Alexander had handed the opportunity to her on a plate. Oh yes, Alexander Rosenholm, you'll soon see I'm not to be fooled around with! I'll write the best story of my life!

In the flurry of clearing the table after breakfast, she slipped outside. Let Knut and Alexander carry out the dirty dishes. She wasn't feeling at all pleased with either of them just now. Besides, she wanted to call Tom in London without being overheard. Automatically, she fumbled in her pocket for her mobile. Gone, of course. Damn, she'd have to phone from Elise's telephone in the hall. But first there was something she had to check out.

The cool fresh morning air blew lightly through her hair, and the smell of the pine trees made her stop for a moment to breathe in the aroma. The whole place was alive with the wings and cries of the seabirds. Questions were whirling around in her head. What was Knut doing last night as he skulked around outside? And why did he lie about what he was doing?

She walked round the house, her eyes fixed on the ground. No traces of people here, only flowerbeds with heavy-headed pink peonies lazily breathing out a soft perfume. Elise must have green fingers or perhaps she had a gardener. Silver crossed over to the flowerbeds on the other side, which were full of yellow flowers, but as far as she could see, there were no fresh footprints or signs of anyone having stood in the loose earth outside last night. She moved round to the back of the house. The kitchen window was thrown open and Elise popped her head out.

'Hello, Silver, we're just making plans for the day.' Her voice was light and happy. The scared woman of the night before was gone.

'I'm just taking a few pictures of the island,' Silver's excuse rose glibly to her lips. 'It'll be a nice souvenir to take home with me and, besides, I need some exercise.' She pulled out her camera and waved it at Elise.

'I'll send one of the boys to keep you company,' said Elise, as she leant farther out of the window.

That was the last thing Silver wanted. 'No, no, don't bother them. I'll be along in a few minutes.' She retraced her steps and deliberately walked away from the house through one of the straggle of ragged pine trees that dotted the island. There was no clear path and she picked her way through the trees at random. It was a long time since she'd tried to track anything, but she searched hard in the tufted grass, not sure what she was looking for. She cast a glance behind her. The window was now closed, so she turned back to the house.

She kept her eyes fixed on the ground, as she circled around. Nothing unusual as far as she could see. She turned the corner to the kitchen window, keeping low. Her eye caught a glint of something half hidden in the grass. A find! She pounced on it. An empty packet of cigarettes, crumpled and thrown down. Silly, really, she was behaving like an old-fashioned detective. The blue, white and gold packet was an unusual brand, with strange lettering. Cyrillic, probably Russian. Where had she seen a similar one recently? It nagged at the inner recesses of her mind. Of course, back on the ship in the owner's suite. She slipped the packet into her pocket, and then noticed two cigarette ends carelessly tossed away. Either Knut had stood outside long enough to smoke two cigarettes, or he hadn't been alone. There was a footprint or two in the soft earth, but did that mean one person with two feet or were there several people outside peering in at her and Elise?

Did Knut have voyeuristic instincts? Why would he be interested in two women pouring over a pack of cards? Whatever his reasons, it was not a nice thought to be the target of a peeping Tom, and why? Knut could just as well have come straight in and joined them.

Could the illegals have been on this island too? Silver shivered at the idea. There were myriads of islands in the Bergen archipelago, so there was only one reason for choosing this one. Knut and his friend Lazlo were the links. Did Elise know about Knut's shady dealings or was she completely innocent? She seemed to live in her own sheltered world with her cats, her tarot cards and her past with her husband. How shocking that she should be implicated in Knut and Lazlo's dirty business.

Silver pondered on Knut's strange behaviour as she walked back into the house to seek out Elise. 'Can I please use your phone?' she asked her. 'I've got to call my editor in London to see if he'll let me stay on in Norway.'

Elise smiled and gestured towards the telephone in the hall. Not very private. Silver would have to keep her call short. She didn't want Alexander to know that she had bigger plans for her article than merely writing about the Rosenholm history. Her starting point for her story was obvious: the influx of illegal immigrants on Alexander's ship. He wouldn't be pleased at her digging into that, but she couldn't help it. Tom would recognise a good story, and her job would be safe.

Tom's abrupt, no-nonsense voice came over the line. 'Yup?'

'Look Tom, I think it can be a big story starting with the stowaways on the ship as you know. You were right, and I've been following up a few leads.' She spoke with a low voice into the telephone.

'Great, Silver. That's what I wanted. Illegal immigrants is hot news. When can you get the story done?' Tom's voice was enthusiastic and it boomed down the line.

Silver looked cautiously behind her, but the hallway was empty. 'It's a great story, Tom. I want to check out the cruise ship I wrote about earlier. There are some interesting developments there. I just need a few more days to track things down, okay?'

'Yeah, Silver, we've been wondering about you. We haven't heard from you. What's happened to your mobile? Permanently switched off?' He gave a bark of laughter at his own joke.

'Sorry, I've had to use this phone today,' Silver said. 'I'll get hold of a mobile and call you later. I can't really talk now.'

'Okay', said Tom. 'Be sure to file your story by Thursday, and then you can take a few days' holiday. Isn't that what you want? You need a break. Sun, sea and sex.' He laughed again in her ear. 'But you wouldn't, would you, Silver?'

'Wouldn't what?'

'Let your hair down like the rest of us!'

'You'd be surprised,' she said coolly.

'Look, about the story – I know a guy who works in the local newspaper there. D'you want to call him? He might have some leads and fill you in on some background. I've got the number, somewhere.'

She could hear him scrabbling about in his papers.

'Try the computer, Tom,' she shouted down the telephone line. 'You know you've typed it in there.'

She could hear the computer keys clicking, then his voice. 'You're right. Here it is. Got a pen handy?'

She picked up the pen from the table. 'Go ahead.'

'His name's Jan Brinchman and the number is five five four seven two nine seven two. He'll help you. He owes me one.'

Silver became aware of someone standing behind her. She spoke into the receiver. 'Thanks Tom, I'll get back to you by Thursday.' She put down the phone quickly.

Alexander! How long had he been standing there? She ran the conversation quickly through her head. What had he heard? Details about the story she was planning to write or the joke about sun, sea and sex in Tom's hearty voice? Because from now on it was strictly business and she was going to keep Alexander at arm's length. She wasn't going to let him play around with her, making her heart beat faster. She had a job to do.

'What's this talk about a cruise ship?' he said.

'So you've been eavesdropping.' Her slight guilt made her overreact. 'That was a private phone call.'

'Look Silver,' he took a step towards her and she backed away smartly. If she didn't let him get too close, she could resist him and stay strong. 'What is it?' she said.

'What was that about cruise ships? You're not going to write about *The Guiding Spirit*, are you?' His eyes pierced her and he looked as fierce as a golden eagle protecting its young.

She turned her back on him. 'I'm not asking you what I can write about. I only report facts,' she said over her shoulder. 'Do you want me to stay with your mother or not?'

'Silver.' Out of the corner of her eye, she saw his hand

stretch out to her and then drop. His voice was resigned. 'Okay, let's get your baggage from the hotel and get you settled in here. I'm going to take the boat over. Christiania wants to get in some food supplies. She likes to do her shopping in Bergen, instead of us bringing it out to her.'

Silver was relieved. Christiania would be a fine buffer and keep Alexander from distracting her. 'Ready in two minutes,' she said.

In Bergen harbour, Silver gave a hand to Christiania, pulling at her plump arm to help her over the side of the boat onto the quayside. 'How will you manage to carry your heavy shopping?' she asked, looking at Christiania's old-fashioned basket.

But Christiania just smiled and nodded. '*Tusen takk*,' she said. It was clear she didn't understand a word of what Silver had said. Behind her, Alexander said: 'I'll go along and help her to carry her shopping when she's finished. We always do it that way.'

'I've got some things to do too,' said Silver, fingering the little note with Jan Brinchman's telephone number, which nestled in her pocket. 'I need to get everything sorted out at the hotel and to pack. It'll take a little time.'

'I'll pick you and your baggage up at the hotel in two hours' time then,' said Alexander, smiling at her. His eyes were tender and unguarded, raising a question in Silver's mind. Maybe he really didn't mean to tease her like that in his stepmother's house. Perhaps he'd been fired up with desire just as she had been, but then he'd felt constricted by all his family around him. She'd have to build up a wall of ice against him if she wanted to survive the next week.

She was quite sure she had to write this story. A pang of guilt shot through her about what she was about to do. But Alexander's abrupt rejection of her this morning had clouded her judgement. Perhaps she should've tried to talk to him. She'd wanted his approval and liking, yet now she was preparing to throw it all away. It was safer that way. In chasing the story, she was only doing her job, and she'd be very careful not to harm Alexander and his family. But the guilty feeling remained.

Silver stumbled and banged her shin as she hurried up the stairs in her eagerness to meet Jan Brinchman in the newspaper offices of *Bergens Post*.

He came towards her holding out his hand in the formal Norwegian way. He was another fair-haired and blue-eyed Norwegian, but not much taller than Silver herself. 'Tom's an old friend,' he told her. 'We usually have a couple of beers together when I'm in London. He's passed on some good leads for stories too.' His English was fluent with an attractive foreign lilt.

Silver settled in her chair, feeling relaxed for the first time that day in an environment familiar to her.

'So you want to know more about the Rosenholms?' said Jan. 'They're a very powerful family. They used to own a few fishing boats, and then Rosenholm senior built up the shipping line from that modest start. Hell of a blow for the family when the old man died.'

'Tell me about that,' Silver said. 'What actually happened? How was he murdered?'

'Nobody really knows what actually happened. But he was alone out on one of the other islands which they own in the fiord. The family had reported him missing and after a day or two, the police found his charred remains in the burnt-down cottage. In fact, they had a hard time proving it was him. But they got his dental records. It seems he was shot first, then they set fire to the cottage to cover up the murder.'

Even though Silver had heard the story from Alexander, it still filled her with horror as she listened to Jan's matter-of-fact voice. Sympathy welled up inside her for what Alexander and his family had been through.

Jan's fingers tapped quickly into the large computer in front of him. He got up from his chair and crossed the big open-plan newspaper office to a printer which was churning out sheets of paper. 'Here's the article we wrote after the stowaways were discovered. You do read Norwegian, don't you?' he asked.

'I wrote the original article myself,' said Silver, smiling at him.

He pushed a pile of photographs towards her and she studied them intently, recognising the scenes from the night when the stowaways were discovered. 'My Norwegian's improving,' she said. 'Even if I can only speak a few words, I understand a lot more. Anyway, tell me more about the Rosenholms.'

'Well, the elder brother, Alexander, is the one who keeps the business running. But you knew that?' He looked at her inquiringly. 'You want to watch out for Knut Rosenholm. He's got a reputation for life in the fast lane and not doing any work. They say he's a real headache for his older brother. He's had to bail him out several times.'

'It can't be easy,' said Silver. 'What about Elise, the stepmother? Where does she come into it?'

'All three of them sit on the board of the company. You can imagine these board meetings. Mother and younger son against the one who does the real work.'

'Really,' said Silver. 'I thought that Alexander was good friends with his stepmother.'

'Probably,' said Jan. 'But he's not her blood son. You can see how family jealousies arise. Little brother Knut feels left out, but he's not prepared to work hard, so he twists mother's arm. He's always short of cash for his gambling.'

'Gambling?' said Silver. 'What does he gamble on?'

'They say he'll gamble on the weather. But seriously, he gambles on everything from the horses in England to the slot machines in the local arcade. Lucky for his brother we don't have casinos in Norway.'

'It must be hard for Alexander trying to hold on to the purse strings.' Silver sipped at the plastic cup of bitter coffee that Jan had brought her and tried to collect her thoughts. She didn't want Jan to see how upset she was about how Alexander's father had died. Alexander had a huge number of burdens on his shoulders. He was to be admired for the way he took care of Elise even though it was becoming clear to her that his stepmother didn't always support him.

'Back to the immigrants on the cruise ship,' she said. 'Can you give me a lead on someone to talk to?'

'Yeah, there's one man who works as an interpreter for these immigrants. All very hush, hush. He's trying to raise money to get his brother over here. Did you know it costs around ten thousand dollars to get a seat on one of these buses that cross the northern border between Norway and Russia? Some people have to sell their houses to raise the cash. They borrow from their relatives – or wherever they can get the money. But if something goes wrong or they're turned back at the border, they've nothing left to go back to. It can be disastrous for them.'

Silver made some quick notes. 'Why do you think these people were on board the ship?'

'I think they'd been told that if they could sneak on board, they could work their passage to America – you know, the promised land. They've probably paid through the nose for that privilege too. You know how it is with

143

these people trying to cross the English Channel desperate to find a new life.'

'It's an even bigger leap to cross the Atlantic,' said Silver. 'Would they really get a job on the ship?'

'I doubt it. Certainly Alexander Rosenholm wouldn't want to get mixed up in anything illegal. He's got enough problems without that. The shipping line is doing nicely too.'

'Then who's behind all this scam?'

'Who do you think? Russian Mafia, perhaps. Certainly they're playing for high stakes. It's a very dangerous business dealing in people. But if any lives have been lost or anybody's got hurt, it's all hushed up very quickly. Talk to the interpreter. Maybe you can get something out of him. That'd be a great story. But you'll have to watch your back to avoid a run-in with these heavies.'

'What's the interpreter's name? Where do I find him?'

'Lazlo Ivanov. You'll catch him on this telephone number...' He pushed a piece of paper towards her.

'Lazlo...I've met a Lazlo. Could it be the same one?'

'Bald, well-fed, with a couple of flashy gold teeth?'

'That's the one.' Damn. It appeared that all roads led to Lazlo. There seemed to be no way of avoiding him. Silver supposed she'd have to chase him up from this new angle as the interpreter. Perhaps he could lead her a step further so that she could meet one of the immigrants. In secret, of course. No names, perhaps even no faces.

Silver looked at her watch as she left Jan's office. Only half an hour to go before Alexander came to pick her up from the Hotel Norge. Lucky that Bergen was such a small town, with everything close to the centre. She began to speed through the streets, her feet pounding the grey pavements until she was breathless and her light cotton top clung unpleasantly to her back in the summer heat. She kept on running. She'd got to be back at the hotel before Alexander arrived as she didn't want him asking any awkward questions about where she'd been. Her mind was made up. She would concentrate on her career, produce a first-class story and not let herself get bowled over by a personable male.

How could she have been so stupid? She supposed she was a bit vulnerable after the death of her mother, and then Mike dumping her like that. God alone knew where her father was. Up the Amazon or perhaps the Zambesi. She never knew where he was. By now, she was used to him turning up for three or four days and then disappearing again for months. The only person she could really depend on was herself. And from now on, nobody would distract her. She was earning good money and she needed to keep it that way. She was doing a good job, and she was not going to let Alexander get under her skin like that.

Now she had reached the door of the hotel. She ran quickly up the two flights of stairs, and shoving the key card in the door, she opened it and entered the room.

She fell back in horror. The hotel wardrobe hung open. Her clothes had been dragged out and tossed all across the room. Even her best friend wouldn't call her tidy, but this was complete chaos. She remembered leaving some of her clothes lying across the bed, but when she'd left the room, most of her clothes were either still in her suitcase or shoved quickly into a couple of drawers. She hadn't brought very many clothes with her, but the way they were thrown around the room made it appear that she'd brought twice the amount.

The door to the minibar hung open, all the small bottles from inside had been pulled out and thrown on the floor. She just avoided stepping on some broken glass. The whole room stank of old whisky and sour wine. Her stomach clenched and a shivering black fright swept through her.

Her knees buckling, she forced herself to walk into the bathroom. There she found her washbag upended and all her make-up spilt out on the floor. Even her tube of toothpaste had been squeezed flat by the intruder. He'd drawn a horrid round face with a sinister smile on the mirror. Silver put her hand over her mouth to stifle a scream.

She picked up her suitcase. It was entirely empty…But she never ever emptied it completely – it saved packing it again when she had to leave.

The knot in her stomach expanded. Someone had clearly been here looking for something. But what? Not only had this person thrown her clothes all around the room, but he, or she, had been picking through her belongings.

Now her cotton top didn't feel so warm as she looked at her strewn garments and wracked her brains, trying to make out if anything was missing. Her laptop. But there it was on the dressing table. She rushed towards it and almost knocked it to the floor in her haste. The cable wasn't plugged in. Hadn't she left it connected as she always did? She shoved the plug into the wall and opened the lid. She pressed the 'on' button. Bing! The laptop grumbled and whirred as it usually did when booting up. With trembling hands, she typed in her password and clicked on the most recent file. Yes, yes, that was the one she'd been working on last…before she came to Norway. Everything seemed all right. Could they have been looking for the stowaway article? But it was published now and out in the open. So it couldn't be that they were looking for.

The Rosenholm article – was that what they were looking for? But it wasn't yet written. She'd only got as far as some handwritten notes, which were not yet transferred to her laptop. Why were these people after her and who were they? This was the second time she'd been got at since she came to Norway.

Her pulse beat erratically. People were able to come in and out of her hotel room. But why? She'd nothing of value except her Rolex and she was wearing that. Thank God, she was moving out. She couldn't sleep in this room now, never knowing if someone was going to suddenly walk through the door.

There was a sharp rap on the door. On shaky legs, she left the laptop and walked over to peer through the security peephole. Alexander stood outside, his broad shoulders blocking the light. She pulled open the door. 'Thank goodness, you've come,' she said. 'Something awful has happened and I'm not ready yet.'

His gaze raked the topsy-turvy state of the room. 'Has someone been in here?' he asked quickly.

Too quickly? Silver wondered.

'Is there anything missing?'

'Not as far as I can see,' she said. 'They've just had a field day searching through my clothes for some reason. But I don't know what they could be looking for. I've nothing of value. It's even more worrying that they haven't taken anything, as they may come back to search some more.'

'Have you called down to tell the hotel what's happened?'

'Not yet,' she said. 'I've only just come in.'

'But you left me hours ago.'

Silver bit her lip, but said nothing. She wasn't going to tell him about her visit to Jan Brinchman. 'I went shopping and things,' she said improvising swiftly. 'I didn't expect to come back to this horrible chaos.'

'Don't worry, we've plenty of time,' he said. 'I told Christiania we'd have lunch together, and she's gone off to see her sister.' He strode across the room as if he owned it. He turned towards her. 'Aren't you going to report this to the hotel and possibly to the police?' He looked at her intently.

Silver's body began to tremble. She bent down and began fiddling with her suitcase, her face turned away from him.

'Silver,' he squatted down beside her. 'I'm sorry if there was a misunderstanding this morning. I didn't mean it that way.'

'Don't give it another thought. I haven't time to play around. I've got work to do!' She laughed awkwardly. 'I think you're trying to make use of me when it suits you.'

Chapter 12

The strains of the last few days had taken their toll on Silver. A surge of irrational anger coursed through her. 'I don't go in for cheap thrills or quick fumbles.' The words tumbled out of her as her whole body shook. She subsided onto the faded pink velour armchair, astonished by her own outburst.

'Silver, Silver,' said Alexander. 'That's not what I meant at all.' His face was white, and he towered over her like a pine tree in the forest. He seized her arm spinning her towards him.

Silver flinched away from him. 'I'm sorry,' she said, her lips stiff. 'My stay in Bergen has got a bit much for me. Right from the start when my passport was stolen at the fair, then I was deluged by the sprinklers on the ship and, on top of that, the scene with Elise last night. And now this!' She gestured towards the spoiled room. 'I ask myself why? Why am I being targeted like this? I feel like some kind of jinx, attracting danger wherever I go. I know nothing special – I'm not involved in any kind of dubious activities.'

She could feel tears pricking behind her eyes, but she refused to let them fall. She turned her head away from him, fighting for control. Swallowing, she rushed on: 'I don't like guns and I think your stepmother is more than a little unbalanced. But I won't let her down and I'll stay with her as promised.' As she struggled to regain her composure, she picked up her clothes and folded them rapidly before shoving them back into her suitcase.

'Thanks, Silver,' Alexander looked relieved. 'I'd feel better if you're with Elise at this time. Believe me, I know we're not the easiest of families.'

He began helping her to pick up her belongings. 'You said nothing was missing.' His tone was sharp. 'No jewellery or valuables?'

Silver gave an uncertain laugh. 'No, nothing. But who could possibly have been here? Not an ordinary thief. And surely not the chamber maids. What could they be looking for?'

'What about your computer?' said Alexander. 'Has anyone tampered with it? Had you written anything about our company on it?' He stood tensely waiting for her answer.

'I think it's okay,' she said. 'I checked it and, besides, it's got extra password security. Unless someone is a really nifty hacker, they wouldn't get past it. Luckily, I hadn't transferred my latest notes onto it. They're still here in my bag.' She crossed her arms over her chest and looked at Alexander. He seemed relieved and walking towards the door of the room, he pulled it open. He hefted her suitcase into the passage outside, then turned back to look at her. 'Look, Silver, I'm not saying that it didn't happen, and now it's up to you. But what good would it do to stir things up if you've lost nothing? We're leaving now. The jeep's outside. Let's just forget it.'

Silver was fired up and ready to argue. Then Alexander's words sank in. Did she really want to make a lot of trouble and hang around a police station while a bored policeman, struggling with his English, noted down that nothing was missing. It was easier just to let it go. She had far too much to think about now. Alexander's hand came up and stroked her face. 'Relax,' he breathed. Silver shut her eyes and leaned against him for a moment.

He fished in his pocket and held out a mobile to her. 'Here's one of the company phones and you can borrow it for a bit. I really think you need it.'

'Goodness, that was thoughtful.' Silver put the mobile in her pocket. 'I'll check it out later.' She zipped up her large carry-on bag. 'Now I'm ready to leave,' she said, picking up her laptop and shoulder bag. She thrust away the nagging doubt that Alexander didn't want anyone investigating into the situation.

'I thought we might have lunch down by the seashore.' He smiled at her and her spirits lifted. 'It'll give you a break from here.'

'That sounds great,' she said, unable to hinder a warm glow flowing through her. Maybe they could take a little time out and just enjoy themselves. This man could play her like a violin, tuning her senses from melancholy low notes to high singing happiness. She'd have to work very hard to resist his assault on her emotions.

Alexander led the way to the other side of the harbour from where yesterday Silver had sat in the café with Knut. The seafood restaurant where they now sat was thronged with tourists as well as some business people, the men wearing crisp open-necked shirts and Bermuda shorts, just like Alexander. It must be the required business wear for the successful executive in summertime Norway.

The tables were covered with pristine white tablecloths, shining cutlery and an assortment of wine glasses. Far above their heads, large white seagulls sailed on currents of air, their wings outstretched against the piercing blue sky.

They sat down at a table overlooking the marina and

the scores of tall-masted yachts moored there. A gentle breeze fluffed up Silver's hair, and she leaned back in her chair absorbing the sun. 'Does Knut come here?' she asked, her eyes half closed. 'Because I don't want to see him or his funny friends.'

'Funny friends?' Alexander handed Silver the large menu. 'Who are you thinking about?'

Silver took a sip of her aperitif. 'Have you met the man, Lazlo, who's running about with Knut? I should ask you: Who is this man?'

Alexander raised his eyebrows in surprise. 'Yes, I've met this Lazlo. He's Russian or Eastern European of some kind.'

'Well, he seems a pretty suspicious character. I just know that he and Knut are involved in some kind of shady dealings.'

'Look Silver,' Alexander leaned forward, his gaze intent upon her. He picked up her hand, sending little thrills of warmth up her arm. 'This is strictly confidential. Off the record, as you might say. You're right. I'm absolutely sure that Knut is involved in some 'shady dealings' as you call it.'

Silver tried to draw her hand away from him. 'Well, it's obvious – it's bringing people illegally into the country. They have a great operation going. And Lazlo and Knut are the kingpins of the operation.'

'If I know anything about Knut, it's a money-making scheme, and Lazlo is his partner. But he's not like Knut's usual smooth friends,' said Alexander.

'I've met Lazlo too.' Silver threw out the words as a kind of challenge. 'When I last saw him, he was down by these old warehouses over on the other side of the harbour.'

'Yes, I know the place. They've been standing empty for a long time. Let's take a look at them after we've eaten,' he said. He was silent for a moment as if trying to reach a decision.

The breeze stirred the white tablecloth. Alexander bent his head closer to Silver, his voice so low it was hard to distinguish it from the buzz of the sound of the other people around them. 'Can I trust you?' His eyes were pools of dark blue earnestness. 'You won't write anything about what I'm going to tell you, will you? You'll keep it strictly off the record as I asked?'

Silver smiled at him. He had swallowed his pride and was almost pleading with her. The combination was irresistible. He appealed to her sense of fair play and honesty. She traced a pattern over his hand. 'Maybe you shouldn't press me to keep secrets, Alexander.'

The waiter's voice broke into their intense concentration on each other. 'Are you ready to order?' How long had he been standing there attentively? Silver didn't know. She withdrew her hand from Alexander's warm clasp.

'You choose.' She pushed the menu back at Alexander. 'You know about seafood.'

'How about lobster? Are you up to dealing with that?' he asked.

'Love it,' said Silver. 'Struggling with a lobster might just have a calming influence on me.' She cast him a teasing glance.

The waiter vanished back into the kitchen with their order, and Alexander stared intently at Silver until she began to move uneasily in her seat. She wondered what really was going on in his head. Was she just a pawn to be made use of or was he genuinely interested in her?

'You'll have noticed that Knut and I don't really get on,' he said.

'That's the understatement of the year,' Silver said, taking another sip of her aperitif. She waited.

It was as if a dam had burst. Words came pouring out of Alexander. 'I'm so worried about Knut. Normally, he comes to me for handouts and, believe me, I give him a hard time before I give him any money, because it always means I have to square it with the accountants, and it's a drain on our company's resources. Usually, it's for a new car, a new speed boat – you've seen the latest – or some other expensive plaything.'

Silver nodded. 'I'd guessed as much,' she said.

'Okay.' Alexander sighed. 'But now it's gambling. He's a compulsive gambler. He spends vast sums of money. Sometimes he wins, mostly he doesn't. And then he comes to me.'

'Oh God, Alexander, what do you do then?' A rush of sympathy for him flooded over her.

'You tell me, Silver. What should I do? He's my brother. I have to try and keep him out of trouble and avoid the family name being dragged further into the mire, not to mention the company finances being decimated.'

'What about Elise? Where does she come into this?'

'Oh, Elise always sides with Knut. Our latest battle is over the introduction of casinos on our ships. I'm dead against it. We'd lose a lot of space in building the casino – space which would be better used as passenger cabins or even a larger range of shops. We're doing fine without adding a casino, which brings with it all sorts of implications.'

Silver looked out down the fiord. 'Have they caught the people who murdered your father?' she asked, trying to fathom what it would feel like to have lost a parent in such circumstances. Sitting in such pleasant, relaxed surroundings, it was hard to grasp the horrors Alexander must have gone through when he discovered his father was dead, and in such a terrible way.

He shut his eyes as if deep fatigue swept over him. 'It's a long drawn-out process,' he said. 'The fire in the cottage obliterated most of the traces of who'd been there. So it's hard to get any leads, so the police tell me.'

Silver repressed a shudder. 'Where exactly did it happen?' she asked. 'Which island? Not the one where your mother lives?'

'Stepmother,' he corrected her gently. 'No, it happened on a smaller island, a couple of kilometres away out in the fiord. The one with the stave church over there,' he pointed far out. By straining her eyes, Silver could just make out the silhouette of the black stave church rising from the grey rock of the island. Hadn't she seen it from the rooftops of Bergen on her unfortunate trip up the mountainside with Alexander?

'That's the one,' Alexander nodded. 'That island was his private sanctuary – it's been in our family for years. My father used to sail out there in his boat to do some fishing or get some peace if he wanted to work on a new strategy for the company. Elise never goes there. It's too quiet and remote and uncomfortable. There's no running water and there's only an old stove for cooking simple food. And an outside lavatory!' He looked at her quizzically.

'What about Knut then?'

'Very seldom. It's too primitive for him. He likes his fast-living lifestyle, as you very well know.'

'What about you, Alexander? Did you go out there sometimes with your father?'

He moved restlessly. 'It's easy to see you're a journalist. You ask so damn many questions.'

Silver sat back in her chair. She wouldn't allow herself to be put off. She was now in full pursuit of the facts. She gazed out over the gentle swell of the sea, thinking hard.

She fixed her eyes on him. 'Just tell me, what happened

on your father's last day? Were you out on the little island with him? Was Knut?'

'As far as I know, nobody was there.'

'But somebody was, and that somebody killed him. These illegal immigrants that broke into your ship – could they have been there?'

Alexander looked at her. 'Desperate men, desperate methods? But how could they have got out there? And why?' His eyebrows met in a frown.

He turned away abruptly to gaze out across the sea, withdrawing from the easy intimacy that was building between them. He was putting up the barriers again. Now she would have to try and coax him out of the dark place of retreat he'd returned to.

A seagull screamed near her ear. She whirled round, startled by the large, well-fed white bird with its long talons. It dropped to the ground and snatched up a crust of bread lying on the smooth stone floor of the restaurant.

'Alexander,' she touched his hand gently as it lay on the table. She leaned forward. 'Why don't we go out to the island and see what we can find?' Against her will, her eyes were drawn to his sensual well-formed mouth.

'I'm very observant,' she pressed him. 'You can rely on me to be an excellent outside witness. Strictly off the record, of course! I've no axe to grind. I was far away in England when it happened.'

His eyes darkened and his broad shoulders seemed to relax. 'Silver,' he said, lacing his fingers through hers. 'You've got a deal. You are irresistible. You're sensible, and maybe you can lift some of the guilt from my shoulders that I should have been out there on the island that day with my father.'

He took hold of her other hand and pulled her gently towards him across the table, neither of them noticing that the white tablecloth was being crushed between them and the knives and forks were skittering out of place.

'Two lobster parfaits,' said a voice, and they sprang apart like coiled springs. The waiter stood beside them, his hands full of dishes. He set them down on a side table and began righting the confusion of cutlery and straightening the tablecloth.

Alexander's hand went up to smooth his slightly dishevelled hair, and Silver caught him having a quick look around at the other tables. She noticed several of the other guests were staring openly at them, smiles curving their lips. She sat up straight and smiled defiantly back.

The waiter placed the lobsters in front of them and withdrew. Silver seized the water jug and filled Alexander's glass and then her own. She took several deep swallows and fanned her face with her napkin. Alexander watched her, something intense flaring from his studied concentration of her face and body.

Silver found she was ravenous. Alexander showed her how to clip the claws of the lobster with the special lobster tongs to extract the meat. The fresh sea-tangy taste of the pink meat was heaven, and Silver soon got the hang of dealing with the hard crustacean shell. She picked delicately at the fresh green salad.

'Skol,' Alexander said, raising his glass of wine to her. He reached across the table and gently curled his fingers round hers. 'To our expedition and to our better acquaintance.' The old-fashioned words rang pleasantly in Silver's ears. Everything seemed so perfect. Maybe too perfect. Silver now wished she hadn't been quite so enthusiastic about going out to the island where Alexander's father had been murdered. What would they find? Charred remains and maybe some violent criminals?

Chapter 13

Silver and Alexander left the restaurant and climbed into the large jeep that Alexander had left parked beside the marina.

Silver struggled with her conscience. She was knee-deep in it now. Should she keep her plans to interview the gold-toothed Lazlo secret from Alexander? If only Jan Brinchman had come up with someone else, she could have avoided this dilemma. But there was no doubt in her mind that there was only one Lazlo, and he seemed to be coming at her from all angles. If she told Alexander about the forthcoming interview, he would throw obstacles in her way to stop her getting her story. For now, she decided to keep her mouth shut as she hadn't yet made contact with Lazlo again. But he might be the link between the stowaways and the island where Alexander's father was murdered.

Alexander swung the jeep in a fast horseshoe round the harbour until they came to the clump of desolate-looking warehouses which Silver had visited with Knut.

'In the old days, the sailing ships set off from the harbour here and when they returned after months away, they stowed their cargoes in these sheds or in the even older ones which have now been pulled down,' he told Silver. 'But of course they're not used any more. They just stand here empty.'

Silver lost her concentration as her eye caught sight of

a battered blue bus parked beside the sheds. Somehow, it seemed familiar. She switched her mind back, wondering where she'd seen it before. Click, click, it all came back to her. Of course, parked very discreetly beside the caravans at the fairground. She'd forgotten all about it.

'Didn't you want to look inside the sheds,' Alexander's voice distracted her.

'Yes, I want to look through the windows.' Silver ran towards the grey square-block building and peered inside.

She scrubbed at the window with a tissue. 'It's difficult to see anything,' she said, rubbing hard. She stepped back, almost colliding with Alexander who stood so close she could smell the freshness of his aftershave. She felt her temperature rising, but with an effort, she shifted neatly away from him to peer through the next window. Her eyes took several seconds to adjust to the dim interior, but all she could make out was a square perimeter of emptiness.

'Perhaps this is the wrong shed,' she said to Alexander. 'There's nothing there.'

'There are two other sheds.' Alexander strode in front of her over to the next square grey building. He put his hand on the streaky pane and rubbed a space on the dirty glass. 'Nothing here either,' he said. 'Except for a pile of rags in the far corner. What are you looking for anyway?'

'Piles of old clothes.'

'Old clothes? Why is this?'

'Yes, like in the stateroom on the ship.' She sped on ahead of him. 'Let's look at the last shed.'

'Come on then, one last look and then let's get out of here.' He caught up with her and took her arm, hurrying her across to the third shed. 'Hey, wait a minute...' he said, vanishing round the corner, leaving her standing.

159

Silver rounded the corner and caught up with him as he stood outside an open door. A man emerged from the building. He swiftly banged the door shut and locked it. With fast footsteps, he crossed the road, keeping his head low.

'That's Lazlo,' Silver said and began to run after him. 'Hey, Mr er...Lazlo, stop!' she shouted. 'Wait! Is this your shed?'

The burly man turned and, with a beaming smile, he came towards her.

'Good day, Miss Silver,' he said holding out his large hand. 'Are you out enjoying the sun?'

'Is that your shed?' Silver cut the preliminaries. 'Do you know anything about all these clothes here?'

Lazlo scratched his head. 'Clothes? No clothes here.'

'Yes,' Silver persisted. 'These old clothes in the warehouse. Do they belong to you?'

'I know nothing about clothes,' Lazlo shook his head. 'There are some old boxes and packages lying there. I will throw them out.'

'Does the warehouse belong to you,' she pressed him.

'No, I rent from man. Not my warehouse.' Lazlo looked at her through half-closed eyes. 'I am new tenant.'

'Who then owns the warehouse?' Silver was like a terrier with a bone.

'You ask too much, young lady. I not answer more questions,' Lazlo huffed, his face flushing red with annoyance.

Silver stood her ground. Alexander was now right behind her, and she didn't want him interfering.

She stepped closer to Lazlo. 'Who owns the warehouse?'

Lazlo looked at her, his eyes inscrutable. 'Go away, lady. Go – not bother Lazlo more.' He made a swatting movement with his hand as if chasing off an irritating fly. With a rush, he jumped into his battered Volvo and accelerated fast away.

She dashed into the road, her eyes following his flight and trying to see which direction he took. A car bore down on her with a screech of brakes.

'Look out, Silver!' Dimly, she heard Alexander's voice. With a terrific effort, she almost flew over to the other pavement, but the kerb rose up to hit her and she fell. A searing pain tore through her, and she crumpled, clutching her leg. 'Ooh, that was clumsy,' she gasped.

'Silver,' Alexander was right beside her, lifting her up. His face was creased with worry.

'Ooh, don't move me. It's my ankle, I must have twisted it.' She took a sobbing breath and leaned against him. 'Give me a minute. God, I never knew it could hurt so much!'

Alexander supported her in his strong arms, his face pressed against her cheek. 'You're crazy, Silver. You could've easily been killed, or desperately injured. Why the hell didn't you look where you were going? I couldn't stand another accident.' His face was white, with deep scored lines round his mouth. He looked down at her sternly. He'd probably have given her a good shaking if she hadn't been resting so limply against him.

'Oh God, I'm sorry, Alexander,' she said rubbing her ankle and trying not to give in to easy tears. 'I didn't mean to be such an idiot. The angels must have been watching over me.' Her voice wavered, and Alexander hugged her tighter, distracting her from the pain in her ankle for a moment.

'My clothes are ruined,' she said shakily, staring down at the dark smudges and long rip down the left side of her light-coloured trousers.

'Just be glad you're not squashed flat,' Alexander

comforted her. 'Trousers are easily replaced. Broken bones taken longer, and lives…' his voice trailed away. He propped Silver carefully up against a stone wall and gave her another quick hug before he strode off to collect the jeep.

Heedless girl, nearly getting herself killed. Alexander's mouth set in grim lines as he walked back along the road. Silver was getting under his skin like a languorous drug that he couldn't seem to resist. What he'd have done if she'd been badly hurt, or even killed, didn't bear thinking about.

He'd told no one about the agony and guilt he'd gone through when his father was killed…murdered. He found it hard even to form the thought…murder. There was no one he could share his thoughts with. He had to be the strong one, for the company and for his stepmother. Besides, Knut had behaved very strangely about where he was on the night of his father's death. First, he said he'd been with a girlfriend, then he finally admitted that he'd been out on the island earlier that evening before the 'accident' happened. But he'd managed to come up with a watertight alibi for those crucial hours when the murder took place. His mobile phone records showed he'd been driving along the main road out of Bergen on his way to his girlfriend. And she'd sworn blind that he'd been with her from ten o'clock in the evening onwards and that he'd spent the night with her.

That was all the more painful, because it was Mariella with whom Knut had spent the night. Alexander's ex-fiancée and daughter of his father's rival in the shipping business. Alexander's mouth twisted at the thought of it. He'd been engaged to Mariella for six months before she broke it off, saying he was too serious and intense. Married to his work, in fact. He never had time to go out and have fun – that was one of the accusations she'd flung at him.

Perhaps it was all for the best, because now he saw clearly that he and Mariella would have fought all the time. There was no way he could imagine himself married to her. It would have been a disaster. What she needed was a pet poodle to string along. She'd have trouble with Knut too, but for a different reason.

The intensity of his feelings for Silver went far beyond what he'd ever felt for Mariella, even though Mariella was a consummate artist in bed. But it was all so damn mechanical between them. And now Silver had entered his life at the worst possible time...fate played a lot of funny tricks.

Switching his mind back to the day's incidents, Alexander thought about what he'd seen through the open door of the warehouse. There were these mystifying piles of clothing that Silver had been searching for. That was just before the man, Lazlo, had slammed shut the door and swiftly vanished. What was the link between him and Knut and all the clothes? It just didn't make sense. And those other piles of clothing in the rucksack that he and Silver had found on board *The Guiding Spirit* nagged at his brain. Some of the clothing was quite good – or so Silver had said. It seemed to him there was little value in people's cast-off clothing, so who on earth was so keen on collecting this...unless it was for refugees? Refugees or in fact illegal immigrants! Alexander was now in no doubt that Knut had brought some of these people onto the ship and even into the owner's suite. There must be big money involved. That made sense, otherwise suave Knut and burly Lazlo made unlikely partners.

Silver watched as Alexander brought the jeep to the side of the kerb and jumped out. Her ankle was throbbing intensely and had ballooned to twice its normal size. She was sure she couldn't walk on it. Stupid, stupid, stupid. She'd forgotten that they drove on the right in Norway, and she'd looked the wrong way as she dashed across the road.

She didn't have time to be laid up with a damaged ankle. A few tears slipped from her eyes in her frustration and pain. She dashed her hand against her cheek before Alexander reached her. She was supposed to be looking after Elise as well as chasing after her own story for Tom. Now she'd really and truly immobilised herself. What was she going to do?

'Hold on tight to my arm and we'll get you back to the car.' Alexander spoke in a deliberately cheerful tone. 'C'mon Silver, we'll soon get you put right.'

Silver gripped his proffered arm as he bent towards her, his voice warm and comforting against her ear. 'I'm going to take you back to my apartment in town, and we'll get you strapped up. That ankle looks pretty painful.'

He supported her as she pulled herself up into the vehicle. He pulled an old cushion from the seat behind to prop up her ankle, and she relaxed, pushing her worries aside for the time being.

He set the jeep in gear and they drove slowly through the town. After some minutes, he turned off into a quiet, leafy avenue with low-slung blocks of apartments placed at careful angles within a broad sweep of green lawns. Several wide-branched trees were dotted across the expanse, heightening the effect of seclusion.

Alexander pulled up in front of one of the apartment blocks. At the top of the flight of stairs, the door was flung open. A young woman, her dark hair caught back in a ponytail, stood there, dressed in blue jeans and a blue blouse.

Silver stared. Did Alexander have a wife after all? Her body went rigid and she felt a deep disappointment.

Alexander's voice in her ear went unheeded, as with a dry mouth she slumped down.

He prodded her with his finger. 'Silver, Silver, wake up,' he said. 'This is my housekeeper, Kari. She's very good at first aid. She'll fix your ankle.' He gave a quizzical smile: 'You thought she was my wife!'

Silver felt her whole body flush in embarrassment and she kept her face turned away from him as she took in his words. An absurd feeling of being let down lingered as she realised that she and Alexander were not to be alone in his apartment. Just try and keep your head, Silver, and don't get too close to him. But she wasn't doing a very good job of keeping her distance.

Alexander helped her to manoeuvre over to the long sofa in the large sitting room and deposited her gently. He propped two cushions behind her head and one under her foot.

'You've done this before,' said Silver teasingly, striving for a lighter note as she began to recover her spirits. She was amused to see that it was his turn to flush, the hot colour rising from his neck and upwards into his cheeks.

'I haven't actually,' he said, awkward as a little boy.

Kari, the housekeeper, appeared carrying ice packs and bandages. With deft fingers she made a neat strapping round Silver's ankle, which immediately lessened the pain. She brought Silver an ice cool drink of freshly squeezed orange. Silver lay back against the cushions feeling more comfortable. She sat up suddenly. 'But what about Elise?' she said.

'Don't worry, we'll sort that out,' Alexander soothed. He bent over her and touched her ankle gently. 'How does your ankle feel now?'

His nearness made Silver's stomach churn pleasurably. She wasn't sure she could force down a single bite of the food Kari was preparing. She lay back on the cushions and shut her eyes, worrying that she was letting Elise down.

Far off, she thought she heard the sound of the doorbell ringing, followed by the sound of voices, and then Kari appeared. 'Your brother's here,' she announced, and Knut strode quickly into the room.

Chapter 14

Knut's hair was standing on end. His dark blue tie, patterned with small gold Viking ships, hung askew. He had collected a bruise on his cheek which was fast deepening to purple.

Silver's eyes shot open. She lay tensely, waiting to see what would happen, feeling like a reclining statue. Alexander leapt up from his chair. 'What the hell's happened to you?' His face was a mixture of irritation and concern.

Knut advanced into the room and threw himself onto the end of the sofa where Silver lay stretched out. He knocked against her, and she drew up her feet, grimacing as he jarred against her injured ankle.

'You've got to help me.' Knut's tone was petulant, like a small boy's. 'I'm in deep shit.' Then he swivelled round to look at Silver. 'Silver,' he said softly. 'What are you doing here?' His dark eyebrows drew together.

'She's here because I invited her.' Alexander frowned at Knut. 'Why are you here, for God's sake, and what trouble are you in now?'

'I don't think we need to involve Silver,' said Knut winking at her.

'If you want to talk to me, talk in front of her,' said Alexander.

Silver watched the drama between the two brothers as they played for power before her. She remained quiet, waiting to see who'd make the next move. Knut did indeed look battered. He must have been in quite a fight. But she didn't think he was drunk, as he leapt to his feet again and began pacing the floor quite steadily.

'Well…?' Alexander prompted.

Knut's words tumbled out in a rush. 'I need money, Al. And now, upfront, on the table. I'm desperate.'

'So what's new?' Alexander sounded tired.

Silver intervened to stop the two brothers egging each other on until one of them lost his temper entirely. The debonair Knut did really look in a bad state. 'Who attacked you?' she asked. 'That bruise is quite a riot of colour.'

His hand flew up to his face. 'I walked into a door. It's nothing.'

Silver wasn't buying that one, so she tried another approach. 'What's wrong, Knut? What do you need the money for?' She kept her voice low and soothing. It seemed to strike a chord with his need for sympathy.

'Silver, darlin'.' He bumped down beside her on the sofa again. 'I knew you'd understand.' He edged closer trying to take her hand, but she moved it quickly away.

'Just tell us, Knut. Get on with it,' she said bluntly. Knut gave her a hurt puppy look. Now she had really placed herself on Alexander's side, like a mature woman against a young careless cub. It gave her a warm feeling.

'It's this great project. It'll bring in bags of money. Dollars. Make us all rich. So I need funds pronto for a down payment.' He gave Alexander a defiant stare.

'What crazy scheme is it now and how much?' Alexander lowered himself into an armchair. 'Why do you think I've got any money to spare? And you're not going to siphon off company funds. You could ruin us, and end up in jail. We've got three new ships on order and I'm not going to let you jeopardise that.'

'But it's a great deal. It's a chance of a lifetime to get hold of half a million dollars, perhaps more. Legit and all that.'

'What is?' Alexander held Knut's gaze relentlessly.

'Helping some refugees get into Norway. They're Russians, like Mother. You'd like to do that, wouldn't you? You always take such care of Mother. Now you can help her persecuted compatriots, and get paid for it.'

'Where are these refugees? Are they here in Norway already?' Silver's mind was working fast. Knut's scheme must have something to do with the stowaways on the ship. She sat up straighter, moving into alert mode. 'You must be crazy bringing a whole lot of people illegally into the country. You do mean illegally, don't you? If they catch you, they could put you behind bars for years!'

Knut's eyes wandered round the room. He didn't answer.

Silver began to put two and two together, and didn't like the answers she was getting. Irrationally, her immediate thought was to curse Knut for turning up to spoil things just as she and Alexander were going to enjoy a relaxing evening together. He was her least favourite person, even if he was Alexander's brother. She was getting hungry too, which made her feel weak and cross, and it was hard to gather her thoughts. Her ankle began to hurt again as her dilemma escalated before her eyes.

Now it was crystal clear – this was the story Tom wanted her to write. It was all here in this room. But if she wrote the story her editor was looking for, she would slap Alexander roundly in the face by exposing his brother. And how far was Alexander himself implicated? This was the story Alexander didn't want her to write. She put her hands to her head and suppressed a deep groan.

Both brothers turned to look at her. 'My ankle's aching.'

She forced a smile. Trying to distract their attention away from her, she pressed Knut again: 'What's happened to your face?'

Knut shot back: 'What happened to you, darlin'?' He gestured towards her foot on the sofa. Silver could see his prevarication needled Alexander, but once again, Knut's enthusiasm for his new project burst through, and the story came tumbling out.

He quickly outlined his plan that if the immigrants could be helped across the border and brought into Norway, they were willing to pay large sums. All that was necessary was a fleet of buses to transport them from the border between Russia and Norway in the north down to Oslo or Bergen in the south. 'We've got one bus already, but it's rather old and unreliable – we can't have it breaking down as we're on a tight schedule between Russia and Norway and the long distance down to Bergen.'

Knut carried on outlining his plans for the illegal immigrants. 'Without waiting too long in this country, they can board fishing boats and be ferried across to Britain or France. We could even set up a scheme where they could be transported onwards from there to the States.' Knut's eyes were glistening with excitement. 'Of course, we would have to arrange for food and changes of clothing while they're waiting to leave Norway.'

Silver looked at Alexander. He looked as stunned as she felt.

'All foolproof and legal,' Knut was triumphant. 'We wouldn't be breaking any laws in Norway, because the refugees are only in transit and, by God, they're willing to pay well for their journey.'

'Knut, it isn't legal. Don't you see that? You're smuggling people both into Norway and out of Norway into other countries. You're playing with people's lives.'

Silver couldn't go on. She couldn't believe that he couldn't understand this. 'It was you who got the stowaways onto *The Guiding Spirit*. I just know you did.'

Knut snorted, but he leant towards her pleadingly. 'But it's giving them a great opportunity to start a new life, Silver. Saving them from oppression. And they're my mother's people.' He turned appealing eyes to Alexander.

'You've been doing this for quite some time, haven't you?' Alexander narrowed his eyes at his brother. 'Why do you need the money now?'

'It's getting more expensive to get people to take them across the North Sea,' said Knut. 'It's harder to get them into other countries, and the fishermen aren't so keen to take the risk unless they're very well paid in advance. There are heavy fines now if they're caught. They could lose their livelihood. So they want a massive insurance. And it's up to us to provide it.' He attempted an ingratiating smile at Silver.

'Who are you working with?' said Silver. 'It's that Lazlo you hang out with. Anybody else?'

'Mind your own business,' Knut was jolted out of his usual urbanity and his eyes were unfathomable as he stared at her.

'The clothes,' said Silver. 'Where do they fit in?'

'The immigrants, stupid,' said Knut. 'They need clothes when they come here. Some of them have nothing at all if they've slipped over the border at night.'

'Do you give them to them, or do they have to buy them from you?' Silver couldn't believe Knut was just being obtuse.

'Well, of course, they have to pay for them. It's very expensive shipping out refugees. I've explained all that.'

Alexander and Silver looked at each other. Their pleasant evening had been shattered by Knut's intrusion

171

and the nefarious schemes he was cooking up. Alexander's face was gaunt, the skin pulled tight over the high bridge of his nose.

It would be Alexander's shoulders that would have to bear the burden of sorting Knut out and trying to put a stop to these schemes. If the Russian Mafia was behind it all, with their claws deeply embedded, it would be extremely hard to shake them off. Silver shivered, just thinking about it. How could two brothers, well stepbrothers, be so unalike? Alexander, probably too honest for his own good, and Knut ready to sink to the depths of evil and human suffering just to turn a fast buck. Maybe it was his compulsive gambling, which Alexander had talked about, that propelled him to such desperate involvement. Or maybe he just liked living on the edge.

'Supper's ready,' Kari appeared at the door of the sitting room. Alexander helped Silver to hop through into the dining room, where three places were laid with heavy silver cutlery, white starched napkins and a bowlful of yellow roses in the centre of the table. The crystal wine glasses were heavily redolent of money.

Silver supposed it was perfectly usual for Knut to turn up at his brother's apartment, even when he wasn't asking for handouts. For her, it was strange to find herself in the middle of a family. She was so often alone. She'd always wished for a sister or brother, but now she wasn't so sure. A brother like Knut could only be a constant problem.

Her mind flashed again to Elise waiting for them out on the island, afraid and alone. She jumped up, sending a jag of pain through her ankle. 'What about, Elise? You know I promised to keep her company.'

'That's all taken care of,' said Kari, smiling in a friendly way at Silver. 'Alexander's asked me to go out to the island. I'll stay with her myself. For once, my husband's at home from the fishing. I can leave the kids with him.'

'How will you get out there,' Silver turned her questioning gaze on Alexander.

'Kari's got her own boat,' said Alexander. 'We're a seafaring people, we Norwegians, remember!'

Silver relaxed. Now the evening would be spent with Alexander and Knut. Well, she was certain of entertainment, but perhaps not the kind of entertainment she'd expected. She wondered how soon Knut would leave them or would he spend the night? He seemed strangely dependent on his brother despite their differences. She tried to read Alexander's expression, but his face was shuttered. He flicked out his napkin as he sat rigidly at the table, the stern elder brother with no time for dalliance.

Still struggling with her conflict of interests, Silver realised she had a great chance to find out more about the illegal immigrants. It was here right at her fingertips, if she really pushed Knut hard. Maybe he could even tell her something about the warehouses down on the quay. And what about the intruder in her hotel room? Had that person anything to do with Knut?

Kari brought in a dish of elegantly stuffed crabs in their shells. The Norwegians were really into seafood. Lifting some salad from the bowl Alexander offered her, Silver mused how healthy she would become with all this lovely food. Her mouth watered and it seemed ages since lunchtime. But first she went on the attack with Knut.

'Is there a rough assessment about how many illegal immigrants cross the border?' she asked.

Knut looked at her quizzically. 'I wondered when our little journalist would get going!'

'Come on, Knut,' Silver persisted.

He couldn't resist boasting. 'About a hundred every two or three months. They're desperate to get to the West to get jobs and earn money. Some of them even sell their houses to raise the money to come.'

'Sell their houses…' Silver was shocked. 'That's really burning their boats behind them. What happens if they're not accepted?'

'Well, there's no way back unless they go to stay with their old grandparents or remaining family. Otherwise, they become stateless here and have to go underground.' Knut's voice was monotonous as if reciting a learned piece.

Silver's blood pounded in her ears. How could anyone be so uncaring? 'Don't you see what you're doing, Knut? You're destroying people's lives.'

Knut blinked and paused, while Alexander joined in. 'What's driving you? Is it the money? You're short again, aren't you?' He sprang up from the table and went to stand behind Knut, his hands pressing down hard on his brother's shoulders.

Knut wriggled uncomfortably, trying to break Alexander's hold. Resentment crossed his face as Alexander leaned forward and spoke close to his ear. 'I've got you out of trouble time and time again. But not this time. Not for the Russian Mafia – you complete fool. Not this time, brother!' He released Knut suddenly and went back to his seat.

Knut straightened his shoulders and tossed back his glass of red wine in two gulps. 'It's not just the money. It's the excitement. The danger of sending these people off at night when no one sees what we're doing, except the bats and the owls.' He gave a harsh laugh. 'My grandfather was a hero of the Norwegian resistance, Silver. He saved many lives and helped people over the border to Sweden to escape the Germans when Norway was occupied. He was a very brave man.' He leaned back and crossed his arms over his chest.

Alexander made a sharp irritated movement. 'Get your feet back on the ground, Knut. Those days are long past. Forget the false heroics.'

'And your partner in this scheme?' asked Silver, wishing she could make a few notes.

'Lazlo, of course. You know that, both of you.' Knut shrugged his shoulders. 'I told you – I'm doing it for Mother. She's Russian. She thinks I'm doing a good thing.' He looked triumphantly at Alexander. 'My mother – not yours Al.' He swigged back a third or was it a fourth glass of wine? Silver had lost count.

Her glance turned to Alexander. How was he taking all this? His brother had really freaked out and now his stepmother seemed to be involved. If Silver wrote the story, it would explode all over the front page. It had all the elements of human suffering and human desperation, with wads of dirty money changing hands. A rich shipowner's playboy son involved in the illegal trafficking of immigrants. What a tantalising mixture.

Alexander's eyes were on her. 'You can't do it, Silver,' he said. 'You can't write the story. You'd betray me and the family. You're a guest in our home. You've eaten our salt.'

His words pounded silently in Silver's ears. The blood drained from her face. The whole wall of indecision was about to topple on her. Then it became blindingly clear. She couldn't do it. She would never betray Alexander. And back in London, Tom would never forgive her. She would be forced to resign from her job. The thoughts churned and hammered through her mind. She could only see two possible choices: either betray Alexander or lose her job. A small mewl of anguish escaped her.

Chapter 15

Silver tossed and turned in the night, despite the comfortable bed and the lavender scented sheets. She was wearing a dark blue silk pyjama jacket borrowed from Alexander. The silk caressing her body was as sensuous and disturbing as if he were in the room with her, and she found it hard to relax properly. He kept intruding on her intimate thoughts.

A myriad of images floated through her mind. It was not only the immigrants arriving in Norway who were stateless. She felt stateless and driven herself. She belonged nowhere. There was no way she was going to give up her job. She certainly wouldn't allow Alexander to put a gag on her. She couldn't be part of Alexander's life and, after today, she wouldn't have a job in London if she made a hash of things and let Tom down.

She swung her legs out of the large bed and stepped gingerly down onto the floor. There were a lot of things to sort out in the day ahead. At least her ankle seemed to be holding up. The strapping Kari had put on last night supported it well and the long night's rest had helped too.

Downstairs, Alexander and Knut were joshing each other in the kitchen over a frying pan of bacon and eggs. It was as if last night had never been.

'Good morning, Silver. We're making you an English breakfast.' This morning Knut was bright and perky. The livid bruise on the side of his face had faded a little, and he had tied a tea towel round his waist. He was altogether a less threatening figure than the night before. It was hard to imagine him dealing in human lives.

Alexander put a plate of bacon and eggs in front of Silver. His eyes were clear and sunny. Silver smiled back at him perplexed. The aroma rising from the plate reawakened her appetite, though the thought still teased at her: how could the two brother act so carefree and normal when the one was so heavily involved in serious crime and the other was still reeling from the shock of his father's unexplained death?

Knut ate hurriedly. He constantly drew out his mobile and checked it. At last, a sharp bleep from the phone made him rise from the table and swiftly leave the room, his shoulders hunched and secretive.

'Are you going to work today?' Silver probed Alexander. 'What about your mother? Shall I go back to stay with her?'

A careworn expression crossed Alexander's face, erasing his thin veneer of insouciance. 'Silver, after what Knut told us last night, I must drop everything and get out to the island where my father was killed. Remember, it was your suggestion. Do you feel up to coming with me today?' His eyes searched hers intently. 'For every day that passes, there's less chance of finding any clues to my father's murder. The police seemed to have got stuck. The enquiry is on hold.'

A warm feeling of gratification bubbled up from the depths of Silver's stomach, chasing away the cold feeling of rejection from last night. So she was needed after all. He did trust her. That only made her qualms of conscience all the harder to ignore, but she couldn't refuse him. She put out her hand and took Alexander's. 'You know I want to help you,' she said, her spirits spiralling upwards.

She was seized by a sense of urgency as she heard Knut coming back. 'When do you want to leave?' she whispered to Alexander.

'Now,' he said.

Alexander manoeuvred the boat carefully out of the marina. Once out in the open sea, he opened the throttle and they picked up speed. She stood close to him as he steered the boat. As they skimmed past, leaving a wide swathe of foaming water in their wake, Silver recognised Elise's house on Rosenholm Island lying to the port side of the boat.

'What do you expect to find?' Silver asked. 'Your stepmother told me it was about three months since…' She couldn't continue.

'Since they found my father? Yes, and still they haven't found the people who set fire to the cottage and killed him. All they tell us is that they think it's a case of arson, but the body was so badly burnt, it's difficult to find any traces of what actually happened. But they did find bullet holes in what remained of his skull.'

Alexander stepped away from Silver, so she went over and sat down on one of the seats in the boat. His face was bleak, the sorrow and shock from that terrible day showing in his eyes. She longed to comfort him.

'Let's see what we can turn up today,' she said quietly, trying to convey her sympathy to him.

He slowed the boat. 'There's my father's island,' he said, pointing straight ahead at a small island where the pine trees grew thickly. High up on the left side of the island, Silver made out the sharply pointed black wooden structure of the stave church silhouetted against the sky like a large sailing ship.

'That's my father's church,' said Alexander, manoeuvring the boat towards the shore. 'He arranged for it to be transported out to this island in hundreds of planks and separate pieces. It was dismantled from a rotting old structure which had been long abandoned in a small village further north.'

'How wonderful to conserve a living piece of history like that,' said Silver surveying the tall structure as they drew closer.

'He was working to reassemble and restore it just as it was in the original state,' said Alexander, a hint of pride in his voice. 'He was so proud of the work he'd done on it. A lot of it with his own hands. It was to have been finished this year. But then he died...and everything has had to wait.'

'What a huge undertaking!' Silver stared at the church in admiration. 'He must have been an exceptional man to take on such a gigantic task.'

'It was his greatest pride,' said Alexander. 'Except for his ships, of course. In fact, I think he was trying to recreate an ancient ship. Same style of construction.'

He throttled back the engine and began to lower a heavy anchor over the side of the boat. The thick chain rattled as it sank into the water and the anchor embedded itself on the bottom. 'There's no jetty on the island, so we can't sail straight in,' he told her. 'We'll have to take the dinghy. You'll have to be careful with that ankle of yours.'

Silver looked down at the water below the boat. Although her ankle was so much better, she didn't think it would bear her weight if she jumped down into the small boat.

The anchor held firmly and, with an easy movement, Alexander dropped a second anchor over the bow of the boat. From under one of the seats, he pulled out a small red dinghy and lowered it over the stern. Silver's nervousness was growing, but the sea was calm and the wind had dropped in the lee of the island. Alexander tied the painter which kept the dinghy attached to the boat and reached out his arms to Silver. 'Come here and I'll lift you down,' he said. 'It's easy. You'll be quite safe.'

'What about oars?' Reluctantly, she moved closer to him and looked down nervously at the small red craft bobbing on the water. It seemed to have shrunk in size since Alexander first lowered it.

'I'll hand them down to you when you're in the dinghy.' He laid a pair of oars on the seat in readiness. 'It's not far and we're very close to shore.' He smiled reassuringly at her.

Silver gritted her teeth and reminded herself she could swim quite well, even if her swimming achievements came from an indoor swimming pool at home in London. It was her ankle that bothered her the most.

Alexander put his arms round her and lifted her high, then eased her carefully over the stern of the boat down into the dinghy. He leant perilously far out from the larger boat to support her. She stood for a moment balanced on her good leg and then dropped down onto the one small cross-beamed seat.

'Grab the oars,' he called, handing them to her one by one. Then he swung himself down the short ladder in the stern and leapt lightly into the dinghy beside her. She made herself as small as possible as he lowered himself down and cast off the painter. Picking up the oars, he began to row with steady rhythmic strokes towards the shore. A few minutes later, he sprang out of the small craft and dragged it up over the sea-washed stones. He turned to sweep Silver out of the small dinghy, whisking her up in his arms as if she was feather-light. She clasped her hands around his neck, the warmth of his body stirring her senses, but he set her down quickly on the grass beyond the small bay and returned to drag the dinghy even higher across the stones.

In the eerie quiet of the island, the only sound being the whisper of the waves, Silver stole a look at Alexander's impassive face. What was he feeling? What memories were stirring in his mind? She looked at the sky, which held lemon streaks among the grey storm clouds that were brewing. The air was heavy on her shoulders and she found it hard to force herself across the pebbly beach.

In front of her, a primitive stairway stretched up between the pine trees. The high, uneven steps were hewn out of the black rock of the island and led up to a flat plateau. Silver pushed herself upwards, trying to conceal that her ankle was hurting again, but Alexander noticed and grasped her hand, pulling her up behind him.

At the top of the staircase, the trees thinned, and they emerged into an open space. Silver's nostrils caught the bitter stench of charred wood as they drew nearer to a wide area of blackened ash. Faded red and white plastic cordons, left behind by the police investigation, hung forlornly, stirring gently in the freshening breeze.

Alexander's face was set in hard lines as he surveyed the scene before them. He dropped her hand and strode on ahead of her.

'There's absolutely nothing left of my father's cottage. The blaze was all-consuming,' he said, his face chiselled with strain. 'There's just this pile of ashes here. It was hard to find any remains of my father. There was just a piece of skull and a charred finger – that's all they said they found. Everything was incinerated in the blaze.' He ran his hand over his jaw and was silent for a moment. 'The police searched for a long time for traces of what might've happened – but they drew a blank and now the enquiry has stalled.' He walked on round the dismal site, his back towards Silver.

Silver stood frozen, surveying the scene. A black depression seeped into her bones at the devastating sight. So pitiful and evil. Yes…the evil was still there, rising from the charred ashes. She could almost smell it. A rook in the tall leafless trees behind the site of the fire cawed a raucous dirge over their heads.

'Alexander,' Silver's voice choked in her throat, 'how could you bear it?'

'I had to bear it,' he said, swallowing hard. 'There was nobody else to take charge. My stepmother fell apart. Knut was useless. He holed up with my stepmother and locked himself in his room for several days, refusing to come out. If we brought him food, he told us to leave it outside his door. He wouldn't speak to anyone. He just left us to sort things out.'

'Left you to get on with it all alone.' Silver clenched her fists in frustration and sympathy.

'Then just as the police were finishing their enquiries and my father's remains were to be released for burial, Knut took off. Elise and I didn't see him for weeks. He'd dashed off to Monte Carlo or somewhere.'

'What about the funeral? Didn't he come back for that?'

'We had to hold it without him. Poor Elise, it made it ten times worse for her. She was distraught, weeping and crying, and scared out of her wits every time the phone rang…even then.'

Silver was shocked. 'How could he abandon his mother at such a time?'

'It brought him under strong suspicion with the police, but he had an alibi for the time when the fire was set. He swore blind he'd spent the night with my ex-fiancée, and she confirmed it. So in the end, I just had to get on with picking up the pieces.' He looked at her and squared his shoulders as if chafing under a burden. 'We never actually found out where Knut had been. He was like a wounded animal that went to ground to lick its wounds.'

'What a mess,' said Silver. She stroked Alexander's arm trying to give him comfort. The bleak desolation of this place scared her. It was a complete contrast to the lively boat life taking place further back along the fiord. The stench of smoke surrounded her, clinging to her skin and clothes, cloaking her in the tragedy.

'Shall we look around first and see what we can find around here?' she said, desperate to be on the move again. The task seemed overwhelming, and the angry yellow clouds were darkening to a deeper grey as a few hissing drops of rain began to fall. Silver shivered in her light clothes, wishing she'd brought a jacket.

'I've searched the site too, alongside the police and afterwards, even though they didn't want me to get involved. We've searched for clues with our bare hands, with gloves, with metal detectors. I don't think there's anything left to find. Certainly not today for us two amateurs with no technical equipment.' Alexander's voice was harsh and raw. 'There's nothing here, Silver.'

'Look, Alexander, we came here for a purpose,' Silver reminded him. 'Fresh look, fresh eyes,' she smiled at him trying to lift his spirits and conceal her own shock at the tragic sight before them.

She tried again: 'Do you have any suspicions about who the murderer was?' said Silver. 'Somebody who had a grudge against your father? A business rival?'

'If only we knew,' he said. 'We've gone over and over it to try and work out who it could possibly be. To make things worse, it was over a day before the fire was discovered…and the little that was left of my father. That was because we were all so used to his need for privacy. There were certain times when he shut himself off from the outside world for days on end.' His face was bleak and Silver stepped towards him. He crushed her in his arms as if drawing strength from her body. But just as quickly he put her from him and pointed up the slope. 'Look up there,' he said. 'That's my father's monument, the church he rebuilt with his own hands.'

Silver's pulses were stirred by his sudden action, but calming herself, she lifted her head and saw the wooden stave church starkly outlined against the grey sky.

'Yes, it's very like a ship,' she said. 'Tall-masted and strong. But it's black. Was it burnt as well?' She shuddered at the thought.

'No, no,' said Alexander. 'It's covered with a special tar to preserve the wood. Thank God, at least it wasn't touched.'

Silver was getting a better picture of Alexander's father. He was an idealist, not just a hard businessman as she'd first thought. He was a person of flesh and blood who didn't deserve to die in this vicious, underhand way. Nobody did. Whoever could have set alight the small wooden cottage with an old man alone inside it? She backed away from the scene of the fire to avoid inhaling more of the dead smoke that lingered like a pall.

'Could anything be hidden in the church?' she asked. 'It seems strange that a person or persons should just burn down the cottage. What did they want to achieve?'

'Not a bad idea to look in the church,' Alexander agreed. 'There just might be something the police have overlooked that might tell us more about my father's death.'

Silver cast a last look at the blackened cinders, which

refused to disclose their secrets. It was a relief to move on to the church. But if Alexander had asked her to sift through the funeral pyre with her bare hands, she would've done it. She pushed her hair out of her eyes, noticing that her hands were heavily streaked with soot. She shivered and willed herself not to think too much about the tragedy and the fear that the old man must have felt when confronted by his murderers. Was he already dead when the flames first licked the cottage?

She toiled up the slope with Alexander, her eyes fixed on the stave church. 'What about a key?' she asked.

'Oh, it's never locked. Nobody ever comes here,' said Alexander.

Silver looked at him, but bit back a retort. The worst sort of people come here, she responded silently.

The rain fell in drenching drops from the leaden skies. The warm Norwegian summer had turned chill. Silver tried to avoid some of the downpour by keeping to the edge of the path and taking cover under the pine trees. Pine needles scraped her bare arms and scratched her face as she pushed the branches aside. The cold air seeped into her bones.

Alexander didn't seem to care about getting wet. He strode tall and strong, straight along the path, his light hair darkening as the rain fell upon it. His shirt clung to him, outlining the muscles of his body.

Up close, the stave church loomed above them, black and sombre. Alexander strode up to the door. Silver followed more slowly as she studied the details of the carvings on the church. Alexander's solid figure filled the small porch, while his fingers grasped and strained to turn the heavy ring. The door refused to budge. 'If I didn't know better, I'd say it was locked.' His face was red with exertion as he gave all his weight to twisting the ring, his shoulder against the door.

The strange wooden construction in all its gloomy grandeur towered over Silver, an odour of tar and turpentine filling her nostrils. She could well understand why Alexander's father had been so passionate about restoring the majestic building.

At last, the heavy door yielded under Alexander's onslaught and he shouldered it open with a loud creak.

Together they entered the dark, windowless interior of the church and stood blinking for a moment as their eyes adjusted. With a sudden rush of feet, three dark figures swept past Silver, shoving her roughly aside. A sour smell of sweat lingered as three men forced their way out of the church.

Silver turned on an impulse and started to run after them, heedless of her own safety. Alexander's voice cut through the stillness of the island. 'Silver, stop! These are desperate men. You don't know what they'll do!'

He strode up to her as she hesitated uncertainly, wondering what to do next. He stood behind her, holding her back, his hands clamped vice-like on each of her arms. 'You're crazy, Silver. There's been one murder here already. Don't stick your neck out and get caught up in more violence.'

Silver tried to break free of Alexander's hold, then realising the sense of what he said, she stopped trying to shake off his hands. It was true, she'd have torn headlong after these strangers without a thought. The three men sped away down to the sea, strung out like marathon runners. Their shoes chinked on the stones of the path as they disappeared into the trees. They re-emerged on the small beach where Alexander had moored the dinghy.

'Stop!' Alexander shouted again, running forward. His hands fell to his sides as one of the men wielded the flashing blade of a knife to cut the mooring line. All three men squeezed into the dinghy, which lurched and heaved, almost capsizing under its awkward burden.

With one man bent over the oars, the dinghy began to make shaky headway through the waves. Alexander swore, but his hand swung round to hold Silver back.

'No chance. Just stay here!' he said. 'Let them go to hell. They won't be able to start the motor boat. The keys are in my pocket.' He patted his side.

Silver jumped up and down in frustration, but she had to accept Alexander's rational thinking. What good would it do to rush down to the shore and shout at the men? The small craft picked up speed as now two of the men pulled at the oars, the third crouching in the stern, their combined weight pressing it low in the water.

'They'll tip round any minute.' Alexander gave a scornful laugh.

'Hey, these are some of the illegal immigrants. There must be a hiding place in the church.' Silver shuddered. 'God, I hope there aren't any more inside.'

She stood transfixed: 'There's your connection!' she said.

Alexander's gaze was riveted on the three strange men as they manoeuvred the overloaded dinghy away from the island. Silver as usual was right. Unerringly, she'd put her finger on it. Though he had to admit he'd suspected something of the same. He wondered what the hell he was going to do. He should never have brought Silver to the island and put her in potential danger. One tragedy had already been played out here. She was getting under his skin and things were slipping out of control. He cursed inwardly that he'd let down his guard a little. He groaned. Silver was so lovely, with her light fair hair, silvery in certain lights, and her great innocent green eyes that he couldn't resist drowning in.

Soon she'd have to return to her own country, and he'd be left alone with the unholy mess of his father's murder to clear up, and the burden of his stepmother and Knut. He stopped short. He'd never thought of his stepmother as a burden before, but after his father's death, she'd changed noticeably. Instead of being the loving, slightly quirky mother as he knew her, she'd emerged as Knut's champion, condoning and encouraging everything that Knut did, however hare-brained the scheme.

She put up with Knut's neglect and careless treatment, while he, Alexander, tried to sort out the business in the aftermath of the tragedy. She'd become very mercenary as well. The company board meetings, with only the three of them as company directors, often turned into violent shouting matches. Knut and Elise frequently sided against his more rational plans for doing the best he could for both the family and the business. Elise would easily revert to screaming fits if she felt he was hampering her. The issue of the casino wasn't resolved yet. Elise seemed almost fanatically enthusiastic about it. Almost more so than Knut. And as usual, she'd voted for some of the company's much-needed funds to be put into Knut's gargantuan, every-ready pockets.

Alexander straightened his shoulders. He couldn't allow the company to be sucked dry. He was fully determined to get a fourth member – from outside the family – onto the board to balance out things. To be chairman of the board in fact – with a double vote. It was clear that one or two members of the family couldn't be allowed to drag down the whole business on a whim.

The black church had a menacing air. Were there more people inside, desecrating it? He remembered his pride in being allowed to help his father in reconstructing the old roof, each panel so exactly positioned. He'd scrambled

188

up on the roof very precariously because the ladder was too short. Astride the entrance porch, he'd tried to get everything to slot into place without the use of a single nail, in the style of the old workmen.

These strangers had penetrated the sanctuary by forcing their way into the church. Alexander's mind went into overdrive. How long had these people stayed hidden in the church? Had they destroyed anything? It had all been so lovingly restored by his father, an expert wood carver who'd carved much of the vine tendrils and winding stems along with the exquisitely serrated leaves of the church decoration round the door. What luck that the intruders hadn't burnt down the whole place as well as the cottage. The tarred wood of the church would have been engulfed by a sea of flames.

Silver tugged at his sleeve. 'Come back, Alexander. We have to make plans for what we're we going to do now. We've got to get off the island somehow.' She shivered under the chilling rain.

She fancied that the carved dragons of the church peered down at her in grim disdain as she stepped back into the wooden porch to shelter under its roof. It was like an ancient pagan temple with its carvings of fearsome beasts protecting it from malediction. But the evil taint still permeated the scene. Surely there would be sanctity inside the church, despite its threatening exterior?

'I'm going in again,' said Alexander. 'Perhaps there are more people hiding in the church. Just wait outside here and keep hidden under the overhang of the roof.'

'Not likely! I'm not being left on my own.' Silver bumped against him in her hurry as he swung open the heavy door. Together they peered into the dark unwelcoming maw of the church. The only source of light was two small round openings high up under the roof. Silver waited for her

189

eyes to adjust to the meagre light of the interior, her heart pounding until it almost choked her. She prayed that no other men would emerge from their dark hiding places.

She strained her ears, trying to hear if there was anyone else around. For a moment, she listened to the sound of short panting breaths beside her, before going limp with relief that it was only her own panicky breathing.

The rain had stopped. Behind her, Silver could see the sun once more stretch its rays like golden fingers through wisps of clouds, casting a faint light inside the church.

'Alexander,' she nudged him, a premonition striking her. 'They won't take the motor boat, will they? If they do, how are we going to get back to the mainland?' The worry teased at her thoughts, blocking out all sensible reflection.

He looked at her, as if coming back from far away. 'I honestly don't know.' He brought out his mobile and pressed some numbers. 'Out of range.' His voice expressed disgust. He shoved it back in his pocket. 'How far can you swim?' he asked her.

'Not very far. The sea's very rough,' said Silver. 'I've only ever swum in a swimming pool in London or on holiday. I've swum in the warm, blue Mediterranean, but in nothing like these untamed waters.' Her stomach sank. 'How long will it be before anyone misses us?' The thought jack-knifed through her, and she shivered again. Why on earth hadn't she brought a jacket? She was beginning to feel hungry too.

She took several deep breaths. 'Let's look through the church first.' Her voice was nearly normal. 'It's what we came for, after all.' She forced her trembling legs to move forward and looked sharply around her, but all was quiet and still.

'Come on then.' Alexander took her arm, propelling her further into the shadowy depths of the church.

Chapter 16

Silver passed reluctantly over the threshold of the strange old church. Again, she was struck by an odour of turpentine and burnt wood which seemed as ancient as the pagan Norwegian gods. Her main fear was that other strange figures would burst out of the dark depths to knock them over or to stab them with a random knife as they passed.

Alexander seemed to have no such qualms as he strode into the interior and stood for a moment looking around him.

'Come on, Silver.' He seized her arm again and almost dragged her forward. 'The danger's over. There's no one here. And I want to have a quick look in the outside passage. The one which surrounds the church.'

Silver followed as he turned into the dark corridor, which ran the full way round the inner wall of the church. The odour of tar and ancient wood was stronger here.

'This is where the lepers used to stand because they weren't allowed to mix with the ordinary congregation,' Alexander told her. 'Look, that's where they used to stand and peer through when the service was taking place.' He showed her a small eyehole. 'The leper's squint,' he said. 'Pregnant women and other undesirables,' he shot her an ironic glance, 'had to stand here as well.'

Alexander's tourist-guide patter was just what Silver needed to calm her nerves and push down the panic that threatened to overwhelm her. Her legs stopped shaking and she grew bolder. She stepped close to Alexander and peered through the small squint.

'If we're going to find any clues, it'll have to be in that old pulpit,' she said, looking through the hole straight at the elaborately carved wooden structure which rose up on the right-hand side of the church. 'It's the only place where anything could be hidden. Let's go back inside and have a closer look.' Together they walked out of the dark corridor and back into the body of the church.

Her gaze swept over the church's bare interior. There were no pews, no organ, nothing at all that could be a place of concealment. 'How did the congregation keep standing upright for so long? Didn't they have pews to sit in?' she asked. 'Have they been removed?'

'No, they haven't. They didn't have pews in these churches. My father tried to keep the interior of the church as accurate as possible. The old preachers could sermonise for hours on end about the dangers of lust and temptation, so the congregation just had to stand and bear it!'

He put his arm round Silver's shoulders, boosting her courage and making her forget where she was for a moment. Together the two of them formed an enclosed little world of their own.

A distant click brought them both sharply back to the present. Silver caught her breath and swung round. 'There was someone else here after all. We weren't alone.'

Alexander pushed her behind him and peered into the empty space. 'I can't see anyone,' he whispered.

'I'll just check the main door,' Silver said, darting across the open transept. She tugged in vain at the heavy ring of the door.

'You try,' she said to Alexander. 'I can't move it at all.' Her heart lurched uncomfortably as she felt herself trapped like an animal in a pen. She mustn't let Alexander see how terrified she was.

Alexander leaned his full weight on it, but once again, the solid wooden door remained obstinately shut. He shoved his shoulder hard against it without success.

Silver watched his efforts, her hands hanging down helplessly. 'If we're incarcerated here, who will ever find us?' she said, a vision of being stuck in a windowless tomb rising before her eyes.

'Okay, okay. Don't panic,' said Alexander. 'There's that other small door at the back. We'll try that.' With swift strides, he crossed the paved stone floor and disappeared into the shadows. Silver rushed across, keeping him in sight. At the back of the church, an almost invisible small door was let into the wall. It was so low that Alexander would have to bend double to creep through it. But the small door proved just as intractable.

'They've locked us in. We're stuck here like rats in a trap.' Silver's voice rose high with fear. 'We'll never get out.'

'I know, I know,' said Alexander, irritated. He didn't seem to be unduly upset by their predicament. 'Let's do what we came to do – search the church. As you said, the pulpit's the place.'

Silver took heart from Alexander's air of calm. 'Right,' she said, taking a deep breath and crossing over to the pulpit. She sat down on the stairs leading up to where the preacher would stand and began to probe with her fingers around the ornate wooden roses and flowers carved on the banister. A hissing serpent so delicately carved that it was almost seemed alive stared at her, its forked tongue frozen in eternal threat. Silver's sensitive fingers slipped easily between the small spaces left between the carvings, searching for one which might make a convenient hiding place.

Alexander mirrored her efforts on the other side of the carved staircase. 'Here's a funny thing,' he said. 'A camera cover! The intruders must have dropped it when they ran away.' He drew out a small canvas cover. 'What is this doing here? It's not the sort of thing you'd expect the priest to use, unless he's taking pictures of his unruly congregation.' He gave a short laugh.

Encouraged by the strange find, Silver climbed further up the stairs and began to probe higher up under the ornate side of the pulpit. But there was nothing there except a dusty old hymn book. 'Do people really hold church services here?' she asked. 'I thought it was just for show.'

'No, truly, they do hold services. Once a month during the summer, a clergyman comes over on a special launch from Bergen and holds a service,' Alexander told her. 'It's very popular with the cruise visitors, especially those from America. We arrange for them to be brought out here.'

'So we'll be found in about three weeks' time,' said Silver. 'Perhaps just our skeletons. But we will be found.' Her lips twisted at the macabre thought.

Her neat fingers began their search again. This time, she slipped her hand under the wooden tip-up seat of the pulpit. Her fingers grasped one of the carved roses and, with a sharp click, a small chamber opened behind the seat.

Chapter 17

Silver put her hand back into the dark hole and scrabbled around. 'I hope to God there aren't any mice in here,' she said with a shudder. 'I'd die if I got a sudden nip on the fingers.'

'Let me have a go then.' Alexander was impatient as he loomed over her. He tried to move her aside, but Silver persisted and pushed him off. 'No, I found it. I'll do it. Besides, the hole is so cramped, you'll never get your hand inside.' She pushed her arm as far as it would go into the yawning black space.

Alexander stepped back, but kept his gaze riveted on the small chamber in the wall which she'd discovered. Silver's fingers were pulling out an assortment of credit cards and old passports, blue, green and red. 'Must be Russian,' she said, looking in particular at the dark blue ones with their strange Cyrillic lettering. She drew out several letters and documents, some written in English, some in Norwegian, which she passed over to Alexander. The heap of valuable documents on the floor grew larger as she dragged out more and more from the secret cache. Then she pulled out piles of paper money, neatly contained in rubber bands. Dollar bills, English pound notes and Norwegian kroner. There was some other money too that she didn't recognise. Cyrillic lettering again. 'Russian roubles,' she guessed.

Alexander stared at the collection of documents and

money lying in front of them. 'As far as I can see, this is a hugely important stash for the police. You're brilliant, Silver. These long tapering fingers of yours!'

'The space stretches back quite far.' Silver's voice was muffled as she bent forward, peering into the dark hole. She felt around the narrow space and continued to hand out more and more documents. Then she turned to the pile on the floor. She searched rapidly through the torn and battered passports, sorting them into separate heaps. 'Just let me look at the British ones,' she said.

After some moments, she sat back on her heels with a yelp. 'Oh God, look at this! I think this is mine. Well, what's left of it. This is my passport that was stolen from me at the funfair.' She held it up to Alexander. 'Look, they've torn off the back cover. That's the most important part, the part with my photograph. Somebody's walking around with my personal details, my face…that's terrifying. Somebody must have made a forged passport out of mine. It's as if they've raped my identity.' She pushed herself backwards and got up.

'We've got to get out of here.' She clutched Alexander's arm. 'We can't stay a minute longer. Just let me have a last check.' Bending down, she extended her arm into the dark hole once more and brought out what seemed to be the last of the stash.

'Look at this.' She dropped her last find in front of him – six packets of white powder.

He picked them up. 'It's not enough that someone's running a nice little trade in stolen documents and illegal immigrants, but now they seem to be drug running as well.' His face took on a graven look, which Silver now knew meant that he was thinking fast. He took out his mobile again and punched in a number, then swore as once again he failed to make a connection.

A cold hand clutched at Silver's heart. Irritated and fearful, she burst out: 'The mobile's hopeless, Alexander. Don't do that!' The non-connection of the mobile only brought home to her how isolated they were. She coughed as the long-undisturbed dust of the old church began to choke her throat. 'I wish we could get a drink of water. I'm dying of thirst,' she said.

'Yeah, and something to eat too. It's hours since we had breakfast,' said Alexander.

Silver sat up and pushed her hair out of her eyes. She rummaged in her pockets. All she could come up with was a dusty sweet and a crumpled tissue.

'Who do you think is behind all this?' she asked Alexander. 'Why can't you tell me more? I know you're holding things back.'

Alexander looked startled. Then he said: 'Fair enough, Silver. I'm not holding anything back, but there's so little to go on. Lazlo has a lot to answer for. He's got to be knee-deep in all this.'

'And...?'

'And...my own brother Knut,' Alexander exhaled his breath slowly. 'You heard him yesterday. It's obvious that Knut's mixed up in this somewhere – and has been for the last few months. He's been acting very strangely.'

'Knut's knee-deep as well – don't excuse him! What about the funny clothes we found on the ship?' Silver prompted.

'Well, of course, they were meant for the illegals too,' said Alexander. 'I'm scared that he's dragged my stepmother into all this, by making her think she's doing something noble to rescue these people. The Russian Mafia's reach is long. And they have very persuasive methods.'

Silver nodded slowly. Now Alexander was courageous enough to put his deepest thoughts into words. It seemed he trusted her completely and a warm feeling of happiness spread through her despite their predicament.

He straightened up, his eyes energetic and focused. 'Come on, it's time to get out of here.' He pulled her to her feet. He'd found a plastic bag somewhere and was now swiftly gathering up all the things they'd found and shoving them down into the bag.

'Have you checked if your credit card is here?' he asked.

Silver fell on her knees again and sifted through the remaining cards. 'No, nothing here,' she said. 'Even though they seem to have grabbed cards from all sorts of different countries – the United States, Britain, Norway, France...'

'Just dump the rest of them in here.' Alexander held out the open bag to her. 'We'll go through it all later. Let's get out in case some of these undesirables come back looking for us. I don't want to be here when they do.'

Silver jumped up. 'Oh no, God knows what they'd do to us if they discover we've found their hidey hole.' She shuddered and tried to repress the flood of scary thoughts that engulfed her. Wild pictures streamed through her mind of rape, kidnapping, stabbing...or the two of them lying there as skeletons entombed forever in the church. She rubbed her eyes, trying to block out the hideous pictures.

She paced around, looking at the black fortress-like walls of the church, solid and impenetrable. Even the little light filtering through from outside was dimming and the walls seemed to creep nearer. Silver was reminded of a horror story she'd once read where the walls drew closer and the roof pressed down on its occupants until they were crushed to death. She tried to quieten her too vivid imagination and saw that Alexander had brought out a large folding penknife.

'What's that? You can't seriously think of using that knife?'

'Just wait and see. It's a Swiss army knife and can tackle anything.' His gaze swept around the church. 'My father was planning to replace some of the rotten planks. There's a weak place somewhere if we can only find it.'

'That sounds really tenuous.' Silver's voice wobbled. She hated herself for sounding so pessimistic. She coughed again, rubbing her scratchy throat.

'Well, have you any suggestions other than burning the whole church down?' Alexander looked at her quizzically. 'For one thing, we haven't got any matches and, for another, even if we had, we'd probably die of smoke inhalation before we could creep out. There's not much ventilation in these old churches. With all this dry wood, it would be like a tinder box.'

'Don't talk about burning.' Silver shuddered. 'Well, you try with your kid's knife. It seems to be the only hope we have.' She tried to conceal her fear with her flippant remark.

Alexander motioned her to follow him into the dark passage circling the interior of the church. He worked slowly, his hands dragging at the planks as he searched for a weakness. Moving past him, Silver crawled along the ground, her sensitive fingers feeling the boards' solid resistance under her hands. How would they ever break through such a thick barrier?

She stopped suddenly. 'Look here, Alexander,' she called. 'See that tiny chink of light low down between the planks?'

Knocking her knee on a sharp stone, she leaned forward to look more closely at the tiny prick of light. Crawling further along, she cried out in triumph: 'Look, there's a bigger chink. Perhaps this is the place?'

'I think it might be.' Alexander squatted down, and the bulk of his body blocked her view. She heard him scraping and picking away at the wood. After some time, he sat back on his heels and began to pull at the plank with all his strength. 'Luckily, they didn't use nails when they built these old churches. It's just plank upon plank,' he said, pulling harder. 'The wood seems fairly rotten here.' He gave a huge tug and toppled backwards onto Silver as the plank broke off with a loud crack, and a splash of light entered the passage. 'Completely rotten!' he exclaimed in triumph.

'You've done it!' shouted Silver, easing herself from under his weight and trying to squeeze past him.

'Wait a bit.' Alexander's strong hand held her back. 'It's not big enough to crawl through yet.' He resumed his painstaking efforts until he'd managed to release a second plank. Silver saw his muscles bunch under his blue shirt as he dragged the plank hard against him. Another crack and the opening became much larger. Light flooded into the dark, narrow passage. Silver breathed deeply, grateful for the fresh air after the suffocating smell of tar and smoke in the old church.

'It's big enough for me to slip through now.' Silver was impatient. 'Then I can help you drag off another plank.'

'Just wait a minute.' Alexander pushed her behind him. 'I'm going out first. We don't know what we'll find out there. Just hold your horses and we'll both be free.'

'God, it's sacrilege what we're doing.' His voice was muffled as he tried to prize loose yet another plank from the church wall. 'But desperate times need desperate action.' He twisted it to the left and with a final wrench, broke it free.

He eased his way through the hole left by the planks, then put out his hand to draw Silver after him. Outside, she stood up and stretched, her bones cracking under the strain of being confined for so long in the cramped passage. 'Oh, it's great to be free again,' she cried, lifting her face up to the leaden sky. A light drizzle was now falling, but the air was soft and fresh.

Alexander stood like a warrior ready to charge as he scanned the sea below them, a worried frown creasing his brow.

'What's wrong?' Silver shook his arm.

'Don't you see? The motor boat's gone. They've taken my boat as well as the dinghy.' Alexander's face was suffused with rage. 'These buggers have taken the boat. We're stranded!'

Silver let out a horrified gasp as she scanned the empty waves. There was no sign at all of Alexander's large day cruiser where it should have been bobbing at anchor. Her heart plunged. What were they to do now?

'We're not free yet.' Alexander was still scrutinising the area around them. He seized Silver's arm in a tight grip. 'Not free yet,' he repeated and cursed furiously. 'We've still got to get off this damned island.' He held her arm even tighter.

'Ouch, you're hurting me,' said Silver, breaking free of his hold. She moved away from him, racking her brains for a way to escape, now that the boat was gone. 'I can't swim far,' she whispered, feeling like a feeble townie compared with the Viking maidens of Norway, who probably were brought up from birth to swim like mermaids. 'I'm really sorry.'

The answer she was dreading came. 'I'll just have to go alone to get help,' said Alexander. 'How could I have been so stupid as to leave the dinghy as an open invitation to these crooks? But it never entered my head anyone would take it. Even less that they were clever enough to jumpstart the engine of the cruiser without keys and make a quick getaway.' He slapped his fist in frustration against his other hand.

'What about making a fire?' Silver said, biting her lip.

'Well, as I said before, if you've got a match, we can try. But everything's soaking from this rain,' he said. 'If you're good at rubbing two sticks together to make a spark, we can try that too.'

Silver bit her lip, realising that his sharp response was his way of venting his frustration at allowing the two boats to be stolen away so easily. 'Don't blame yourself.' She spoke soothingly. 'I'm sure the island is normally a safe haven for boats. No one ever expected a group of immigrants to emerge from the church. It must be a first in Bergen's history.'

'You're right, Silver. It's always been so safe. Bergen's just a provincial town, no big crimes, no excitement. Until now – I should have been better prepared.' Alexander frowned in concentration. 'The point is that this is such an isolated arm of the fiord that hardly anyone sails down this way, except us...It could be days before we're discovered.'

He straightened his shoulders. 'Well, we can't hang about regretting our mistakes. We'll just have to get on with it. I'm going to walk quickly round the island to make sure there's nobody else here and then I'll swim across to that island over there.' He pointed to another island across what seemed to Silver like a very large expanse of water. 'Some friends of ours have a summer house and boathouse there, so maybe I'll have to do a little more breaking and entering, and try and borrow or steal their boat. Perhaps I can even get to the telephone, if it's still connected.'

Silver's shoulders drooped. She didn't want to spend any more time at all on this island. But it seemed that the only way out was for Alexander to swim over to the other island on his own. They couldn't hang about on the off chance of a boat appearing. She would only hold him back if she even managed to swim halfway. Every time she looked at the other island, it seemed to recede yet further across the water.

'Wait here,' said Alexander. 'Keep out of sight.' He set off down the path.

Silver retreated to the lee of a large rock. After about quarter of an hour, Alexander returned. 'There's nobody else on the island, as far as I can see. You'll be safe until I get back. You can hide in that thick pine grove over there. There's a bit of shelter and it's unlikely that anyone would go looking for you there.' He hugged her hard against him, as if to draw strength from her nearness. 'Don't worry, I'll be back soon.' But his words failed to comfort her.

Together they walked down to the pebbly shore. Alexander handed the plastic bag full of all the treasures they'd discovered over to Silver. It hung like a dead weight on her arm.

'A bag of misfortune,' she said, looking at it with distaste.

'You must hide it well – among the trees or behind some rocks,' Alexander cautioned, as he stripped off his clothes and laid them in a neat bundle on the shore. Now he was ready for the swim. 'It's about half a kilometre across to that island. I'll be across in no time.'

'It's quite far,' said Silver, inwardly thinking that it looked as far away as France is from England across the English Channel. She compressed her lips to stop herself from blurting it out. No point in adding to Alexander's problems by telling him of her fears. It would be a long, arduous swim for him and a long nerve-wracking wait for her left alone on the island.

He stood before her in his boxer shorts, the rain gently sparkling on his tanned shoulders. A light covering of fair hairs spread across his chest, tapering to a vee under the line of his shorts. 'A golden man,' thought Silver.

Alexander's arms were around her and he gave her a quick kiss. 'Wish me bon voyage, Silver!'

Silver's heart turned over. What if he didn't make it back? What if he drowned? She'd never get over it. The moment of truth was upon her. She'd never get over it if she lost Alexander.

Then he was gone, cleaving through the grey waters at a steady crawl, his figure diminishing fast until he was almost swallowed up by the white-crested waves. It was hard to keep track of him as he drew further and further away. Now he was just a very small black shape bobbing in the waves.

She couldn't leave the beach to go up to the pine grove. She had to keep her eyes pinned on Alexander, her tiny link with the outside world. Her tee-shirt was soaking and her sodden hair dripped water down her neck, but she never took her sight off Alexander. She sat down on a rock to wait. The damp and cold seeped through her thin clothes, so after a few minutes she jumped up restlessly. The bag of passports and credit cards dragged on her wrist. She'd have to find a place of concealment as far out of the rain as possible to preserve this vital piece of evidence of the criminals' activities.

Knut was heavily involved in the immigrant scam. And how much did Elise know about the operations? Silver couldn't be sure. But Knut? Foreigners would not have come to this island unless someone had shown them the way. The location was ideal. It was so remote that it would be easy to hide people trying to dodge the police or the authorities. She'd have to investigate some more when…if she got back to the mainland.

Alexander was quite enjoying his swim. It was years since he'd pushed himself so hard physically. Downhill skiing, marathon running, a round of golf – all these were controlled sports, but nothing like the exhilaration of pitting himself against the untamed sea as now. He and Knut used to swim like fishes, diving from a large rocky promontory below the house at Rosenholm.

Once Knut had nearly dragged him under the water, using a heavy rope from one of the boats, which he twined round Alexander's ankles. He'd nearly succeeded too. Alexander had struggled in panic for what seemed like hours, as he sank lower and lower in the water. Eventually, he broke free and surfaced gasping for breath, his tortured lungs sucking in life-giving air. Alexander had never told anyone about this. It was too humiliating that his younger brother had almost won control over him like that, and yet another incident that ensured he was always on his guard with Knut.

He moved along at a smooth easy crawl, the waves supporting him, a gentle current urging him along. The rain had warmed the water and it caressed his body. Silver might have managed it, but it would have been too much of a risk. It was over a kilometre to the island with the boathouse. He hadn't dared tell Silver the true distance. He touched his trusty Swiss knife that he'd tied round his neck with a piece of cord he'd found lying in the church passage. It was his only tool if the boathouse was locked. That was another thing he and Knut used to practise. Opening locks. It used to give him a guilty thrill to open some of the drawers at home that his father kept locked, although there was nothing exciting to be found. Only old photographs and some of his own mother's old jewellery. He suspected that Knut was far more adroit at opening locks than he was.

Sometimes he and Knut would sail round the fiord calling at the different islands and trying to pick the locks of some of their friends' holiday cabins. He'd been pretty wild in those days, but he'd grown up, settled down and taken his responsibilities seriously. It seemed though that Knut was still in search of dangerous thrills. He hadn't given up his boyish pranks. He was still hell bent on pushing the boundaries for cheap excitement, always balancing on the edge of the law. Now it seemed that he'd finally tipped over to the wrong side.

Alexander lifted his arm and looked at his watch. He'd been swimming for half an hour now and the island was getting closer. The boathouse lay to the left and he hoped to God he could get inside and get the boat started. Poor Silver. How was she? He hoped she'd had the sense to go and keep herself hidden in the pine grove where no one would find her. It was always worst for the one left behind. Time expanded and the seconds crept by on reluctant feet.

He knew. He knew how it was to wait. He'd spent long enough waiting for his father to come home and comfort him after the death of his mother. But he'd never come. Not then. Only many years later after he'd grown up, they'd had quite a good relationship, as father and son. But he never forgot the waiting. Was that why he tried to compensate Knut all the time, so that he would never know the pain of being excluded and waiting for someone who never came? And Elise too. Was that why, he, Alexander, was so grateful to her, because she'd always made time for him? He'd always tried to pay her back for all the good things she'd done for him and forget the unpredictable, bad things.

Silver had burst into his life at the worst possible moment, when he was at his lowest ebb. Funny how she'd wormed her way in under his defences. He'd tried to keep her at arms' length, but her feistiness and persistence had broken down the barriers he normally erected. He pictured her as he'd left her, her face tired and strained. Black marks streaked her delicate pink and white skin. He wondered if she felt the same way about him. He trod water for a moment to save his breath. He wasn't usually so introspective. Normally, he just got on and did things. Silver coming along like that had forced him to confront certain aspects of his life. To wonder why he felt compelled to take such care of Elise and Knut, when they offered so little in return.

But the chill of the water was forcing him to slacken his pace and he was losing the rhythm of his easy crawl. The cold had penetrated his skin and he found his legs wouldn't obey him. They were stiffening up. His muscles started to knot and an excruciating pain ran up the calf of his left leg. No panic, for God's sake. He tried to breathe steadily in out, in out, in an attempt to regain the rhythm of his strokes. His left leg was like a rigid stick, refusing to bend. He bent down to rub his toes and start the circulation, but took in a mouthful of salty water, which made him choke. The shores of the new island loomed up in front of him. He wasn't sure if he could make it. Then he focused himself and increased his efforts, propelling himself along with his good leg. Nearly there, just one final spurt, he urged himself on. The beach was straight ahead. Three more strokes, and his good foot found the rocky bottom of the fiord. Fighting to drag air into his lungs, he pulled his chilled body out of the water and collapsed onto the sharp stones of the beach.

After a while, he pulled himself up into a sitting position. Seawater rained off his shoulders. He shaded his eyes with his hand, trying to catch a glimpse of Silver on the far island. But a light mist swirled over the fiord, hiding the other island from view. He hoped to God she was safe and that the strange men hadn't returned. Now if only he could find a boat to get them off the island.

Silver shook her watch, convinced it had stopped because the minute hand seemed glued in position. The cold of the night seeped into her bones and it was impossible to make out any sign of Alexander in the waves. In fact, it was better not to try, because she only scared herself that something had happened to him.

The pine grove was a little warmer, and Silver found a secluded hollow among some rocks. There was an overhanging branch where the rain hadn't penetrated. She wished she had a rug or something to put over her. The incessant dripping of water from the trees was getting on her nerves.

She decided to take another look at the documents that they had collected from behind the pulpit in the church to see if she could make some sense of them. It would help to pass the time too. Her stomach rumbled, reminding her that almost ten hours had passed since she last ate. She could at least cup her hands to gather moisture from the trees and get a drink.

She began pulling out the documents from the plastic bag, careful not to get them wet. The fallen pine needles provided a soft, dry carpet in the little hollow where she sat. The light was poor and tiredness made her eyelids droop, so she gathered up the documents carefully and returned them to the plastic bag. Where could she hide them? Her fingers felt carefully along the ridges of the rocks until she found a crevice deep enough to conceal the precious bag. No one would find them unless they knew exactly where to look. She slid the bag carefully into its new hiding place.

Shutting her eyes, she conjured up Alexander's image as she'd last seen him in front of her, his body tanned and broad-shouldered, and his arms warm and comforting around her. She sat still for a moment as a flood of fear swept over her. Oh, Alexander, don't let anything happen to you!

Chapter 18

Silver awoke with a start and sat up hastily, trying to orientate herself. She'd wrapped herself in Alexander's discarded clothes to try and keep warm, but it hadn't helped. She was chilled to the bone. The night was dark and full of shadows except for a whitish phosphorescence rising off the sea. She must have slept for some time. She tried to read the hands of her watch, but the darkness was too enveloping. She uncurled her legs and got stiffly to her feet, rubbing her hands up and down her arms to try and put some warmth in them.

The full realisation hit her. Where was Alexander? Surely he should be back by now? She pulled herself to her feet and began to totter on her unco-operative legs towards the sea. Perhaps she could catch a glimpse of Alexander from the shore and surely the light from the sea would illuminate her watch.

She wished she didn't feel so empty and nauseated. How long was it since she'd last eaten? Impossible to tell. She moved out of the pine trees and looked down on the small bay where she and Alexander had come ashore. That was yesterday, she supposed.

Then her body jolted into full alert. There, in front of her disbelieving eyes, a tall white motor boat rode at anchor. Alexander was back. Why hadn't he come to look for her? Relief flooded over her, but why had he been so slow in coming to find her? She slithered on the wet pine needles in her haste to get to the beach. Closer to the boat, she became uncertain because it seemed larger than the one they had sailed on yesterday.

Two men were standing there. Two? Silver held back for a moment. Had Alexander found a companion? Oh no, perhaps it wasn't Alexander. She crouched down and began to move back as silently as possible, but the branches of the trees rustled as she edged away. She kept a watch on the two men while raindrops from the pine trees dripped down her neck. Even in the darkness, she felt exposed and vulnerable to anyone who came to the island. What had happened to Alexander?

She strained her eyes, peering at the two shapes moving across the shore. By the silvery light rising from the sea, she could just make out two dark heads. There was no sign of a fair one. Alexander, where was he? Her nostrils caught the sharp tang of a cigarette. If it wasn't Alexander, who could it be?

Silver's eyes adjusted to the gloom and she made out a stack of large cardboard boxes piled high on the shore. '*Herring boxes without topses.*' The stupid rhyme ran through her head, but she was sure the boxes didn't contain anything as innocuous as fish. The two men continued to pile up the boxes, their voices an unintelligible mumble. They moved easily back and forth carrying their burdens and didn't seem to be making any effort to conceal themselves.

Silver gripped the pine frond tightly, holding it in front of her as feeble protection. Why would two people come here in the middle of the night close to where the murder of Alexander's father had taken place? There must be some connection. One murder had taken place here and if she wasn't careful she could be the next. Fear ratcheted up in Silver's mind. Something must have happened to

Alexander. She was sure he would have come looking for her if he had arrived back safely.

She shivered. It was time to beat a retreat before the two strange men caught sight of her. Her heart was pounding so loudly that she was afraid it might reveal her hiding place. She looked upwards and wondered if she should return to the old church, now a solid black mass of shadow on the hill. But it glowered at her, more of a threat than a safe haven. She inched backward, still holding the men in her sights, when suddenly the wet pine fronds released a loud splash of cold water over her shoulders.

One of the two men stopped working and raised his head like a dog sniffing the air for a strange scent. Silver tried to stop breathing.

The man moved towards her hiding place. She froze, mesmerised like a rabbit. Then, unable to stop herself, she broke cover and ran as if a pack of hounds were snapping at her heels. She turned back sharply to check if she was being followed and her foot caught in an exposed tree root. She pitched forward, hitting the ground. The breath was knocked right out of her, and she lay there tense and rigid, unable to think or move.

Hands seized her arms and pulled her roughly to her feet. For a long moment, she thought she'd never breathe again. Then she choked and coughed, and her lungs began to fill with blessed clean air.

'Silver!' A man's voice broke through her trauma. 'What are you doing here?'

'Oh no.' The words were forced out of her in a deep groan. She wrenched herself free of the restraining hands. Knut was here. She turned her gaze to the right. And Lazlo. Her two least favourite people. 'Better the devil you know, than the devil you don't.' She realised she was speaking aloud.

Lazlo's eyes were small and feral as he regarded her. He licked his lips, his face a mixture of fear and lasciviousness.

Why should he be scared of her? Silver puzzled over the question. A rank smell of fear rose from his body and nagged at her nostrils.

Knut, the urbane, slipped his arm around her and then swiftly withdrew it as he felt how damp she was. 'Well, little Miss Curiosity, what are you doing here, and where's my esteemed brother?'

Knut's put-down riled Silver. In just a few short moments, she had passed from the depths of fear to fury at Knut's irritating remarks. A surge of adrenaline pumped through her veins, giving her courage. She gave Knut a great push on his chest so that he staggered back with a surprised grunt.

'Hey, no need for that,' he said, regaining his footing. 'What are you doing here, Silver? And how did you get to this island?'

'By boat.' Silver's answer was curt. She knew it would annoy him.

'By boat, of course. But who brought you? Alexander, I suppose. What've you done with him?' He turned to scan the island to the east as an arc of orange light rose from the sea. Dawn was approaching.

Lazlo stepped forward. 'What shall we do with her?' Silver noted his furtive glance at the pile of cardboard boxes.

'We can't leave her here,' said Knut, grabbing hold of Silver's arm again. Silver looked at him. She thought she could break free of him, but she was afraid she'd be no match for burly Lazlo.

'Then we'll just have to take her with us and dump her overboard.' Lazlo's face was full of black menace.

Knut appeared shaken. His fingers tightened on Silver's arm. He didn't seem sure whether Lazlo was joking or not. 'Give over, Lazlo. Are you crazy? This is my brother's girlfriend. We can't just dump her overboard. There'd be hell to pay.' His voice rose with irritation.

Despite her woes, Silver felt a secret thrill run through her at Knut's words. Alexander's girlfriend!

'Hell to pay anyway,' said Lazlo. 'She see too much. She tell brother. Come on, missy, you poke your nose in too much. But you got very nice boobs!' He threw back his head and his coarse laugh reverberated through the trees. His eyes glittered as he studied Silver. 'Come, we go now.' He seized Silver's other arm and pulled her over to where a black plastic dinghy was dragged up on the shingle.

'You fix packages.' Lazlo flung his words over his shoulder at Knut, who was trailing uncertainly after them. 'I take girl.'

The words were ominous, making Silver's heart skip several beats. Just suppose Alexander did return in the middle of the stowage operations – he would be caught completely unawares.

She was freezing cold and her damp tee-shirt clung to her chest in a revealing way. She seemed to have lost Alexander's shirt, not that it would shield her much from Lazlo's gaze. Uneasily, she tugged at the small tee-shirt, trying to stretch it while Lazlo's ever-watchful eyes enjoyed her struggles. She had no intention of getting into the dinghy alone with Lazlo. Knut provided only flimsy protection, but he was better than nothing. Where was Alexander? Why hadn't he come back? But in the cold relentless sea, anything could have happened to him. Suppose she were left behind alone on the island by Lazlo and Knut? She could be marooned for days. And what if those strange foreign-looking men that she and Alexander had seen row away from the island returned?

If only she could get back to the mainland, she could

get hold of a boat or send a search party out for Alexander. She took a deep breath trying to gather strength and fight against the shivers sliding down her spine. She was so cold and tired, it was hard to think straight, but of one thing she was certain. 'I'm not going anywhere without Knut,' she told Lazlo firmly, planting her feet securely on the ground, her hands on her hips.

Knut eyed Lazlo uneasily. All the bright swagger seemed to have been knocked out of him. It was clear he was Lazlo's puppet.

Lazlo jerked Silver down to the shore. She turned back: 'Knut...' She was annoyed to hear the tremulous pleading in her voice. 'You're coming too, aren't you?'

He stood, hesitating. Then, picking up one of the cardboard boxes, he walked down to the shore as Lazlo's iron-hard arm forced Silver towards the small black dinghy. Silver and Lazlo splashed outwards, the shallow sea covering their ankles. Lazlo shoved her roughly into the small craft. She tripped and sprawled down onto the bottom boards of the boat, scraping her face.

At last, Knut was galvanised into action. He ran down over the shingle. 'Stop there, you can't knock her around like that, you stupid bastard.' A hint of authority crept into his voice as he grasped the rim of the dinghy and held it back. 'Sorry, Silver, this should never have happened, but you should never have been on the island.'

Now all three were on board the small craft, which listed hard to the port side with Lazlo's heavy weight. 'Sit down, for God's sake, man,' said Knut. 'You know nothing about boats.'

The two men glared each other. The boat lurched again, taking in water.

'Sit down, sit down at once,' Silver screamed desperately, clutching the side.

But it was too late. With a shattering splash, the little craft capsized and neatly ejected its three passengers.

Silver found herself face down on the seabed, her face against the sea-washed stones. Involuntarily, she gulped a dose of salty water, but stubbing her knee on a larger stone, she heaved herself to her feet. She coughed and spat, trying to get rid of the water.

She looked around her. Further in towards the shore, Lazlo lay spluttering on his back like a cumbersome whale, his stomach protruding from the waves. But Knut lay face down, as Silver had done. With a stab of fear, she saw he was inert, making no effort to raise himself. His body swayed like seaweed with the movement of the rippling waves.

'Knut.' Silver's voice was croaky. She coughed to clear her throat. 'Knut, are you okay?' Heedless of her injured knee, she splashed her way over to him, wondering if he'd hit his head on a rock.

Lazlo cursed up a storm in a guttural language. With an ungainly movement, he pulled himself to his feet and waded back to the shore.

Silver dragged at Knut's body, which moved limply in the water but showed no signs of life. With a supreme effort, she managed to push and turn him. She gasped as she saw that his face was grey and ashen, with a bruise appearing near his left temple. He didn't appear to be breathing.

She slipped her hands under his arms and began towing him towards the shore. His body got heavier and heavier as they drew closer to land and the buoyancy of the water decreased.

She looked across and saw that Lazlo had slumped down on a rock, his head in his hands. 'Lazlo,' she called sharply. 'Come here at once.'

He mumbled something unintelligible.

'Lazlo, if you don't come down here at once, you'll have a murder on your hands.'

Like a zombie, the large man levered himself off the rock and wavered his way down to the shore. A long wave rippled in from the fiord and, with Lazlo's help, Silver drew Knut's inert body up over the shingle. She was trembling hard and her teeth were chattering.

God, she knew very little about first aid or resuscitation techniques. But it was obvious that he was in a serious state and would die if she didn't do the right thing. His face was turning a nasty bluish pallor, which terrified her.

'Help me or he'll die,' she said to the reluctant Lazlo. Where the hell was Alexander? She shouldn't be dealing with this situation alone. Annoyance tugged at the back of her mind, giving her the courage to struggle on.

With Lazlo's clumsy help, she straightened Knut out and managed to turn his head to the side. That much she knew. He lay as still as a long-dead mummy.

'Get your hands on his chest, Lazlo, and press for all your worth,' she commanded. 'We've got to get him breathing again.'

Fat Lazlo seemed to have shrunk and his face was grey with fright. He put his great fleshy hands on Knut's chest and pressed gently.

'Harder, harder, or we'll lose him!' shouted Silver. 'Damn you, Alexander, get back here!' Her frustrated cry floated away on the freshening wind. She bent down and tried to blow air into Knut's mouth, waving her hand to try to keep Lazlo working in synch with her.

'Come on,' she shouted, then blew into Knut's mouth again. Three more times they strove together, then Knut's eyes flew open and his chest stirred. Silver stepped back quickly as he vomited a stream of greyish water onto the shingle. His chest began to rise rhythmically and after some minutes, he moved his head to look around him.

Silver got behind him and helped him up into a sitting position. He groaned and put a hand to his head.

'Bugger you, Lazlo, what've you done to me?' His eyes were dark and bloodshot as he stared at his henchman. Then he caught sight of Silver. 'What're you doing here?' he asked querulously.

'Lazlo and I probably saved your life,' said Silver, now encased in a strange calm. After all her desperate efforts with Knut, she was exhausted. She looked out over the broadening strip of light between sea and sky. Hope mixed with fear sprang in her heart. A black launch was approaching the island.

Chapter 19

Silver stood transfixed, unable to take her eyes off the powerful-looking launch speeding towards the island in a cloud of spray. The word *Politi* was painted in large white letters on the side of the black vessel, which was unmistakably official. She put a hand out to support herself on a rock, feeling dizzy and disorientated. Straining her eyes, she could just make out someone waving to her with great sweeping gestures.

'Silver!' A deep male voice floated across the waves.

Silver's heart lifted with joy. 'Alexander, oh thank God!'

He didn't wait for the boat to reach land, but launched himself over the side and splashed his way onto the shore. He must have borrowed some clothes because he was wearing washed out jeans, several sizes too small for him and exposing a long expanse of tanned bare leg. The shirt he was wearing was the most garish red check Silver had ever seen. It was also far too short and left his flat midriff bare, but Silver had never seen anything so beautiful or sexy in her whole life.

She hurled herself at him and his arms came round her, drawing her against his warm strength. She raised her head to look at him, fighting back tears of relief. 'What took you so long?' she asked.

He drew her head against his chest and his hand

smoothed her hair back from her damp face. His fresh breath warmed her cheek. She pressed close to him trying to hide herself in the depths of his comforting presence. She felt his lips brush hers and tasted the salt on them. Silver's feelings flickered from relief to love, to deep fatigue and hot desire.

Time stood still. Then Alexander released her gently. She looked around and focused on the scene behind her, taking in the fact that Detective Chief Inspector Berg and a leather-jacketed, uniformed constable had arrived in the police boat with Alexander. The two policemen had tactfully walked over to talk to Knut. DCI Berg was bending over him, talking earnestly. The inspector helped him into a sitting position with support from the young police constable. Knut still looked very shaky. A twinge of horror ran through Silver. How near Knut had come to drowning. It had been touch and go before he began to breathe of his own accord. Suppose they hadn't managed to save him! She closed her eyes for a moment, shutting out the horror.

But where was Lazlo? She caught a glimpse of him moving on stealthy feet back toward the old stave church.

At the same moment, Alexander noticed Lazlo's slippery movements. Immediately, his voice rang out: 'Stop there! You're not going anywhere!' He chased after Lazlo, who speeded up and set a cracking pace for such a fat man, his short legs pounding up the path. But Alexander's long strides soon gained on him and his arm went out to grab him. With a blood vessel-bursting effort, Lazlo squirmed loose from Alexander's fingers.

Silver's hand went to her mouth as, with a swift movement, Lazlo dived under Alexander's outstretched hand and doubled back towards her as she stood watching him from her position down on the shore. Panting, his face red and eyes popping, Lazlo ran up to Silver and seized her arm. He brought out a long knife with a serrated blade that looked as if it could butcher a horse with ease. In triumph, he stood his ground, his arm round Silver's neck. His harsh hands held her as a shield in front of him. With a light pinprick of his knife blade, he touched the tender skin of her throat and a splatter of small red dots dropped onto her tee-shirt. A cold shudder of fear ran through her.

Alexander stood watching in horror, his body taut with tension. The two policemen had abandoned Knut and now stood behind Alexander. The three formed a group frozen in inaction.

Lazlo said nothing, but twisted Silver's arm behind her. The pain was agonising as she felt her muscles crack. She bit her lip, forcing herself not to cry out. Silently, she tried to make herself smaller and more passive to avoid startling Lazlo into a mad reaction. Trying to keep calm, she fixated on Alexander, and on hope and help from the two policemen. Did any of them have a weapon? Lazlo's cramping grip around her and his hot excited breath scared her into a near faint. Once more, she fought the waves of dizziness rolling over her.

Alexander's foot crunched on the shingle. 'If you injure that woman...' he rasped.

But Lazlo broke in fiercely. 'Keep back,' he ordered, jerking Silver hard against him.

Alexander's face was ashen. Silver wept inwardly. In a blinding beam of clarity, she realised how much she loved Alexander. With all her heart and soul – just as she was to be snatched from his arms by this filthy fiend. She managed to stop herself turning her head and spitting on Lazlo. She told herself to lie low and do nothing until there was an opportunity to escape.

Puffing and sweating, Lazlo half dragged her along the

path leading up to the church. He touched her temple with the long blade of the knife and she flinched back. It would be easy to lose an eye! She dared not resist.

She cast a surreptitious glance back at the men on the shore, but they remained like petrified stone in a sculpted group around Knut's reclining figure on the shingle.

Anger and frustration were building inside her but she kept them concealed from Lazlo. Men – had they no imagination? Here she was being hauled away like a sack of potatoes and all they could do was to stand around. The surge of adrenaline gave her more courage and she began to visualise the interior of the church. If she could break free of Lazlo, were there any places where could she run and hide? The pulpit? No, too risky. If she ran up those stairs, he would bar her from coming back down.

At the top of the path, they reached the old wooden church, and Lazlo released one of Silver's arms and gave the heavy black door a rough push. It creaked open and a stream of light ribboned into the dark maw of the church.

Lazlo's voice sounded low and sullen in Silver's ear. 'You're not going to spoil our operation, you trouble woman. Why did you poke your nose in? Money, lives, you spoil it all. I am to be rich and you come here and destroy.' His eyes were burning with suppressed fury, and he shoved her so hard that she slipped down on her knees onto the cold flagstones of the floor.

She gasped with fright as the heavy door banged shut behind them. Twisting her arm behind her, Lazlo clicked the lock and darkness enveloped the church. She tripped and fell on the floor. Everything happening outside was blanked out. Even if she screamed, the sound would be muffled in the church walls. Again, a picture of Alexander crossed her mind. She tried to hold onto it like a talisman and dug her nails into the palms of her hands as she lay curled up on the cold flagstones.

Gradually, her eyes adjusted to the gloom. She turned her body slowly round, hoping Lazlo wouldn't notice her stealthy movements. The centre of the church was a wide open space. If only it was like an ordinary church with pews where she could conceal herself or dodge behind them. Her eyes were nearly shut as she peered through her lashes at him. Lazlo moved away from her and brought out a flat bottle from his pocket, which he uncorked. He took a couple of quick swigs from it.

Silver strained her ears. Was that a stealthy rustle outside the building? Lazlo took several more swigs from the bottle and pushed it toward her. 'Good French brandy. Very expensive in Norway.' He threw back his head and laughed. 'Drink, drink,' he said, his face suddenly full of bonhomie as he shoved the bottleneck almost into her mouth. She wrenched her head sharply away. His knife clattered to the floor. She looked at his glittering, excited eyes, and her blood chilled.

He snatched the bottle back and took another pull at it. 'You and that brother snob Alexander laugh at poor Lazlo. You too fine people. But Knut, he Lazlo's friend. He need money. Lazlo give Knut money. Lazlo big man, he got megabucks. He rescue many people and bring them here to Norway. Fine wines and liquor too. Ha, ha, ha!'

Silver's mouth was dry. Lazlo's uncontrolled laughter was even more terrifying than his sullen rage. He stepped forward and caressed her cheek. She managed not to flinch from him. He pinched her cheek gently between his finger and thumb. 'Soft like baby,' he said. 'Lovely angel hair. You beauty, all for Lazlo.'

Silver held herself rigid. The danger was greater than ever. If she wasn't murdered, she would be raped by Lazlo.

Which was worse? She strained her ears trying to hear if there was any movement outside. Was it just the wind brushing against the side of the church in a series of raps against the wooden walls?

Lazlo didn't pay any attention. He took another drink from his bottle. and then picking up his knife, he strolled over to the pulpit.

He stopped short. 'Who's been here?' he roared, rounding on Silver. 'You steal my things!'

This time, she failed to keep a steady mien. 'No, no, I never touched anything.' Her fear forced her to lie.

He strode over to her and forced her head down to look at the empty space where all the passports and credit cards had lain concealed. 'You and that Alexander brother swine take my things!' His brandy-fuelled breath almost choked her. Silver tried to break free, her stomach churning with revulsion.

Outside the church, Alexander's attempts to open the heavy main door were futile. It rebuffed all his efforts. Silver, now the most precious thing in his world, was incarcerated inside the unyielding bastion of the church. DCI Berg had tried to make several calls to the mainland for reinforcements, but failed each time to make the connection.

'Three of us together can surely manage to overpower one man,' said Alexander. His face hardened. 'We've no choice.'

He remembered the way Silver had looked when she'd first come to visit him at the office. So delicate and pretty in her green dress. She'd got a good story out of him too, even though he usually refused to speak to the press. Then he recalled how the water had drenched her on their disastrous visit to the cruise ship in the harbour.

She was so plucky, she'd simply laughed it off.

The strongest picture of all floated through his mind of how she'd stood nervously and waved him off to swim across to the next island. She'd been cold, wet and shivering with fear, but with a valiant smile on her lips. If anything should happen to her, it would be his fault. He twisted his mouth in anguish. What had he brought upon her? The Rosenholm connection had been catastrophic for her. She'd probably never want to see him again. He pushed his hair back from his forehead, then squared his shoulders. He would get her out of the church come hell or high water, away from that bloody madman that Knut had got tangled up with. People smuggling, money laundering and even drugs. Whatever possessed his brother to get in with people like that?

He set his jaw. Give him ten minutes and he'd be inside that church! If he lost Silver now, his life would be an empty sham.

The young constable slipped on some loose stones, sending them rattling down the slope. 'Be careful,' snapped DCI Berg. 'We don't want to reveal anything to the people inside.'

'It's a double wall,' Alexander said. 'I doubt they can hear us through that.'

All three of them looked back at Knut, now propped up against a rock and in as sheltered a place as they could find for him. Alexander realised there was no help to be gained from that quarter, and anyway what could he expect from Knut, who'd brought Lazlo into it from the beginning. He thought of his stepmother, how shocked she would be. It might even destroy her, although he now suspected her of being involved in whatever illegal immigration operation Lazlo was running with Knut. He thought of his father. Rage almost blinded him as he recalled his father's needless death, probably at the hands of this villain. In fact, he was sure of it, even though the police hadn't come up with any proof.

He walked over to DCI Berg. 'What's the latest on my father's murder? We've heard nothing from you for several weeks. Have you uncovered anything new? You must have by now.' He clenched his fists and almost shouted at the man in his frustration.

DCI Berg's face reddened. 'We are still waiting for DNA tests from the laboratory in England – it takes some time for these to become available. But it seems that there were two or three people on the island who torched the cottage. I can promise you, you will be the first to be informed of the test results.'

Get a hold of yourself, man! Alexander muttered to himself trying to tamp down his emotions and analyse the situation coolly. A plan began to form in his brain. Tracking back round the church, he searched for the small gap where earlier he'd loosened the planks to allow him and Silver to escape. He walked carefully back and forwards, bending down to drag at the planks, but they seemed firmly fixed in place. He searched harder, now crawling on his knees, his trousers soaked by the moisture from last night's rain. He dragged more frantically at the planks until one gave way a little under the pressure of his eager hands.

At last – there was the place! He sat back on his heels, pausing to size up the space. It would be hard to scramble back inside such a small hole without making a lot of noise and alerting Lazlo inside. Then the bastard would probably stab him as he tried to enter.

He racked his brain for a better idea, but the tall church, with its carved demons, seemed a near-unassailable fortress. Somehow, he had to get through the impenetrable outer wooden wall and into the dark corridor which surrounded the church. He knelt down to examine the planks more closely.

He would save Silver, even if he had to kill Lazlo with the man's own knife.

If only he hadn't left Silver alone on the island. He could've seen off Lazlo with ease. What a stupid decision he'd taken. Trying to play hero to impress her. Although he'd really had no choice if they were going to get off the island safely. But if he lost her now...?

Silver watched Lazlo. He was down on the floor, his large bottom sticking out as he felt inside the hidden cavity behind the pulpit. The empty bottle of brandy rolled across the floor and his foot gave it a flying kick. He sat up quickly and looked around him. Silver was motionless, waiting for the explosion to roll over her.

'Stupid bitch, you take them!' Lazlo's face was black with rage. With two steps, he crossed over to her and yanked her to her feet. A stream of wild curses flew in her face and his spittle sprayed her cheek.

Then he shut his mouth. It was all quiet in the eerie church. A greater fear rose in Silver's throat. She watched Lazlo as he studied her. What would be his next move? A smile spread over his face, illuminating the cruel lines running from nose to mouth. He picked up the knife again, sweeping it across her neck and between her thighs. 'You lovely angel,' he said again. 'You want big cut? Or you be kind to Lazlo?' He stroked the knife across her stomach, his breathing thick and fast.

Silver turned numb. She tried to distance herself from her own body, to escape into another dimension. This couldn't be happening to her. But he grasped her arm hard, drawing her to him and fingering her nipples. He dropped the knife and began undoing his belt, pulling it slowly off. His tongue slipped out from between his lips and his eyes were black with concentration.

Silver whirled and wrenched herself free from Lazlo's hold. The church was dark and she was afraid of tripping over something, but she ran like a Valkyrie, her feet hardly touching the ground. She sped along, desperate to find the entrance to the outer dark passage which ringed the inner space of the church.

Once inside the passage, she'd got to keep out of his reach. She'd got to find the place where Alexander had loosened the planks. She breathed fast, sweat breaking out on her brow. Keep calm, keep calm, she exhorted herself – in her panic, she mustn't dash past the only escape route. Would Lazlo's fat beer belly slow him up enough for her to elude him?

There! She caught sight of the entrance to the passage and dodged swiftly into it. She slowed a little, trying to catch her breath. Then she heard Lazlo's heavy feet pounding after her. He shouted something, but the words were muffled by the wooden walls.

She noticed a faint ray of light penetrating the dark passage. Was that the place where she and Alexander had managed to get through? Her breath was coming in short gasps and she had a huge stitch in her side like a sword stab.

Lazlo was gaining on her. He had more stamina than she'd expected. It was now or never. She crumpled up into a small ball and rolled towards the planks.

Luck of luck, Lazlo hadn't noticed her. He pounded on, past her curled up body, wheezing and short of breath, past her shallow hiding place. As his footsteps died away, Silver crept out and began pulling back the tarred planks. The weight of the planks resisted her, but she continued to tug and pull at them, heedless of the splinters tearing at her fingers. Sweat poured in rivulets down her back. The last plank moved to the side, and she almost fell backwards, jarring her injured ankle. She stifled a cry of pain. But at last she'd forced open a narrow space, large enough for her to squeeze through. Even though she was so slim and lithe, it was a tight fit. The torn planks scraped against her side and tore at her clothes as she wriggled her way through. Then with an awkward movement she caught her arm on a large splinter of wood, which embedded itself in her arm. Once more, she bit down a cry of pain.

The bright daylight almost blinded her and she hesitated for a moment. Blinking, she could just make out Alexander coming toward her. Then from behind, a hand clamped down hard on her ankle.

Chapter 20

Silver screamed as Lazlo's fat hand clamped on her ankle and dragged her back from the small ray of daylight which shone through the gap in the external wall of the church. Alexander rushed towards her and seized her fingers. Silver's muscles cracked as she formed a living rope between the two men. The pain was excruciating.

She kicked with all her might at Lazlo. Alexander released her hands and forced his way through the loosened planks. Silver's wild kicking didn't make much impression on Lazlo, but his stout girth hindered him from moving backward. Alexander's long arm shot out and seized Lazlo by the ear, while Silver scrambled to her feet and wriggled out of the way. She pressed against the wall trying to make herself as small as possible.

Alexander took a firmer grip on Lazlo whose face was red with fury and shiny with sweat. He shouted to the two policemen to come and help.

Silver slid past Alexander and slipped out through the enlarged hole. She inhaled desperate lungfuls of fresh air then forced her unsteady feet to move towards the men on the shore. 'Help,' she cried, but her voice came out as a hoarse croak. She tried again: 'Help! Oh, please help us.' This time DCI Berg looked up and ran swiftly towards her.

'It's Lazlo. He's fighting with Alexander. Oh please, go up to the church, round the back.' She subsided on the ground gasping for breath. The pain of her stretched muscles rose up and overwhelmed her, and she slumped onto her side. Dimly, she heard DCI Berg calling to the police constable he'd brought with him and together the two men ran up the slope.

Silver lay on the ground, hungry, cold and hurting. She wondered if they would ever be free. She longed for a soft bed to lie in and a large bowl of thick warming soup. Tender loving care, that's what she needed right now. TLC from Alexander in particular. She floated off into a protective haze, her eyes closed and her head pillowed on Knut's lap.

On Knut's lap? Her eyelids snapped open. How did he get there? She didn't want him close to her. He had caused all the trouble. She wanted Alexander. She beat at Knut childishly with her fists.

He bent over her and whispered in her ear. 'Be quiet, little Silver! You're safe with Uncle Knut now!'

Silver stared up at him. He resembled a rakish pirate, with his stubbly beard and dishevelled hair. Rage shook her at his patronising words. She shoved him away hard and jumped to her feet. 'Where's Alexander? Why don't you go up and help him?' She pointed up the slope to the church.

Knut remained in the semi-reclining position she'd pushed him into. She regarded him more closely. His face was a pasty cream colour. Perhaps he wasn't up to walking? Did he remember how they'd pumped the water out of him? Probably not. Anyway, Silver was too tired to care. She lay down on the grass again well away from Knut, waves of dizziness rolling over her.

She didn't know how long she'd lain there. It could've been three minutes or three hours. Through the fog of fatigue, she heard Alexander's voice. His arms slipped under her and he carried her close to his warm chest. Dimly, she heard him call to Knut. 'Get up, Knut. We're going back to Elise's house. You've got a hell of a lot of explaining to do and so has she.'

Silver opened her eyes again just as Knut stood up. He swayed a little and put his hand to his head. Then he followed Alexander as he carried Silver down to the boat. Bringing up the rear was Lazlo, his arms firmly gripped by the two policemen.

Silver sighed and rubbed her head against Alexander's scratchy red shirt. He smelt of the sea and of good masculine sweat. He dropped a kiss in her hair and clutched her tighter against his chest. A hazy, numbed comfort swept over her.

With Silver in his arms, Alexander waded out towards the black police boat, followed by Knut and then the two policemen, who shoved the chastened Lazlo into the vessel.

Alexander deposited Silver on one of the wooden side seats and grasped the rudder, while DCI Berg started the engine. Knut was slumped in the stern. The younger policeman sat beside Lazlo, and Silver noticed that the fat man was now linked to him by handcuffs. The inspector manoeuvred the boat into deep water and soon they were streaking their way over the white-tipped waves to Bergen.

Once back at the marina in Bergen harbour, they split naturally into two groups. The two policemen put Lazlo into a waiting police car. As they drove off, Silver caught his baleful stare through the window.

Alexander was left with the two walking wounded, Silver and Knut. He helped them both into the parked jeep and gave out orders. 'Okay, Knut, it's off to the hospital for you and no protests. You're damned lucky the police let me take care of you, you fool.'

Knut lifted his hand in a weak wave of assent.

Having left Knut in the capable hands of the local hospital for a full check-up, Alexander turned to Silver and said: 'Okay, now it's out to Rosenholm and Elise.' She leant back in her seat, glad that he was in full command. Her eyes kept closing, despite her efforts to stay awake.

The short voyage out to Rosenholm in a borrowed boat passed in a blur. Alexander once again took the rudder and ferried the two of them over to the family island.

After a night of coma-like sleep, Silver stirred, woken by a knock on the door. It was hard to open her eyes to the bright sunlight that was filling the yellow bedroom where she'd stayed the last time at Elise's house. She struggled out from the warm cocoon of her duvet. Her muscles still ached, but her nostrils were tantalised by the aroma of fresh coffee. She sat up, pushing her hair out of her eyes and looked at Alexander, who'd entered the room bearing a breakfast tray.

At the sight of him, not yet shaved, but dressed in a light blue open-necked shirt and grey chinos, she came fully awake. She raised her face to his as he bent over to brush her lips with his. The crockery nearly slid off the tray into her lap.

She pulled back hastily and laughed as Alexander tried to right the cups and plates. 'That was a near thing,' she said.

'A very near thing.' Alexander laughed with her, but his blue eyes smouldered. His gaze held depths of meaning that made her pulses spin with desire. But his hand came down hard on hers as he appeared to control himself with an effort.

'We have things to talk about, you, me and Elise. Knut as well. He's refused to stay in the hospital. So now he's back here. Can you be ready by lunch time?'

Feeling slightly let down, Silver looked at her watch. Eleven o'clock already! She must have slept like the dead.

She nodded. 'I'll be ready.'

Alexander left the room for a moment. Then he came back with a stack of clean clothes. 'Elise found you these,' he said. 'Just look through them and borrow what you'd like.' Then he withdrew, shutting the door behind him.

Silver was ravenous. She fell eagerly on the breakfast tray, demolishing cereals, a soft-boiled egg and buttered rolls in record time. She savoured the hot coffee and poured herself a second cup. Holding the cup in her hands, she wondered what it was that Alexander intended to talk about. Could he be open with his stepmother about what had happened on the island? And the problem of Knut? How far was he involved and in what? Or was there a lot more? She threw the duvet off her legs. It was time she got up.

Standing under the shower, she let the needles of water stab her into a state of alertness. It was getting to be a habit, her borrowing clothes from Alexander or at least from his stepmother. Her muscles still ached despite the warmth of the shower. Her light wisps of underwear had dried overnight, so she put them on and then slipped into an elegant striped blouse belonging to Elise, which was several sizes too big for her. She approached the pile of clothes wondering who they all really belonged to. She had a feeling of distaste, as the different garments reminded her of the clothes they'd found in the owner's suite. All intended for the illegals. But she forced herself to pick out a blue skirt with a belt, which she could pull tight round her waist. Her trainers, which she'd kicked off in a heap last night, were still a little damp but she pulled them on. In the round brass-framed mirror, her green eyes looked back at her, huge in her pale face above the too wide neck of the blouse.

Someone seemed to have taken her wet and torn clothes away, and with them her lipstick. She bit her lips to try and make them redder.

She ran downstairs into the sitting room, but only Elise and Alexander sat there. Between them on the table stood the inevitable pot of coffee, which all Norwegians seemed to need if they were to function properly. Cups and saucers were stacked up on the table as well.

'Where's Knut?' Silver glanced through the door to the kitchen.

'He'll be down in a minute,' said Alexander. 'He's probably still snoring his head off. He looked pretty rough last night.'

Elise moved uneasily in her chair. 'Yes, he looked worn out last night. What have you done to him, Alexander?'

'Never mind Knut just now, Elise,' Alexander's voice was curt. 'I'll go and stir him out of his bed in a minute. I want to talk about your part in the affair and Silver is here to help us.'

A warm glow spread from the pit of Silver's stomach and up through her body. Alexander needed her. Just as she needed him. Her eye caught him studying her. He seemed to find it hard to wrench his eyes away from her too. 'Now to business,' he said. 'What about these Russians you've been helping, Elise?'

Elise's face was strained and there were dark rings under her eyes, but today her hair was caught back in a sophisticated chignon, and she was wearing a blue tailored blouse and skirt and a pair of elegant high heel shoes. There was a long pause. Then she said: 'How did you know about that?'

Alexander pressed on: 'We've been talking to the police, and we've met Knut's new friend, Lazlo. It isn't hard to piece things together.'

Elise spread out her hands, palms up. 'These people are my compatriots. I want to help them to freedom and to start a new life.' Her voice trailed away.

'But don't you realise what you're doing is illegal?' Alexander's tone was patient.

Elise's voice was staccato: 'But Knut said...that they are Russians you know, just like me. Knut said I must help these poor people. The only thing I don't like is that Lazlo he's always with. He's Ukrainian really. I think he bullies Knut. But Knut never listens to me. He bosses Knut around and tells me not to interfere.'

'What were you actually doing?' Silver tried to get Elise back on track.

'Knut told me if I gave him money for them, it would help the refugees to get across the border from Russia into the safety of Norway.' Elise wrung her hands. 'Don't you know how these people suffer? They've hardly enough money for food. They live in extreme poverty.'

Silver put her hand on Elise's arm. 'I know you only wanted to help them. But what else did you do for them?'

'I made up some parcels of clothing for them too. Knut said they had very little. Just like I'm lending these clothes to you now, Silver. Where's the harm in that? I was only trying to help as you said.' Elise dabbed her eyes with a white linen handkerchief, her shaking fingers twisting it into a crushed rag. 'I collected some cast-off clothes from my friends as well. They were pleased to give them to me. I got a really large collection of winter clothes.' She gave Alexander a proud look.

'All these piles of old clothes in the owner's cabin on board the cruise ship and in the shed down by the harbour.' Silver nodded. 'So that's where they came from. From you, Elise, and your friends.' Silver's thoughts turned to the speeding car, which had all but run her down. Could that have any connection with Lazlo's shading dealings?

'These people are illegal immigrants, Elise,' Alexander said. 'Lazlo seems to be leading a big operation to help them over the border from Russia into Norway. Some of the people have sold their houses back home to raise money to pay for their tickets. Then they find out they've entered illegally and nobody wants them. But they can't go back because they've no money left.'

'You must see – I was only trying to help these poor people,' said Elise plaintively.

It was all falling into place. 'Is Lazlo the leader of the operation?' Silver asked Elise. 'And what about these people on the island with the stave church? They must have been some of the immigrants he was trying to hide.'

Elise sat mutely, shaking her head.

'Of course. Why do you think they ran away from us? They're all in hiding from the authorities because they have no proper papers to show. It's a complete mess.' Alexander sighed. 'And Knut is knee-deep in all this shit.'

Silver's mind was working furiously. Was that why Alexander's father was murdered? Had he disturbed the immigrants in their hiding place on the remote island? She'd better not say it aloud as she might hurt Elise in dragging it out into the open.

'Where's Knut?' Elise looked worried. 'He should be up by now.'

'I'll go up and drag him out of bed.' Alexander rose and left the room.

Elise looked at Silver and spread her hands wide. 'Really, I've done nothing wrong, and neither has Knut. He's so soft-hearted, you know. It's not his fault. I've always had to protect him. You do understand, don't you, Silver?'

Elise looked pleadingly at Silver, but there was a flash

of calculation in her almond eyes that were so like Knut's. Maybe Knut's mother wasn't as simple and fey as she tried to make out. Silver hardened her heart against Elise's entreaties. Could Elise possibly be involved in the cigarette smuggling and the other scams too?

'Coffee, Silver?' Elise had a fixed smile on her lips.

Silver held out her cup to Elise as Alexander strode back into the room. 'He's not there. Nor is he in the bathroom. In fact, I've looked all over the house and the garden too. He's vanished. Yet the boat's still there, so he can't have left the island.'

The coffee spilled all over the table as Elise gave a small cry. She stifled it quickly.

'He can't have gone far without the boat.' Alexander spoke in a soothing voice. He turned to Silver. 'Come with me and we'll find him.'

Silver jumped up. She winced as her strained muscles protested, but she was glad to be doing something useful. 'I hope Knut hasn't slipped over the cliff. He looked really ropey when we left him at the hospital last night.'

'He didn't look too good this morning either,' Alexander said. 'But he insisted he would be down to talk to us.'

They walked out of the house and down the slope leading to some wooden outhouses at the back. He strode ahead of her and pulled open the first door they came to. Silver peered in through the opening, but it was very dark and hard to make out what was inside. 'Knut,' she called. 'Are you in there?' She pushed past Alexander and called again: 'Knut, are you okay?' All was silent and Silver could just make out some old tables and chairs piled up on top of each other. There were rows of skis and ski sticks leaning against one of the walls, but no human figure was to be seen.

'Well, he's not here,' said Alexander, waiting until Silver had emerged. He locked the padlock, which hung on the door.

'Come on,' he said, breaking into a run. 'I think I know where he is.' He rounded the side of the next building. There were two strange-looking trapdoors which lay slightly raised from the ground. Alexander dragged on the ring to open one side and revealed a flight of steps which led down into another dark interior. There was a glimmer of moving light. Silver pulled on Alexander's sleeve and he bent down to hear her whisper: 'There's someone down there.' He nodded without speaking and silently lifted up the second trapdoor to allow them to enter.

'I'll go first.' His breath stirred her hair. 'I want to see what he's up to. And you're my witness, Silver.'

Silver followed him down the stairs as noiselessly as possible, but their feet scraped against the stone steps. Knut was piling up some logs, but he moved slowly and painfully. He jerked round as they appeared, his face a study in fleeting expressions of surprise, anger and resignation. 'Well, dear brother?' He had lost none of his aplomb, even though he now had a large piece of sticking plaster on the left side of his forehead.

'Oh, Knut, I didn't know you had taken a knock on the head as well.' Silver looked at him in surprise.

He tried to put his arm round her, regarding her with a kind of irritated affection. His breath smelt strongly of alcohol. 'I have to thank you, Silver, for saving my life. Without your quick actions, I'd have been a goner, and my dear brother here, sole heir to the family business. Maybe that'd make it easier for you?' He shot a calculating look at Alexander.

Alexander didn't answer but drew closer to the enormous pile of logs. 'Well, you certainly have been collecting logs for the winter.' His tone was puzzled. 'What are all these for?'

Knut blinked his eyes blandly at Alexander. 'I thought it would be nice for Mother if we could come out here sometimes during the cold season as a change from living in town. It's always freezing here and you refuse to install central heating. Now we can have roaring log fires.'

'Roaring log fires? But we don't even have a proper chimney in this house. You'd set it all alight. You're mad, Knut. I don't believe you. Let me look.' Alexander pushed Knut aside, making him stagger.

'Hey, be careful, Al. Don't knock down a wounded man!'

Alexander took no notice. 'However did you get all these logs across to the island?'

'Oh, I've been working hard over time.' Knut smiled disarmingly at Alexander. Silver stood watching the two brothers. Knut's manner was overly polite and deferential to Alexander. Something wasn't quite right.

'I suppose Lazlo helped you.' Silver stared at Knut.

'Well, of course he did. He's used to humping things about in his country. They don't have advanced machines like we do to do the heavy work.'

Silver moved behind Knut and began to rummage in the pile of logs. 'What's this?' she asked, pulling out a bottle and waving it in Knut's face. 'And this, and this!' She was pulling out more bottles until she held five of them in her arms.

'My God, there's more!' said Alexander. Behind the logs that Silver had dislodged, a stash of white styrofoam containers was uncovered.

A flush of colour washed across Knut's pale strained face. 'Nothing to do with you! Get out of my way!' He tried to insert himself between the pile of logs and Alexander.

The two brothers scuffled together as Knut tried to snatch the bottles from Alexander, who fended him off with one large, strong hand.

Silver rushed forward and tried to take the bottles from Alexander, but two of them slipped from her grasp and fell to the ground with a crash of splintering glass. A heavy smell of alcohol wafted across the room as the liquid spilled in a dark spreading stain.

'Neat alcohol!' Alexander sounded furious. 'Where the hell did you get all these bottles. I bet there are hundreds more, stashed around here. For God's sake man, what have you got mixed up in now?'

Silver shut her eyes. She wanted to believe there was a simple explanation. But it seemed unlikely that it was going to happen that way. She could hear it in Alexander's voice.

Chapter 21

Silver drew closer to the tall pile of logs stored in the half-light of the cellar. The smell of freshly cut wood was sharp in her nostrils. The edifice of logs in front of her had been carefully stacked almost to the ceiling.

Alexander got to work, swiftly demolishing the front pile of logs that formed a wall of concealment. Silver gasped as he moved them away, uncovering row upon row of white styrofoam containers, like glistening blocks of snow. Each of them held four bottles of some kind of alcohol.

'Look at this!' Alexander's face was thunderous as he pulled out the containers. 'Organised smuggling if ever I saw it. How on earth did you get all this over to the island unseen?' He spoke over his shoulder. 'I can't believe that Elise never noticed anything.'

Knut leaned against the cellar wall, with an enigmatic expression on his pallid face. He pursed his lips and slid down into a sitting position against the wall. He made no effort to hinder Alexander.

Alexander worked efficiently, his broad shoulders taking the strain as he restacked the logs in another part of the cellar. Gradually, he laid bare the hoard of alcohol. His shirt hung open showing his tanned chest and a V-shaped patch of dampness spread down his back.

'Where did all this alcohol come from?' Silver asked.

She found it hard to comprehend that the transport of such volumes of alcohol could go unnoticed.

'Don't worry your little head, Silver. This has nothing to do with you. Just don't write any stories about it.' Knut held up his hand dismissively. He seemed to have shrunk and lost his sparkle.

'But why did you get involved in all this, Knut?' Silver persisted. 'Didn't you know it would lead to trouble?'

'Ask my dear brother about that.' Anger seemed to stir Knut from his apathy and colour flooded his face. 'He always keeps me short of money and asks endless questions about my expenses. He treats me like a child. If he could ban me from the Rosenholm office he would. He's to blame.' He slanted a furious glance at Alexander.

'You know you're never more than a few hours behind your desk. Then it's off to the unknown. You never leave a message.' Alexander's voice was full of exasperation. 'We can't ever depend on you.'

'You've always got my mobile to call.'

'It's usually switched off. And if you're out of the country, you can't attend any meetings we've set up.' Alexander sighed and rubbed the back of his hand across his forehead, leaving a black streak.

'I'm a good ambassador for Rosenholm wherever I go.' Knut was calmer now.

'Even in the casino?' Alexander's patience snapped. 'Hell, Knut, don't you understand you're a bloody criminal. This is smuggled alcohol. The police are after you. It's a wonder they didn't arrest you yesterday. Your bloody fool actions have brought disgrace on the family name. You'll very likely end up in jail.'

He dropped the white container he was holding. 'I don't know how we're going to sort it all out. But we're going back to the house now and you're going to explain it all.' He strode across the cellar and grabbed Knut's arm, pulling him to his feet.

Knut shuffled forward like a condemned prisoner. He gave Silver a mischievous wink.

Silver stifled a smile. Knut was incorrigible, yet he could face the world with jaunty courage. He thrived on danger and living on the edge. And that could well be his downfall.

Alexander waved Silver ahead of them and still gripping Knut's arm tightly, he locked the door of the cellar. Together the three of them walked over the flagstones back to the house.

'*Fanden ta deg*, Alexander!' Knut swore as his composure broke and he twisted out of Alexander's grip. He ran up the slope and past the house.

Alexander made no attempt to stop him. He stood watching Knut's progress as he sped down the path to the boathouse. A few minutes later, Knut's flashy day cruiser backed out of the boathouse with him at the helm. He looked back for a moment and lifted his hand in a sweeping wave above his head, before setting course for the open sea. Soon there was nothing left but the churning white waters from the wake of the boat.

'You let him go?' Silver was worried, even though a sense of relief washed over her.

'Am I my brother's keeper?' Alexander's face was haggard. The strain of the last few days was etched clearly in the fine lines running between his nose and mouth. 'It's worse than I thought. Aiding illegal immigrants, forging money and passports, and now alcohol smuggling. On top of that, there's Elise. How deep is she involved in all this?'

'And your father's murder,' Silver added.

'I hadn't forgotten.' The shutters were down and Alexander's face was an expressionless mask. He had retreated into a place beyond Silver's reach. He strode towards the house without looking back.

Inside the hall, Alexander turned briefly to Silver. 'You'd better get back to the mainland. This is no place for you.'

'But...'

'Silver, you've got to go. The Rosenholms have only caused you trouble. We're completely submerged in it. You're better away from us all. You're a foreigner in Norway and that makes you more vulnerable. And don't you dare try to write anything about us or I'll slap a law suit on your newspaper.'

Silver stood stunned. This was total rejection. Alexander's face was stern and unapproachable like one of his implacable Viking ancestors. The day-old stubble on his chin heightened the effect.

Her voice was choked as she tried to remonstrate with him. 'Alexander, I only want to help.'

'You can't.' His reply was curt. 'I'll get one of the men to ferry you back to the mainland and rebook your hotel. Kari will pack your things and get them delivered to Hotel Norge.'

'What about the clothes I borrowed from Elise?' She wouldn't let the tears fall. She wouldn't let him see how he'd stabbed her in the heart.

'Not important. Just get back home to your own country and forget you ever met us.' Just for a moment, she caught the pain reflected in his eyes. Then he strode away, leaving her standing in the hall.

'Goodbye for now, Alexander,' she whispered to his retreating back. Her misery was so acute, it bowed her spine.

Arriving at the Hotel Norge, Silver checked in as quickly and impersonally as possible, only asking for a different room from the one she'd had before. She failed to return the receptionist's friendly smile and good wishes for a pleasant stay. In her new hotel room, Silver tore off the clothes she'd borrowed from Elise. She kicked off her sneakers, which were badly ripped and gashed, and bundling the discarded clothes and shoes into a corner of the room, she grabbed fresh underwear and a clean shirt and jeans from her suitcase, which had been brought from Alexander's apartment. After pulling them on, she found a pair of flat-heeled shoes to wear.

A throbbing headache threatened to overwhelm her and her eyes were burning with unshed tears as she gathered up the rest of her belongings and shoved them into her suitcase. She unpacked her toothbrush, nightdress and clean underwear, moving round the room to a litany of 'Damn you, Alexander!'. Her laptop was already in place on the hotel room desk.

She stopped for a moment. She'd forgotten about her passport. She couldn't leave the country without it. She snatched up the phone and rang the British Consulate, only to hear that the new passport wouldn't be ready before tomorrow. Now she was stuck in Bergen for at least another day and she'd have to change her flight.

Time stretched out empty in front of her. It was impossible to sit cowering in her hotel room. She got to her feet and walked over to the window. The sun was shining brightly. It was enough to tempt her out of doors once more, though she still felt shaky from her ordeal in the church yesterday. Automatically, she picked up her camera and slung it over her shoulder.

Out on the street, she looked for an open-air café to have a light lunch. She found a table under a large sunshade. In the distance, the fiord was sparkling blue, and the small ferries shuttled back and forward across the water to the outlying islands. It was probably the last time she'd ever visit Bergen. It would be too painful to return. Yet the thought of leaving it all, the beautiful clear light and the majesty of the hills surrounding the city, tore at her heart. She rubbed her hand across her hot face and took a couple of sips from the glass of light beer in front of her.

An image of Alexander's haggard face teased her thoughts, yet it seemed that they disagreed on the very nature and meaning of love. Okay, so she was in love with him. Wildly, madly, irrevocably! So what was she doing rushing off back to London when she could stay and perhaps help him uncover the mystery of his father's death?

Alexander had saved her twice. Once when her passport and credit cards had been stolen from her at the funfair in the park, and yesterday when he'd released her from Lazlo's clutches. That must mean he cared for her a little. Or would he be as gallant to any woman under attack? Probably she was grasping at straws.

Lazlo was safely under lock and key, she supposed. He was probably being grilled by the Norwegian police right now, but she was sure he hadn't been running the show alone. It was such a huge operation, with so many strands of crime. He must have had helpers. Elise was tangled up somehow in his web too. How far down the slippery slope had she gone?

Silver picked up her open sandwich covered with delicate pink prawns and smothered in mayonnaise. She'd miss that too! At least she hadn't lost her appetite, although her body was still dealing with the vagaries of shock and lack of food from the day before. Her muscles ached with fatigue. She ordered another sandwich and a second glass of beer to try and get her strength up. The world was rapidly becoming a friendlier place as her energy returned.

Thanks to the passport problems, she'd been given extra time and now she could spend it trying to unravel a little more of the Rosenholm mystery. *I don't give up so easily, damn you, Alexander!* She sent a defiant message to him.

Her spirits lifted as she began to plan what she could do to help Alexander, even though he'd probably accuse her of interfering. But that was better than doing nothing at all. His face rose before her as she'd seen it last, his eyes full of pain and fatigue, his well-shaped mouth set in a grim line, yet he exuded masculinity and power. If he'd crooked his little finger, she'd have run to him.

Silver's thoughts returned to the funfair. That was where it all started, at least for her. Would the stalls and amusements still be there in the park? Fairs often moved on quickly. If it were still there, perhaps she could uncover some link to explain to how her passport and all those credit cards had landed out on the island of the stave church. Perhaps she might even find out more about what happened to Alexander's father. A long shot perhaps, but worth trying.

Leaving some notes to pay for her lunch, she set off at full speed to the fairground. Impatiently, she jogged from one foot to the other as she waited at the crossing for the traffic lights to change to green.

It would be safe enough in broad daylight to visit the fair, wouldn't it? It was only when it was dark that it was dangerous. Small children went there all the time – with their parents, of course. In spite of the sun's bright rays, she shivered at the memory of her last visit to the fair, but that didn't deter her.

In the early afternoon, there were only one or two people wandering around the fairground. A few men stood smoking roll-ups, propped against their trailers.

They watched Silver with lazy, hostile eyes. Some of the stalls were boarded up with heavy shutters. The whole place had a jaded and unwelcoming air, but Silver pressed on searching for the exact place where she'd been robbed. This time, she took the precaution of looping her small rucksack in front of her to keep it in sight.

She approached the area apart from the rest of the fairground where the fair people had parked their caravans under the heavy leaves of the elm trees. There was a dank, miserable smell that she hadn't noticed before. One of the curtains twitched as a pale face peered out at her from a caravan window. But the blue bus was no longer there. She'd last seen it down at the warehouse where Lazlo had stored all the clothes for the immigrants.

Silver hunched her shoulders uncomfortably, feeling like an intruder. She passed along the silent caravans, some of them showing bright pretty curtains and flowers in pots on the window sills.

All was quiet. Was she just wasting her time? What could she do that the professionals couldn't? She was foolish to have believed she could do anything to help. She turned towards the shining waters of the lake some hundred metres away from her.

Suddenly, a bike skidded in front of her as the rider braked, then veered smartly away. She pulled up her ever-ready camera and clicked the shutter, once, twice, three times, her hands shaking as she tried to hold the camera still to get good shots. She wouldn't ever forget that hooked nose and deeply tanned face under the baseball cap.

Even though she'd only caught a glimpse of him before in the fairground when he'd snitched her valuables, his angular face was unmistakably etched in her memory. Her voice was hoarse as she shouted 'Stop, stop!' as she sped after him, stumbling over empty beer bottles and a child's toy. But he stood hard on the pedals of his bike and took off between two large caravans.

Silver's heart thumped in a mixture of fear and exertion. She strained her eyes trying to catch sight of him again, but he had vanished.

A broad-shouldered man emerged from one of the caravans, accompanied by a woman with dark, straggling hair, who was carrying a child. They stared unblinkingly at Silver until a tight knot of fear formed in her stomach. The man spoke in an angry voice to Silver.

'I'm sorry, I don't understand.' She backed away nervously.

'Get out of here. This private place!' The man stabbed his finger in the air.

'Go away, missy,' shrieked the woman, hefting the child on her hip.

Two other men appeared round the side of the caravan. One of them stepped toward her, menace showing in his thin-lipped smile. Silver ducked under a branch of an elm tree and found herself on the asphalt path leading to the lake.

She walked away quickly, trying not to run. She cast a glance behind her, exhaled the breath she was holding and fanned her hot cheeks. At least no one was following her. She'd been stupid and foolhardy to approach these people alone. She'd better go back to the hotel. But could the man with the hooked nose provide a key to Lazlo's operations? Or even to the murder of Alexander's father? That seemed to have been pushed under wraps. Or was Alexander keeping information from her? Fair enough. She wasn't family and she wasn't entitled to know.

She continued along the path wondering what to do next. Her instincts screamed at her to walk over to Alexander's office, while her rational side told her to leave him alone. She set off down toward the lake, telling herself she was going to admire the snow-white swans that drifted majestically across the water. But this is the way to Alexander's office, a niggling small voice murmured in her ear.

Silver concentrated hard on the swans as they sailed away from her with supreme indifference, their black legs just discernible beneath the ripples. Suppose she walked down to the harbour just to see if *The Guiding Spirit* was still there.

Some distance away, Silver could see the distinctive blue and white stripe of the funnel on the Rosenholm cruise ship. The ship lying in its berth towered over the tree tops. So she hadn't sailed yet. Silver quickened her pace and reached the harbour slightly out of breath.

The tall white ship rode easily on the water, but there were only a few people on the quayside. As Silver approached, the ship's siren sounded, the engines started to throb and the majestic ship manoeuvred sideways away from the quayside. Silver stood watching and she raised her hand to wave back to the passengers lining the high decks. The ship turned in slow deliberate motion and headed out to the open sea.

Silver's heart plummeted. Irrationally, she felt that her last link with Alexander was severed. She'd arrived too late. Her eyes followed the churning waters in the wake of the large ship and her throat tightened as she tried to swallow her unreasonable disappointment.

Chapter 22

In the study of Elise's island home, Alexander sat at his father's finely carved rosewood desk. He had accumulated a stack of print-outs and was studying them carefully. Although his father had used his laptop daily, some of his accounting never got as far as a computer spreadsheet. Alexander rubbed his brow. There were certainly some big discrepancies here. There were several substantial payments that he knew nothing about. Presumably to Knut. But there was no underlying paperwork to confirm them – the money had just vanished. He supposed that Knut had played the role of the younger, misunderstood son as he usually did to perfection. Alexander found it hard to believe that his stern father had allowed this slipshod style of accounting to continue. Well, it was all water under the bridge. His father was no longer here and, at present, Alexander didn't feel like confronting Knut about past accounting. He knew his younger brother would simply bluster and evade any questions. There were more pressing things to be dealt with now.

Alexander stretched his long legs out in front of him and eased the stiffness in his shoulders. It was impossible to concentrate. He'd have to work with the auditors to sort it all out. He was exhausted. Never before had he let his emotions bubble up and take control over him as he'd done today. The catalogue of his impulsive actions was long. He'd stabbed

Silver in the back, chased away his brother and made an enemy of his stepmother. A deep groan escaped him.

How could he have threatened Silver with a lawsuit if she should write about the shipping company? That was not her style. She was the most ethical person he'd ever met. In any case, that was the least of his worries with the lid about to blow off on the Rosenholm scandals. Would she understand that he had been goaded into it?

He gathered up the papers and pushed them back into the drawer. Rising from his chair, he decided to have it out with Elise straightaway. He strode through the sitting room and found her sitting outside on the terrace, playing with the cat. The essential cup of coffee stood on the table beside her. She raised her head as he walked toward her, but avoided his eyes.

'Why did you send Silver away?' Her voice was accusing. 'I liked having her here. She's kind and understanding.'

Alexander flinched. Then, born of guilt, his anger spilled forth. The words poured out of him: 'You and Knut are to blame for the mess we're in – Knut for embroiling you in his dirty schemes, and you for spoiling Knut from birth. No one said 'no' to him ever. It made him believe he was untouchable.'

Elise cringed back in her chair, but Alexander threw restraint to the winds. He was tired of being buttoned-up Mr Reliable. For the second time in the same day, he let rip. 'Silver couldn't stay here when the whole facade was rotten to the core. I had to send her away. I didn't want her to be tainted by Knut's nefarious schemes. The whole family is going to be dragged down into the mire. There was no place for Silver here.'

Elise let out a little whimper, her face ashen. She clutched the cat high on her breast as if seeking protection from its furry body.

Alexander bent over the table. 'Look at me, Elise.'

She raised her head and began to sob hysterically.

He sat down in a chair opposite her, his iron control back in place. 'Elise, we have to get these things sorted out,' he spoke in a soothing voice. 'My first question is...'

Elise wiped her eyes quickly and blew her nose discreetly. She picked up her coffee cup. 'Will you ask Christiania to bring some more coffee and some cakes? It'll make you feel better, dear.'

Taken aback at her swift change of mood, Alexander didn't allow himself to be diverted. 'Just tell me about Knut and Lazlo, and for that matter you and Lazlo.'

Elise's hands fluttered in agitation. Her voice was hoarse as she blurted out: 'We needed money to pay Knut's gambling debts. Your father always helped Knut out. But you wouldn't help us, even though I begged you many times. And then Knut ran across Lazlo. Lazlo knew St Petersburg. He spoke Russian to me. He knew the very street where I grew up. That's how it all started. He said he had a project and we could help him. We could earn money for ourselves.' A tear squeezed out from the corner of her eye and she cast a calculating look at him.

Alexander got up and began to pace across the terrace. He turned to face her. 'But Elise, didn't you ever stop to think? The list of criminal activities you are involved with is long. People smuggling, alcohol smuggling, forgery... and murder!'

'No, Alexander, it's not true. Not murder!' Elise jumped up from the table, knocking over her coffee cup. The cold brown dregs seeped over the wooden table like slow-moving blood. She began to sob hysterically with loud gasps and shrieks.

Unmoved, Alexander watched the performance. 'Just tell me how far you are involved,' he said calmly. 'My father's murder hasn't been solved. Let's hear what you know about that.'

Elise sat down suddenly as if her legs had given way. Her face was as white as frozen snow and her hands were trembling. 'No, not murder, never murder. How can you accuse me of murdering my husband? That's really wicked.' She was sobbing in earnest now. 'How could I know that Frederick would be out on the island that night?'

A quick twinge of sympathy rushed through Alexander. Maybe he shouldn't press her any more. He knew how devastated Elise had been when the police had discovered the body out on the island of the church, but he was intent on discovering the truth.

'Maybe not you, Elise, but Knut was the last person to see Father alive. He had no convincing alibi.' Alexander's words stabbed through the air. 'Do you know where he was on the night of Father's death?'

Elise sobbed harder than ever, her voice muffled.

The shrill sound of the telephone struck across the room. He ran out into the hall.

Silver couldn't pull her gaze away from the high-prowed white ship as it drew away from the quayside. As it slowly executed a turn in the water and the tugs pulled away, Silver fancied that she could see Knut waving to her from the upper deck. Or was it her fatigued brain creating non-existent images? She strained her eyes trying to make out who it was, but the vessel gathered speed as it headed out to sea. The passengers dwindled into unrecognisable black dots on the mighty decks as the ship sailed down the fiord.

She blinked back tears and swallowed the lump in her throat. She'd come to Norway for a new beginning. She'd had such high hopes and good intentions. The interview with Alexander would have given a great boost to her career. She'd wanted to push Mike out of her life. Well, she'd achieved that at least. Her trip to Norway had erased him completely from her mind. But then she'd rushed headlong into deep involvement with Alexander. What chance was there of her writing an unbiased article about the Rosenholms? No chance at all. Probably Tom would fire her when she got back home to London, and then she'd be jobless and penniless. Her shoulders drooped as she retraced her footsteps and walked past the warehouses on the quayside. She dawdled on her way back to the hotel, passing the now deserted fish market, a fishy smell still lingering in the air. Then back on the street, she stood for a long time staring with unseeing eyes into a shop window, disquieting images of her recent experiences racing through her mind.

She became aware of a tall presence behind her. She whirled round and found herself gazing into Alexander's brilliant blue eyes. His hands came up to grip her arms and a tingling sensation rushed through her. Her heart hammered as she tried to summon up her defences against him.

'Silver.' The deep timbre of his voice stirred her pulses even more. 'I've been trying to get in touch with you. But you weren't at the hotel. And what about the mobile I gave you?' His eyes searched her face.

She waited, trying to project a cool exterior.

'Detective Berg wants to see you. He wants you to make a statement.'

So he hadn't come to look for her after all. He was only delivering a message. Her anticipation turned to disappointment.

She stuck out her chin. 'Why couldn't he contact me himself?'

'Because I said I would find you.' Alexander's grip

tightened on her. He drew her closer, but she stiffened, refusing to allow him to overwhelm her.

'I haven't much time left. I'm leaving for England.' She was pleased to hear how nonchalant she sounded. She slipped out of his grasp and folded her arms across her chest.

Alexander's arms dropped to his sides. He took a step back. Although they were standing within three feet of each other, an emotional gulf yawned between them, measured in pain and rejection.

'You told me in no uncertain terms that you didn't want anything more to do with me.' Silver held her head high, her voice was clear and reasonable. 'So where do we stand now?'

'I made a bloody awful mistake. In fact, I made a whole bloody awful chain of mistakes.' He studied her face intently. 'But it was for your protection.'

'And so where does that leave me?' Silver turned away from him.

He stepped close up behind her, the heat of his body stirring her pulses. She fought to compose her features and to remain calm and immune to him.

'Let me explain,' he said, taking her gently by the shoulders. 'God knows I should never have sent you away. I was out of my head. You entered my life when it was in a state of complete chaos. I had to question everyone and everything around me. Who I could trust? And who was playing false? I had to keep the Rosenholm problems under wraps as much as possible, or the whole company could literally sink to the bottom of the sea. I'd planned to give you that interview just to show that the company was in good heart – financially at least.'

'You wanted to use me then?' Silver flung the accusation at him.

His fingers tightened on her shoulders, and she felt the strength of his hands and the desperation in him. 'Yes, I suppose I did. It's been hell on earth trying to keep the business running on an even keel. I'm determined to do anything to preserve my father's reputation.'

Silver turned to look at Alexander's strained, distinguished profile. Her heart constricted as she understood what a burden he carried. Impulsively, she pressed her lips against his smoothly shaven cheek. He caught her against him in a tight embrace. Time lengthened and spiralled. Silver was the first to recover. She opened her eyes and forced herself back to reality. Pushing him gently from her, she took a deep breath. He straightened and smoothed his tousled blond hair with one hand.

'Let's go and see DCI Berg and get it over with.' His voice was husky. He kept his arm closely around her as he steered her down the tree-lined street toward the police station.

In DCI Berg's office, the air was stuffy and enclosed, with a trace of stale cigarette smoke. The windows were shut and the decor was brown and dismal. Abandon hope all ye who enter here. Silver hid a smile at her thought. She looked around her and imagined the stream of people who had been summoned to meet the detective. Some criminals, some witnesses of crimes, not to mention the victims of crimes.

The solid, square-faced detective chief inspector gestured to her to sit in one of the hard-backed chairs. Alexander sat beside her. He leaned toward her and brushed her hand with a feather-light touch.

A young uniformed policeman came in through an adjoining door. DCI Berg spoke to him rapidly in Norwegian. Then he turned to Silver. 'We have recovered the pile of passports and credit cards from the island.

Now I want you to make a witness statement about what happened out there yesterday. What you observed. Who was there. And the things you discovered concealed in the pulpit of the church. Constable Moe will take your statement. His English is very good.'

'Rosenholm, I'm going to have to talk to you about your brother. Do you know where he is?' DCI Berg turned back towards him as Silver and the young constable walked through the doorway into the next room.

Silver bit her lip. Somehow, she didn't want Knut caught even though he'd got himself embroiled with criminals. He was weak but not entirely evil…and he was Alexander's brother. Besides, she couldn't be sure her eye had caught him on *The Guiding Spirit*. She was probably mistaken. But Lazlo. That was quite another matter. He was evil through and through, and if they didn't stop him, he'd drag other people into his disreputable schemes and destroy them.

The young constable shut the door between the two offices. Light filtered in between the dusty slats of the Venetian blinds on the window and threw bars of shadow across the young constable's face. A young policewoman slipped unobtrusively into the room as Silver sat down on a hard wooden chair across the table from the two of them and began to answer Constable Moe's painstaking questions. He took out a pen and notebook, and switched on a small recorder. He probed her about the men on the island who'd run away when she and Alexander arrived. About the credit cards and the forged and damaged passports they'd found there. And about the clothes and the money that she and Alexander had discovered on board *The Guiding Spirit*. It was a relief for her to tell the story. Her words came tumbling out so that he was hard pushed to keep up with her account.

'There's one clue I can give you,' she said, leaning forward. 'I saw the man who stole my credit cards and passport last week when I visited the funfair. I walked up there today to have a look around and I caught a good glimpse of him. He probably works there. I took a few photographs of him, but the people of the fair chased me away. I didn't dare to stay any longer. But I could point him out to you.'

The young policeman nodded and smiled. 'Perhaps you can show us your photographs?'

'Yes, of course, and I'm sure you'll find a link at the funfair.'

An hour and a half flashed past. Silver's mouth was dry. The bitter, black coffee in the cup beside her on the table had grown cold. 'Could I have a drink of water, please,' she asked the young constable. He sprang to his feet and went to fetch her a drink.

There was a sharp rap on the door. Alexander and DCI Berg walked into the room. 'The police have uncovered new evidence about my father's death,' Alexander told her. 'It seems to be linked with Lazlo's scams with the illegal immigrants. My father must have disturbed some of them in their place of concealment when he was out on the island on his own. They panicked and shot him. Then they set fire to the cottage to hide the evidence. They took a burning log from the fire in the grate in my father's study to start it!' Alexander's mouth was tight and he rubbed his hand over his temples. 'The old wood of the cottage ignited into a terrific blaze.' He found it hard to keep his composure.

'But thanks to your discoveries on the island, a lot more evidence has been uncovered, which should help us with our inquiries,' said DCI Berg.

'Maybe there's a better chance of my father's murderers

being tracked down from this.' There was a note of hope in Alexander's strained voice.

'Miss Fairfax has a photograph she believes might help,' said Constable Moe.

'Yes, I took several shots of the man who stole my credit cards – I saw him again at the funfair today.' Silver lifted her camera out of its case. 'Can you download the pictures onto the computer here?' she asked the young constable. 'I'm honestly sure that man has some link to the whole affair because of all those credit cards and passports we found on the island. That's why he snitched mine.'

The pictures having been successfully downloaded for the police to examine, Alexander and Silver walked out of the police station. Out on the street again, Alexander turned to her and said: 'Thank God, that's over. And let's hope all this trouble can soon be cleared up.' He paused for a moment, his eyes dark and unfathomable as he appeared to wrestle with some inward dilemma. Then he sighed and took Silver's hand in his warm fingers. 'Silver, please come back to my place and I'll cook you dinner,' he said.

Silver felt a warm glow flow through her. 'Of course I will,' she said.

Alexander smiled at her. There was a promise for later smouldering in his eyes.

As they crossed the road leading to the exclusive complex where Alexander's apartment was situated, a luxurious black car slowly inched toward them. Alexander stopped short and dropped Silver's hand. He stepped forward as the driver rolled down the window: 'Elise, what are you doing here?'

Elise gave a low laugh. She seemed completely composed as she stepped out of the car to meet them. She shut the car door, locked it with a quick movement of the remote and walked determinedly towards them. She wore a dark blue linen suit with gold buttons that whispered top-class designer and her hair was swept up in an elegant coiffure.

'I want to talk to you both. I'm so glad you're here too, Silver.' She kissed the air on each side of Silver's face in a wave of expensive perfume.

Alexander caught Silver's eye and she blushed. She was sure he could read the disappointment in her face that the two of them were no longer alone.

They walked into the sitting room and Alexander offered them a drink. He went into the kitchen to get some glasses and some ice. Elise put her long, flat handbag down on the sofa beside her. She crossed one smoothly stockinged leg over the other. The heels of her dark blue shoes were at least three inches high. Silver sat down opposite her in an armchair, sinking into its comfortable depths.

Elise began to speak in a rapid and authoritative voice. As Silver regarded her intently, Elise sat up and took command of the room. This was a new Elise, ruthless and unstoppable. She was unrecognisable – gone were the flowing clothes and the fey, other-worldly manner. This was a woman capable of anything. They had all underestimated Elise.

Chapter 23

Alexander came back into the sitting room carrying three glasses on a silver tray. He poured two glasses of white wine for Silver and Elise, and a malt whisky for himself. '*Skol*,' he said, raising his glass to the two women. Then he waited for Elise to explain why she was there. Her sudden change of personality spelt trouble, and she seemed in complete control of the situation. No hysterics now. He was on his guard. The silence in the room lengthened and the tension was palpable. He saw Silver clasping her hands tightly, her eyes flicking from him to Elise.

Suddenly, Elise jumped up from the sofa where she was sitting and paced the room. She whirled round to face Alexander and Silver, her eyes flinty. 'I'm selling Rosenholm!' she announced, with a low laugh.

So that was it! Anger erupted in Alexander, but he kept his face calm. 'Well, you can't, Elise. It's family property and we've owned it for generations,' he said.

'Your father left it to me in his will to do what I like with.' Elise's voice was cool and her carefully arched eyebrows drew together in a frown.

Alexander sighed inwardly. Elise was up to her old tricks of dramatising a situation for maximum effect.

'But why?' He kept his tone equally cool. 'You're not short of money. You get a very generous allowance paid out from my father's estate.' He had made it a point of honour to ensure that Elise's allowance was paid out regularly and in full, even before his father's will went to probate. Many times, he dipped into his own pocket to top up the payments.

'That's not the point,' Elise sighed in exasperation. 'I no longer need Rosenholm. My husband is dead and it's time for me to move on.'

Her callousness was stunning. But a clearer picture was emerging. She was an even greater master of histrionics than he'd realised. He was convinced that she had some secret agenda of her own. In fact, after recent events, he wouldn't be sorry if she did move on. When he looked back, he could see how the apparently loving mother of his childhood had gradually changed over the years into a manipulative, scheming woman.

He remembered the screaming rages, when his father would emerge hurriedly from the room and vanish for hours. Yet in a lightning change of personality, Elise would turn as nice as pie, and behave in a sweet and loving way to her husband and two sons, binding them to her with tenderness and charm. On the whole, she had made little distinction between him as her stepson and her own son, Knut. But the pattern was always the same. After walking on eggshells for a few days, the family would relax and harmony would be restored. That was, until the next hysterical outburst.

Could Elise have a kind of Dr Jekyll and Mr Hyde personality? He wondered how he could have been so blind. Perhaps he had simply avoided facing the reality. But now in his maturity, he understood how she had inveigled his father into marriage and how she had manipulated him all through their married life.

How dangerous was Elise? Could she have been milking the company accounts? She had been his father's most trusted personal assistant for several years before they got married. She still insisted on seeing the company's accounts every month. And he, Alexander, had never stopped her. He had some noble idea of maintaining the status quo. Could she possibly have had access to doctoring the figures? She was very close to his father's chief accountant, now semi-retired. He frowned as the realisation hit him that they might have been in cahoots for years.

Silver ached as she watched Elise queening it over Alexander's good nature. The thin veneer of dutiful wife and caring mother had cracked, revealing a ruthless woman who would stop at nothing.

Elise resumed her pacing, her heels striking sharply against the parquet flooring. 'I'm not keeping a house that held me prisoner for nearly thirty years. Always playing the obedient wife to a man who was more interested in his ships than in me. Do you think I liked living on that island isolated from other people, with nobody but you two boys to talk to? Well, I hated it!' She gave an angry laugh.

'Why didn't you tell us that you were unhappy?' Alexander asked. 'I'm sure my father would have done something about it if only you'd told him.'

'I told him and told him, but he never listened. He was off round the world visiting New York, Miami, Singapore, Tokyo or wherever. He didn't care what was going on at home.' Elise's eyes sparked fire. 'If he was at home, he was preoccupied with his hellish church or carving furniture for the house. He never had time to speak to me.' Elise paused dramatically.

'My father gave you everything you wanted. You only had to point at something and it was yours.' Alexander spoke evenly, clearly keeping his temper in check.

Elise tossed her head. 'Look, buddy boy, now it's your

264

turn to do the same. I need the cash. Give me the title deeds and then just bugger off!'

Silver was surprised at Elise's sudden descent into vulgarity. How had Elise managed to deceive them all for so long – even she, Silver, who as a journalist prided herself on her insight into people's personalities, had failed to pick up how weird Elise was.

Elise continued her rant against Alexander's father, then she turned on Alexander. 'And you, the cherished elder son. What a model son! My own poor Knut was always left out.'

'That's not true and you know it!' Alexander's face was haggard, but he still appeared to be holding his temper. 'Father always treated his sons equally.'

'Well, now you've chased away Knut, and broken the bond between mother and son. I'll probably never see him again. And you're going to pay for that, Mr Cool Head.'

'Look, Elise, you're very upset and that's understandable after all you've been through. Why don't you just sit down again and relax. Here's your drink.' Alexander picked up her glass and held it out to her. Elise's threat seemed to wash over him and he remained in control of the situation. He put his arm round Elise and led her back to the sofa.

Elise sat with bowed head. 'You took Knut away from me. You're just like your father, always telling me what to do!' She sobbed, dabbing her cheeks with a freshly ironed handkerchief.

Silver glanced at Alexander's stern face. She made up her mind. It was about time that Elise answered some questions. She got up from her chair and approached Elise. 'You knew Lazlo well. What did he make you do?'

Elise sat up and sneered. Her eyes were dry and her mascara unsmudged. 'Lazlo didn't make me do anything.' She jumped up again from the sofa and stabbed a red lacquered finger at Alexander. 'Just get this clear. I was in charge of the whole operation. Lazlo's a mere lackey. You, Alexander, were the stumbling block. I needed the money because you and your father kept me on too tight a rein. I needed the money for me and for Knut. Do you get it now?' Her voice became more and more high pitched, and her eyes glittered fiercely.

Silver felt a shiver of fear run through her. Alexander's spacious sitting room suddenly seemed very small and enclosed. Elise's jerky movements and pent-up rage against the Rosenholms scared her. Elise's voice went on rambling in a confused diatribe against Alexander and his father.

Silver pushed down her fears. She mustn't miss the opportunity to get some more information out of Elise. She sat forward in her chair and fixed her eyes on Elise. 'First things first,' she said. 'We found a lot of mutilated passports with their pictures cut away, as well as a whole heap of credit cards. Do you know anything about this?'

Alexander drew in his breath sharply, but remained quiet, his mouth clenched in a tight line.

'Do I know anything about this?' Elise's eyes glittered. 'Of course I do.' She laughed scornfully at Silver. 'It's to help all these poor Russian people who want to come and start a new life in Norway. Poor Russian people like me. Lazlo knows a man who can make new passports out of the old, though it's really hard getting the passports to match the people who need them. Some people are too old. Some too young. Some the wrong sex. It's like a giant jigsaw.'

'What...?' said Silver and Alexander in the same breath.

Elise preened. 'I think we've helped at least fifty or sixty people with new identities.'

Silver shivered at the eerie way in which Elise took

266

pride in helping illegal immigrants to slip into the country. 'But Elise,' she said. 'Didn't it matter to you that you were breaking the law?'

'No, no, that's not true,' Elise said. 'I'm only helping my fellow Russians to make a new life. Did you know my grandfather was a White Russian and a count?' She beamed at Silver in a friendly way.

Silver floundered in a maelstrom of uncertainty. Elise slipped in and out of personalities so quickly that Silver found it hard to keep up, but she persevered. 'What about all that neat alcohol stowed in the cellars of Rosenholm?'

'Oh, that's Knut's business, not mine.' Elise waved her hand airily. 'Lazlo and Knut were the ones who took the risks. Not me. I just told them what to do. So you see, I've not broken any laws. Everything I touch is magic.' A smile spread over her face. She paused and looked at Alexander, who was leaning against the mantelpiece of the open fireplace. 'Where is my Knut? And where is my husband?' she demanded hoarsely. 'What have you done with them?' The dark person was back, rage burning just below the surface.

Silver was in anguish. Should she tell Elise about the person she'd seen on the deck of *The Guiding Spirit*? She twisted a button on her shirt with nervous fingers. Nausea rose in her throat at the struggle going on inside her. Suppose it wasn't Knut she'd seen. But had she the right to suppress even this tentative knowledge and keep it from his mother? Yet if she told her, Elise in her fragile state might spring on her in an unbalanced rage.

She blurted out: 'Do you know anything about Knut's departure?'

Elise glanced at her coldly. 'I wouldn't ask if I knew.'

'Could he have been on board the Rosenholm cruise ship?'

'Don't be stupid, Silver. He would have told me.' Elise's tone was dismissive. 'Of course he would've told his mother.'

Silver sat back. At least she'd tried to tell Elise. Probably she'd made a mistake about the figure on the ship anyway.

But Alexander was watching her, his eyes questioning. 'You never told me this, Silver,' he said. 'Did you tell the police anything about this?'

Silver looked down at the floor. 'No, I didn't because I didn't see the person clearly. I was so exhausted that I thought my eyes were playing tricks with me.'

Elise let out a hiss of rage and opened her handbag, her hands fumbling inside. 'You shouldn't have told the police anything, Silver. I thought you understood.' She pulled out a black object.

Silver found herself looking into the muzzle of a small black pistol.

'Neither of you should've told the police anything.' Elise's voice was emotionless. The pistol in her hand veered between Alexander and Silver.

Silver almost choked with fear. She shrank against the back of her chair, panic rushing through her. Dimly, she heard Alexander's calm voice: 'Where did you get that pistol, Elise? Is it my father's?'

'It's mine now.' Elise spoke in a monotonous tone, which chilled Silver further. 'And I intend to use it.'

'Don't be silly, Elise. You've no need to do that. Why don't you sit down again and we'll try and sort things out.' Alexander's voice was soothing and he stepped closer to her.

Elise jerked away and waved the pistol at him. 'Get back there or I'll shoot you. I want to know what you and Silver told the police.' Now she held the pistol in an unwavering hand, pointed straight at Alexander.

Silver swallowed down the metallic taste of fear on her

tongue. Was the pistol loaded? Or was Elise just trying to scare them?

'What did we tell the police?' Alexander was unruffled. 'Why everything you told us. It's in their hands now.' He leant forward. 'Give me the gun, Elise.'

'You stupid fool,' Elise spat out the words. 'You talk too much.'

'Silver.' Her voice was soft and light as her attention focused on Silver. 'You were the one who saw Knut last, yet you never told me. We're going down to the ship together, you and me. He liked you, you know.'

'But the ship's…' Silver caught Alexander's eye as he shook his head.

'Come, Silver.' Elise's voice was insistent. 'You must help me find Knut.' She seized Silver by the arm, jammed the gun in her back and pushed her toward the door.

Silver looked back at Alexander. His face was chalk white and he was mouthing something to her. He stepped toward her, but Elise turned sharply towards him and pulled the trigger of the small pistol. The bullet whizzed past Alexander's shoulder and embedded itself in the wall. Elise cursed and fired again. This time, the bullet skimmed Alexander's hair.

In a panic, Silver writhed and struggled, trying to break free of Elise's hold. She was more afraid for Alexander than herself.

'Don't struggle,' hissed Elise in her ear. 'I'm not afraid of using the gun.'

'Stand back, Alexander. Please don't do anything.' Silver's hands were cold and clammy. She was terrified that Elise would aim at him again and, this time, he might not get off so lightly.

'I'll come with you, Elise.' Her voice was soft and soothing as she tried to appease the older woman.

Elise's cold eyes raked over her. She jerked Silver's arm. Although she was smaller than Silver, she seemed to have a superhuman strength, emphasised by the gun she poked in Silver's back.

Elise propelled Silver forward and struggled with the catch on the outer door. Then they were out on the quiet street. 'Come on,' Elise hissed as she pushed and pulled Silver into the passenger seat of the large limousine. Then she whipped back round to the driver's seat, the pistol in her hand still pointing at Silver's head.

'If you try to escape, I'll have to shoot you,' she told Silver in the monotonous voice Silver had come to dread. She gave a low, dry laugh which chilled Silver to the bone.

Elise started the car with one hand and held the pistol in the other. She pulled out jerkily onto the road without looking behind her. She looked at Silver and laughed once more, a cold, humourless sound.

Silver cast a stealthy glance back to the main door of the apartments. Alexander stood in the doorway, his mobile clamped to his ear, his other hand jabbing the air. Silver leaned back against the seat and concentrated on tamping down the screams that threatened to tear from her throat.

The car veered from side to side on the road, but as yet there was no sign of other traffic or pedestrians. Silver clutched the sides of her seat with both hands. Elise looked at her and the car lurched violently.

'Keep your eyes on the road!' The words were torn out of Silver.

'We've got to get to Knut before the ship sails.' Elise stamped harder on the accelerator.

'But…' Silver swallowed her words. No point in stoking the fires of Elise's anger by revealing that the ship had left. She risked a quick peek behind in the wing mirror. A large jeep was keeping a decorous distance behind them. She couldn't be sure who was in the driving seat.

Elise had the car under better control, and Silver ventured a question. She'd read somewhere that it was better to keep a calm mien and the lines of communication open between hostage and abductor. That way, perhaps she could avoid falling into the role of shivering, cringing victim.

'What will you tell Knut when you see him?'

'Tell Knut? Why tell him to get Lazlo away from the police. And that he must help Lazlo's brother, Vladi.' Elise's profile was stern and concentrated.

'Lazlo's brother?'

'Yes, he's very poor. He works at the fairground and they have to move on in a few days.' Elise seemed to have slipped into a more sane and reasonable frame of mind. 'He was born in St Petersburg too, you know – like me!'

Silver digested this information. Was he the hooked-nose man who'd snatched her passport at the fairground? She took another quick peek in the wing mirror. The big jeep was still keeping a steady distance behind them.

'I like you, Silver. That's why you have to come with me.' Elise beamed at her. 'But you meddle too much. You poke your nose into things that don't concern you.'

A rush of fear invaded Silver's stomach. Elise in friendly mode was creepier than when she was making threats.

'Do you like my Knut? He likes you a lot.' Elise's tone was conversational. If they hadn't been travelling at breakneck speed, with the cars coming in the opposite direction whooshing past, they could be two women just having a casual chat.

Silver cleared her throat. 'Of course I do. He's full of fun!'

'Well, he's going to help us now.' Elise nodded her head sagely.

The big jeep had drawn closer to them. Was that Alexander's blond helmet of hair? If only Silver could be sure.

Elise stamped on the accelerator again and they shot round the last two bends on the approach to the harbour. Several ships loomed up in front of them as they tore down the final slope. Elise pumped on the brakes again and again. The big car slewed round at an angle blocking both sides of the road before it came to a juddering halt. Elise peered out of the window and screamed, her face suffused with rage. 'Our ship's gone. You tricked me, Silver!'

Silver held up her hands to ward off Elise's rage. She prayed desperately: Please let it be Alexander behind us. And please let the police arrive in time.

'You told me Knut was on the ship, and it's gone! You lied to me!' Elise jammed the pistol hard against Silver's ear.

The reality of the situation hit Silver. Trapped in the car with this madwoman, she might be dead within minutes.

Chapter 24

Mounting panic almost suffocated Silver. One false move and she was sure Elise would pull the trigger of the gun and blast her into the next world. She had to calm her down. But her breath came in short gasps so that it was hard to speak.

'Elise, don't...!' Her voice came out as a thin thread of sound. Elise's eyes were fixed on the empty berth where *The Guiding Spirit* had been moored. Silver took the chance of moving her head slightly away from the muzzle of the pistol. Cold rivulets of sweat trickled down her spine as she huddled against the seat.

Elise turned and stared at her with glittering eyes. 'You fool,' she said. 'Because of you, I've lost my son!'

Silver stared back, her lips dry and trembling. A vision of Alexander, his broad shoulders and determined face rose before her. How reassuring he'd looked when he arrived back on the island wearing those awful borrowed clothes. Her lips curved in a smile. Then suddenly her panic eased and she entered a new dimension of calm. She didn't care any more what Elise might do to her. She just had to get out of the car. She fumbled with the door handle, pushed open the heavy door and tumbled out into the sunshine. On stiff, unsteady legs, she headed for the low square building that was probably the Customs Office.

Another car braked with a grinding screech and burning

of rubber a few yards away from her. She flattened herself against the wall. The big jeep which had been following them slid to a halt alongside some warehouses on the quay. A man jumped down from the driver's seat. Silver's heart gave a great leap of joy as Alexander dodged behind a row of pallets stacked on the quayside. If only Elise didn't see him and react too fast.

Silver looked around her, searching for a means of escape. At all costs, she must avoid leading Elise to Alexander. Her eye caught a small day cruiser moored at the end of the harbour, where a man was bent over the side, laying out fenders. Could she, who was younger and stronger, outrun Elise? After all, Elise was wearing high heels. Or would Elise fell her with a gun shot? In a split-second decision, she took off like a racing hare, a decoy leading Elise away from Alexander.

Someone shouted, but she paid no heed, concentrating on speeding towards the day cruiser. A shot rang out, but she didn't look back. She reached the boat and flung herself over the side, collapsing on the deck in front of the shocked eyes of the boatman.

She sat up and looked back. Several metres away Alexander was grimly holding on to Elise as she desperately tried to break free of his grip. He held her with one hand while his other arm dangled limply by his side.

Silver gave a gasp of horror. She scrambled out of the boat onto the quayside again, leaving the boat slapping hard against the water. 'Sorry about this,' she flung at the startled boatman, who stood speechless trying to keep his balance in his rocking craft.

She tore across to Alexander. 'Has she hurt you?' she screamed, terror squeezing her heart as she saw blood oozing through the sleeve of his shirt.

'Pick up the gun, Silver.' Alexander nodded to where

it lay half hidden by the pallets. His face was white and strained, but he kept his tight hold on Elise. 'Why did you dash off like that?' he asked Silver. 'She could've shot you dead, or at least injured you.'

'It was for you, Alexander. I wanted you out of the line of fire. I couldn't bear anything to happen to you and I had to get away from her. She couldn't keep me hostage forever.' Cold shudders chased through Silver's body at the thought. She held the gun in her shaking hand, pointing it downwards.

Elise stirred. Her black eyes burned with hate mingled with triumph. 'I did it, you know.'

Alexander looked down at her.

'Did what?'

'I shot your father. He was meddling in our operations. I had to save Knut.' Elise's frenzied laughter burst forth. She seemed unable to contain it. 'I had to save Knut,' she gasped again.

Silver stood transfixed in horror. 'You, Elise. How could you kill your husband?'

But Elise was beyond sense and sanity. She twisted and writhed in Alexander's grip, muttering and giving an occasional small scream. Her dark hair had slipped out of her elegant coiffure and her eyes flickered wildly. Now she resembled a gypsy fortune teller at a fairground. One of her elegant shoes lay forlornly on the ground, its heel broken.

The rhythmic shrieking of police sirens rent the air. Two police cars swept through the steel gates, blue lights flashing. Doors opened and the quayside became alive with men in black leather jackets and peaked caps. A wave of relief washed over Silver, causing her knees to buckle.

After a flurry of explanations from her and Alexander, two policewomen took Elise gently by the arms and led her to one of the police cars. Elise, now apathetic, looked back with empty eyes at Silver and Alexander as they stood watching her.

The car swept away. Like a homing dove, Silver flew into Alexander's one-armed embrace, not caring that her clothes got smeared with his blood. Her voice was full of sympathy. 'I'm so sorry, Alexander. It's unbearable. She's completely mad.' Then she stopped, feeling that she was only making things worse. Elise's actions were too horrific for words of comfort.

Alexander's face was strained, white lines running from nose to mouth. Silver looked up at him, seeing the vulnerability in his eyes. 'Oh God, Silver, when she snatched you off in the car, I thought I'd lost you.' His voice was husky and his hand caressed her cheek.

'Alexander,' she whispered. 'We must get you patched up, you're losing blood and we don't know how serious it is.'

A policeman stood behind them. 'There's a police car waiting to take you to the Accident and Emergency,' he said.

Half leaning on Silver, Alexander got into the back seat of the police car and Silver took her place beside him, and they swept away to the hospital.

Several hours later, back in his own sitting room, Alexander sported a large sling. His shirt was pulled tight and puckered over his shoulder where fresh bandages covered the wound where Elise's bullet had entered. He was numbed by the discovery that she had killed his father. Yet, in some way, he wasn't surprised. He had had his suspicions for a long time, too dreadful even to admit to himself. He exhaled and blanked it out of his mind for the time being.

He stretched his long legs out in front of him on

the sofa and gazed at Silver sitting opposite him in the big armchair, so fragile and beautiful, yet she had been prepared to risk her life for him.

He rose and walked over to the window, staring down the steep slope leading to the fiord. What had he got to offer her, but a disgraced family and a damaged soul? Soon it would be time for her to return to her own country and her own life. She'd have to put all this behind her and move on. Norway would be the last country she'd ever want to return to.

He didn't know how he would go on living without her. Without her bravery and good sense. Without touching her silken skin, her delicate features, her kissable mouth. His mouth twisted in anguish.

Silver slipped silently across the room to stand beside him. Together they watched the orange rays of the evening sun touch the mirrored water of the fiord. Her nearness was balm to his troubled thoughts. He turned towards her. 'How long can you stay, Silver? You know I need a nurse.'

She flinched at his words. 'Is that all you need me for, Alexander?'

He crushed her to him with his one good arm. 'Of course not. I just wonder how long you'll stay with me.' His thumb caressed her lips.

The house was waiting and silent. Tension between them burned and shimmered.

He fought against the blaze of need in his body until the words formed themselves. 'Come upstairs.' His voice was low and husky.

Like thistledown, she moved in front of him. The sun, slanting through the window, highlighted her silvery gold hair like a blessed halo as she mounted the stairs.

Cursing his useless arm, he passed ahead of her and pushed open the door to his bedroom. He tossed back the coverlet of the large double bed and they sank down on the cool, fresh sheets, their bodies fitting together in perfect accord.

Silver stirred. The sun shone brightly through the uncurtained window. Troubled thoughts intruded and would not let go. Could there be any future for the two of them? Alexander carried so many burdens. Could he ever break free of the family taint? And another more immediate and mundane concern nagged at her. Tom!

Alexander awoke and drew her against his warm body. She turned and laid her face against his chest.

'Silver?'

'I've got to go back to London.' Her voice was husky and she touched his jaw gently. 'I haven't done so well here. I can't write about anything of what's happened. Maybe I haven't even got a job.'

'Silver, we've just made the most earth-shattering love together and immediately you talk about leaving. You can't be thinking straight.'

Silver felt a burning behind her eyelids. She couldn't be about to cry, could she? Together they'd shared the most intense experience of her life. Her emotions were raw and confused. 'My life is in England. My job and everything. I've got to get back.'

'And what about me? Does this mean you don't want anything more to do with me? I wouldn't blame you because my family's a complete disaster. A murdered father and a mad, murderous stepmother, not to mention my half-brother. And maybe you feel I've nothing but trouble to offer you.' Alexander's face was devastated. Then he squared his shoulders and looked at her, his eyes brave and proud. He picked up his clothes from the floor and began pulling them on.

Silver drooped. Alexander's perception had put all her fears into words. Her heart knotted in her breast as he clattered downstairs away from her.

Chapter 25

Silver descended the stairs slowly. All the joy had gone out of her. She'd have to get back to the hotel and pack her belongings ready to leave. How could everything have gone so wrong?

She heard Alexander moving about in the kitchen. Maybe she should have one last cup of coffee with him instead of rushing out of the house like a kicked spaniel. And wasn't it she who had done the kicking?

She walked to the kitchen door. He swung round to look at her as she asked: 'Can we at least have a drink of morning coffee together?'

He came forward and cupped her face in his hand. 'Are you really going to run out on a wounded man?' He smiled at her and she melted under his deep blue gaze.

'What about my job?' she faltered.

He raised an eyebrow, his emotions seemingly well under control. 'What about it then?'

His mobile jangled in the sitting room. He strode through the hall and Silver could hear him speaking English to the caller. Not the police then. He came into the room again, the mobile in his hand. 'It's your editor in London. He's tracked you down.' He handed her the phone. She took it half in anticipation, half in dread.

'Silver, you'd better get back. No more swanning about in the midnight sun,' Tom's robust tones resounded in her ear. 'I've got a couple more jobs for you here in London, so get on the afternoon flight and back here pronto.'

'Tom, I'm so sorry about the Rosenholm story, but I can't possibly write it. There's no way I could do an unbiased story.'

Alexander's head jerked up, and he smiled.

'Well, you'll have to sort it out somehow – you can't let me down. I need that story. What about Jan Brinchman? He can do it without any conflict of interest. You got far too close to your sources – a very bad move! We'll have to talk about that and I hope you'll learn from it,' Tom told her, in an unusually stern voice. 'Call up Brinchman, and get back here. You've work to do.'

Silver sagged with relief. At least she hadn't lost her job. 'I'll be there,' she said, and put down the mobile. She turned to Alexander: 'How did he find me?'

'He's been calling here and the Rosenholm offices every hour. It was only when I switched on my phone again that his call could get through.'

'He says I've got to catch the afternoon flight back to London, so I'll have to get ready to leave,' said Silver. 'At least I've got my new passport.' She sighed heavily and sank into an armchair as despair over a bleak future without Alexander overwhelmed her.

'You're not leaving.' Alexander towered over her sternly. 'Or if you do leave, I'm coming with you to London. I'm not letting you out of my sight. You'd only get into trouble.'

He moved behind her chair. Silver felt his warm breath on her cheek and looked up at him. Maybe there was a solution after all. She leaned back against him and his arm slipped round her waist as he drew her to him.

Once more, his mobile shattered the peace. He spoke in Norwegian and Silver felt him grow rigid as he listened to the caller. 'It's the police,' he mouthed.

Silver detached herself from him and went over to the sofa. Alexander's face was grim and his voice was stern as the unintelligible conversation flowed over her head. It seemed interminable as Alexander gave short sharp replies and, at one point, punched his fist on the table. His face became more and more gaunt. Finally, he laid the phone on the table.

'Things are coming to a head,' he said. 'Lazlo has admitted that it was his brother Vladi and two others who started the fire on the island to cover up the shooting of my father. Anyway, Lazlo couldn't wait to incriminate his brother so that he could whitewash himself. So he poured out excuses and explanations. He said Vladi and his accomplices started the fire to hide the incriminating traces of my father being shot. They took a log from my father's own fireplace and threw on some petrol taken from a petrol can they carried in their boat. The old wood of the cottage was ignited easily and the blaze exploded into an inferno within minutes.'

Alexander bowed his head for a moment. 'And then there's Elise. Lazlo didn't hesitate to dump the blame on her. It seems there's no doubt that she was out on the island with the immigrants. She ranted and raved that my father would stop her activities. She was in a frenzy – no one was going to hinder her lucrative operations, not even her own husband. She was completely out of control.'

Alexander swallowed, finding it hard to go on. In a strained voice, he continued: 'Lazlo admitted they were all terrified of her for she frequently threatened to expose them. She said she was an important woman and untouchable. She laughed in their faces. Nobody would believe she was involved. Helping her Russian compatriots brought in a lot of money and she thrived on the danger.

The police say she was the kingpin, and Lazlo and his cohorts were all under her thumb. That day out on the island they were looking for hiding places for the Russian immigrants. Unfortunately, that was the day my father had sailed out to the island – innocent, unsuspecting, but he got in her way. That signed his death warrant. She panicked and lost control. So with the gun in her hands she pulled the trigger and shot my father. Her own husband! My poor father!' Alexander's eyes looked inward at some indescribable horror. 'Oh, what a horrendous mess!' he groaned.

Silver sprang up, full of sympathy. 'Where is Elise now? What will they do with her?'

Alexander raised his head. 'Elise is in hospital in a special secure unit. She'd reached breaking point and flipped completely. DCI Berg told me, off the record, of course, that probably she'll never be fit to plead in a court.'

'And Knut?'

'Nobody knows anything about Knut. We've called *The Guiding Spirit* several times, but nobody's seen him there. He seems to have vanished off the face of the earth.'

'Well, I wasn't even certain if I did actually see him on the ship, or if it was just a trick of the light.' Silver was sure that whatever Knut had done, he'd wriggle out of it and land on his feet again. He wouldn't be kept down for long.

Alexander straightened up. He seemed to come to a decision. 'Come, Silver, if we're going to make the flight to London this afternoon, we'd better look smart. I've been too serious, weighed down by family cares for too long. I have to restart my life.' He gave her a quick hug and moved her away from him. 'I'm going to break free of the past and have fun. Time for a new beginning!'

Just wanted to have fun? Like Knut? A new beginning with...or was it without her? Silver felt a sinking sensation in her stomach. Was it just fun for him? She breathed in shallow, quick gasps and then saw he was studying her.

'God, I'm making a hash of this,' he said. 'I want to have fun with you Silver and I want a long-term commitment...'

They sat in silence for a moment. Silver's thoughts tumbled round in confusion as her mind sped back to all they had been through. Murder, near murder, people smuggling, forgery, madness, deceit and treachery. It was a long list of crimes and they were lucky to be sitting here safely. Both of them had come near to losing their lives. Thank God, Alexander had escaped with only minor injuries.

'It's a pity you live in smog-choked London. What an unhealthy place!'

'London's not smog-choked.' Silver's voice was indignant. Then she caught his teasing glance.

'Silver, sweetheart, I know you've not been given a very good impression of Norway over these last few days with all that has happened. My father was murdered, my step-mother's been arrested and my brother's vanished into the blue waters of the ocean. You are my anchor – my lifeline! Please stay.'

Silver looked at him, a smile spreading over her face. 'Well, maybe...' she said.

THE END

I wish to thank Susan Gault, without whose proofreading and support this book would not have been published.

Lightning Source UK Ltd.
Milton Keynes UK
UKOW02f0018281215

265414UK00001B/50/P